Dead On

Dead On

Ann Kelly

iUniverse, Inc.
New York Lincoln Shanghai

Dead On

iUniverse, Inc.

For information address:
iUniverse, Inc.
2021 Pine Lake Road, Suite 100
Lincoln, NE 68512
www.iuniverse.com

ISBN: 0-595-32664-1

Printed in the United States of America

Main Entry: **jour·nal**
Function: <u>noun</u>
Etymology: Middle English, service book containing the day hours, from Middle French, from <u>journal</u>, adjective, daily, from Latin <u>diurnalis</u>, from <u>diurnus</u> of the day, from <u>dies</u> day

April 5, 1903

April is the cruelest month. I don't resent March because March is always unpredictable and you know that going into her. But April; April is a different story. She catches the sun in your eye then darts behind snow clouds. She breathes warmly against your cheek then disappears, laughing, in the final sting of winter's ice-clad breath. You hope for the sun's warmth, expect it more and more each day, then wake up to find snow curling and twisting and piling itself on tree branches one last time. Makes me think of ice-cold fingers tangled in dark hair.

Her middle name is April. Her daffodil-blonde hair skates around her shoulders hinting of the sun; her startling blue eyes hold silver-gray crystals of warmth; her smile holds the promise of new beginnings. You can see them if you really look. I suddenly find I'm in no mood to write about anything more. I'm sick of the gray shadows skidding across the sky. I'm sick of the cold. I'm sick of the boredom. I think I'll go down to the lake. It won't be frozen now; just gulps of brown toffee water shifting to the surface and breathing again. I sit on the bank and feel the wind reveal its secrets. When it stings my skin, I have the strangest feeling I've lived before, and it wasn't good. Like I am shades of all those who came before me, shadows and twists of things. Lately, when I look out across the lake at blonde shadows scratching black water, I feel a premonition. I don't know what it is, but it makes me shiver. It makes me fear for April and the coming of spring.

Prologue

May 31, 1865
Virginia

The afternoon was warm and bright; the sky shimmered above the earth like soda glass. He'd been home for three days. He hadn't really felt like he was home until she was standing next to him.

"The war's really over," she said, the words sounding more like a question on her tangerine-peach lips. "We've both changed so much." She smiled prettily. "I hardly feel as if I know you anymore." She looked at his left sleeve, the stump of his arm. Her lovely tawny eyes bore pity. There was no indication she'd been impressed by his faded blue uniform. It was itchy and he was sweating, but he wanted her to see him in it.

Sweeping a tendril of auburn hair from her cheek, she looked away from him. "I'm sorry…I…I never meant to give you the wrong impression in my letters…"

Night was falling purple-clad as they looked out across the lake where they had first met as children. This time last year he'd lost his arm, fighting Confederate forces not far from the tiny village where he grew up. After three years in hell, could you return to heaven? Could you feel the prongs of hope digging into your chest and not *die*? He longed to tell her how he felt, about the things he'd experienced—the demons he couldn't chase away, the dark secrets of his childhood. How her letters had been his only source of courage, the only reason to live through each day—when the shot was raining like hail, the bodies of dead and wounded men falling all around him like leaves in the autumn. He couldn't now.

It's not too late. It can't be too late.

"There's someone in my life now," she went on cheerfully. "He's a wonderful man. A surgeon. We're to be married next week. I can't wait for you to meet him. I told you about him in my letters. He's the one I met in Washington."

He'd faced death many times; her memory the only thing keeping him alive, the only thing that assured him he was still among the living as another day curled into the endless, deep ink stain of night. He'd fallen in love with her in her letters. He thought she loved him too.

Something inside him snapped.

1

Love is as strong as death. Our dead are never dead until we've forgotten them.

They had been children when he'd left. He looked at her face, her smooth skin, the lovely new curves of her body. Rage and injustice welled within him. He *didn't want* to be forgotten. He took her small hand in his and squeezed it gently, as if he understood her naive sentiments. A slight breeze moved over him, as soft as his mother's voice.

Great love is a current that flows on forever, restless and circling, as fragile as glass yet as strong as death; and death is never satisfied.

In his head, he heard the tin beat of the drummer's drum like a pulse, the gold, courageous notes of a young bugle stretching across summer earth like skin over a youthful body. Firm. *Soft.* He heard the legion steps of boys and men marching together toward death. He believed in the immortality of the soul—that it was born again and again and again.

"June is at your doorstep," he breathed. "But I won't forget you in December." She looked at him, confusion in her eyes.

As he knelt beside her lifeless form, he kissed her childlike lips. He removed her engagement ring then yanked the delicate gold chain from her neck, turning it in his hands so it glinted in the sunlight. A swan made of mother-of-pearl dangled from the chain, its black onyx eye silently condemning him. He stuffed it in his pocket and ran his fingers along the slender curve of her cheek.

"Death will bind us as life could not. I'll remember you. I'll find you again, my sweet. I promise."

It was a dark promise.

1

June 2004
Doylestown, Pennsylvania

The first time he'd done it, he'd thought it would cleanse him, make him feel better. But two days later, the dark shadows returned. Something was unfinished.

She wasn't the one.

He was visiting her now. It was dark and drizzling, but he wore no jacket. He didn't even feel the rain.

I bet you wish you hadn't been so mean to me. I bet you wish you'd been a little bit nicer. Now look at you.

He trembled with delight as he remembered their first meeting. She'd been easy prey, but physically stronger than he'd given her credit for. She'd been sitting alone at a table in Chambers. The small restaurant was always dimly lit, even at the lunch hour, but when she turned her head a certain way the lamplight caught the ash-blonde highlights in her hair.

She'd looked up absently a few times, and he'd finally caught her eye. She had smiled rather sternly, as if she weren't used to it, wasn't expecting someone to notice her. Her nails were long and manicured, her clothes tailored and expensive-looking. He guessed she was in her late forties, and lonely. She wore a lot of make-up, but there were telltale shadows beneath her eyes—the black paint of a lonely woman with self-imposed burdens.

He'd been patient. He'd seen her a few times in the restaurant, each time discreetly watching her, memorizing things she told the waiter, whom she appeared to know very well. Her voice was strident. He didn't like her voice. *As if everyone wants to hear what you have to say.* She always ordered the same thing, Buffalo Chicken salad, plenty of rolls and butter, a glass of Chardonnay, topped off with Key Lime pie. Sometimes, after she was through, she walked to the corner of Main and State, crossed the street, and got a mocha latte at Starbucks. He guessed that was why she was on the heavy side. *Pampered rich girl. Daddy spoiled you rotten.*

He'd enjoyed reading about her disappearance in *The Intelligencer.* It had been front-page news in the local paper. No one in the small, eclectic town could understand how a successful businesswoman, active in the community and charitable causes, could simply disappear. It helped that she was recently divorced. Her husband had not been publicly named as a suspect, but the police were questioning him.

His head started to ache, and he knelt down in the shadows and the damp grass cradling it with his hands. The voices were whispering, and his head felt like it was on fire.

You know what son? You're just like your good-for-nothin' mother. You ain't got what it takes to stand up to me and you never will. No...He wouldn't listen. He *wouldn't.*

He doesn't have that kind of power over me anymore. He concentrated on the sound and the feel of the rain through the tree branches, now heavy and drenching. Then <u>he</u> was there, the other voice, that stronger part of him. <u>He</u> always laughed at him, told him he was weak.

The precious uniform. Great, great, great Granddaddy's uniform. The one you took. The one from the secret closet. I'm just waiting for the right person. She'll wear it to her grave and we'll never have to look at it again. All you have to do is find her.

He reached into his pocket and gripped the crumpled newspaper clipping. He was only going to savor it for a few days and then throw it away. It was dangerous to keep it. Especially now that he'd put her body by the field. He knew that. But he couldn't throw it away. Not yet. He realized he liked reading it. He would read it over and over. But first he would go to the church and pray for his pitiful soul—a soul his father said was as black and damned as a river in hell. There was something about the stained glass of the oblong windows of the church—rose, coral, apple green, and sky blue—that made him feel like he was enclosed in the wings of a butterfly. The glorious, fluttering wings of one of nature's perfect creatures—a creature who tasted with its feet, he remembered, as cold rain water and mud sucked at his shoes and socks.

I'm tasting with my feet too. I'm tasting death.

In the church, the voices were smaller. Yes, he would pray. Then put flowers on his mother's grave. His mother would tell him where to find the next one. His mother would help him because she had never meant to leave him.

◆   ◆   ◆

Late afternoon. For early June, it was unusually warm. Recent rain had made the grounds behind Fonthill Museum soggy. To Ann Yang, medical examiner for Bucks County, it felt more like July. As she climbed out of her white four-wheel-drive Jeep Cherokee, she grabbed her black leather medical bag, a box of disposable latex gloves, and her camera. She was also going to need a white body bag, neatly packaged in plastic, bearing the warning: *Use universal blood/body fluids precautions with all patients.* Ann preferred the white bags to the black; they picked up everything, carpet fiber, specks of paint, strands of hair. They helped the dead to speak.

At 5'3", with shoulder-length glossy black hair, deep brown eyes, and nerves of steel, she was an oddity of the homicide unit. Because she was an attractive woman with an even brighter mind, she'd been called all sorts of things, by the men <u>and</u> women she worked with: intelligent, ambitious, cagey, elusive, a bitch. There were times when she had to be all of those things. It was due to her recent and bitter divorce proceedings that she found herself working a crime scene in Doylestown, Pennsylvania; she'd left New York and Peter behind months ago. She'd ended up here because her sister Bo and her grandmother Nai Nai both lived in the area, and she was at a time in her life when she needed to be with family.

This wasn't the kind of crime that happened in Doylestown. She'd been making her way back to her office from Starbucks, fresh coffee in hand, when she got the call on her cell phone. A body had been found in a field and it appeared to be a brutal homicide.

She trudged across the wide cushion of grass between Fonthill Museum and the woods, her white blouse sticking to her skin. Located in the former home of industrialist Henry Mercer, the museum was a concrete castle decorated with beautiful tiles and full of treasures from around the world. The tips of her tan khakis swept damp grass; her tiny silver earrings jangled and kept time with her hurried pace. Ann signed in at the crime scene and looked at the tops of the trees edging the wooded clearing; it would be dark soon. Several uniformed officers, a captain, and a detective were present. Three police cruisers with their lights flashing were parked to the side of a wide swath of yellow police tape, wheels muddied by the wet field. EMTs stood by waiting.

Everything smelled damp, sticky. At least it wasn't raining anymore. Ann soon discovered who was first on the scene, a young officer named Jeff Stevens with a full head of blonde curly hair and a boyish face; he was new to the force and looking very pale.

"Dr. Yang," he said, sweat starting to bead on his smooth forehead. "I was the lucky officer today—closest to the scene. I didn't know it would be so…it's bad. I mean, she's just lying there, for everybody to see." He looked like he was going to vomit.

"You notice anything unusual?" Ann asked.

"No, ma'am. Guy walking his dog found her. The scene's been roped off with controlled access."

"Anybody else been in out out?"

"Not since he called it in."

"Good. I've had problems before with contamination of scenes. I need to preserve the chain of evidence. Thanks," she said, quickly walking toward the body lying at the edge of the field.

Ann was thankful the museum was closed. It would make things easier—no crowd of museum-goers—most likely school kids on an outing, their teachers, and supervising parents—gawking at the swarm of officers, yellow police tape, emergency vehicles, lights and equipment, not to mention the body. It would be easier to protect the scene from destruction or contamination by onlookers, and curious police officers too. The latter were usually curious to see things for themselves, and the less experienced left behind items that were then mistaken as important evidence. And then there were the obnoxious reporters, eager to be the first to break the story, the first to break a family's pain wide open for the whole community to see.

Personally, Ann couldn't stand reporters. Especially TV reporters. They were so pompous; thought the world hung on their every word, and thought every word they spoke was news. Ann had come close to physically assaulting a reporter who'd managed to get past the barrier of yellow tape and men in blue inside the home of a murdered woman and her three children; the reporter and his cameramen were so busy capturing this family's grief for the 6 o'clock news that they unwittingly destroyed evidence.

The area around the victim had been cordoned off, divided into manageable sections to be searched individually. So far, no cameramen were present. A pathway had been marked off with string and flags to be used as the sole entrance and exit to the scene until the search was finished. Several officers were already out canvassing the neighborhood for information, potential witnesses, so Ann was sure the news vans would be there soon.

She heard Chief Hyde before she saw him; he had a loud, rasping voice. The local community was divided on how he ran things—some thought he was a bully. You either did things his way or he made it difficult for you. The newspaper editorials about him were interesting. Ann was still taking his measure. So far, he was doing his job containing the crime scene.

Wearing white latex gloves, she bent down and examined the body lying face up not far from the run-down remnants of a boarded-up shack in the woods, where local teenagers came to smoke pot and drink cheap beer. She looked at the ground surrounding the body then looked up—nothing but a canopy of green leaves.

The woman was fully clothed in a pair of dark blue tailored slacks and a rose blouse; both were soaking wet. There was a large, glittering diamond ring on her finger, so the intent hadn't been robbery. Without moving the body, she looked between the arms and legs, the hands and fingers. No visible defense wounds; nothing immediately visible under the immaculate fingernails, painted a glossy pink. The body was lying about 300 yards from the museum parking lot. Ann examined the face and neck. The vessels were occluded, the face and neck dark red. There were bruises and contusions. Her eyes protruded, the conjunctivae showing petechial hemorrhages, small bright red spots resulting from increased pressure in the veins and capillaries. It was obvious the victim had been strangled.

Ann tried to quell the sadness that rose up inside her. What a senseless waste of a life. Her job always showed her firsthand how short and fragile life was. She felt the familiar ache to bring the grieving family members and friends of victims some sense of justice, some sense of closure.

She gently placed her hand on the cheek. It was cold to the touch. The muscles in the jaw and neck were already stiff. She'd been dead at least 12 to 24 hours. There was something odd about the set of her jaw. The lower side of her face had dark discoloration. She pressed it with her fingertip and it blanched pale. When she'd finished making notes about the appearance of bruises, the direction of blood flow patterns, the external appearance of the body and clothing, noting the tiny folds and rolls indicating that the body had indeed been dragged, and all the photographs had been taken, she carefully examined the inside of the woman's mouth.

Chief Hyde approached the body. "What you got, doc?"

"Victim was strangled. Probably with a cord or clothesline. Muscles still stiff, so she's been dead at least 12 to 24 hours. She was killed and then her body was moved here."

"Shit."

"Killer left a calling card. Some sort of button." After it was photographed in the victim's mouth, she removed it, turning it over. It was brass with an eagle imprint. It glinted in the butterscotch sun poking through the clouds as it leaned toward dusk. Someone had deliberately placed it under the woman's tongue. Ann felt a terrible dread brush her soul. This was no ordinary homicide case. One-time killers didn't leave calling cards. Neither did professionals.

The button appeared to be some sort of military button. She handed it to the gloved team supervisor. "Bag it."

2

Ann viewed Beverly's unclothed body as it lay on the cold table inside the forensics facility. Actually, the facility was housed in a funeral home. Ann's agenda included building a brand new forensics facility but that was a few years away. A toe tag rested on Beverly's foot, a small, tasteful tattoo of a yellow rose on her ankle. Ann would perform the autopsy on the body as well as collect blood samples and other bodily fluid samples that might be used as evidence in a criminal case. Ann adjusted the microphone attached to the front of her green surgical scrubs then picked up the chart with gloved hands and started to dictate. "Case number 65 dash 2321, Beverly Wilcox. The body is that of a well-developed, well-nourished, fifty-eight-year-old white female with dark blonde hair and blue eyes. The body is 65 inches long and weighs 175 pounds."

Ann put the chart down and moved beside the body. X rays, multiple photographs, measurements, and weight had all been obtained earlier. Her clothing, the wrapping sheet, and trace evidence had been sent for analysis. It was time for the external examination and internal dissection of the body. Bright overhead lights bathed the table and steel instruments in a gray-yellow glow.

"Rigor mortis present in the extremities. Skin normal texture." The autopsy was under way. Detective Jeff Stevens, who'd been one of the officers present at the crime scene, and Chief Hyde observed.

In this particular case, Ann believed the person or persons responsible for her death wanted her to be found; her wallet, containing credit cards, money, and emergency phone numbers, was found 30 feet from the body in a loose tangle of weeds. And then there had been the button. The borough had an overconfident killer on their hands, possibly a serial.

She spoke into the microphone. "Presence of substantial lividity on right side of victim's body, including right arm and right side of face." She clicked it off and spoke to Jeff without turning around. "That means gravitational settling of blood after death."

She clicked it on again. "Victim had probably been lying on her right side for a minimum of 4 hours prior to the discovery of her body. Fully developed lividity on victim's back; victim likely to have been lying in that position, on her back, for an additional 2 to 3 hours before discovery of her body was reported. Two fresh bruises on the right side of victim's body, probably caused by blunt-force trauma. Absence of purge or vomit. Post-mortem discoloration and skin slough-ing in the area of mouth is probably a result of the face being vigorously rubbed or cleaned after victim died." She clicked the recorder off and opened the body with the usual y-shaped incision, observing a 1-inch hemorrhage in the left chest. Two fractured ribs. She cut through the ribs and cartilage to expose the lungs and heart. She lifted the rib cage. After she took a sample of blood from the heart, she carefully removed each organ and weighed it, examined its external surface, and sliced them into sections to evaluate structure and damage.

"Victim's heart stopped, probably due to seizure."

Mechanically, she continued removing and weighing organs. "Stomach con-tents consist of blue-gray fluid, no digested food as part of stomach contents; no food particles present." Ann collected the blue-gray fluid from the stomach and took samples of the peripheral blood, heart blood, vitreous humor, and liver tis-sue. She also collected samples of lung tissue for further testing. "It is the opinion of the chief medical examiner that victim's body was moved after death to a face-up position after lying on her side."

She turned the recorder off again and thought about what she was seeing, what she wasn't seeing. The genitalia were swabbed; samples would be sent along with blood and hair to the lab for DNA typing. The urinary bladder was removed, the urine sent for toxicology. She probed the eyes for hemorrhages, knowing she would find them. Finally, she examined the head and brain.

"The tongue, epiglottis, and larynx show evidence of injury"—not a surprise, considering the ligature marks on her neck indicating she'd been strangled with a cord or rope. Odd bruises, too, that looked like they were from fingers. A partial fingerprint had been recovered from the scene; it appeared to be the outer por-tion of a finger, however, and the chances of a successful AFIS search were doubt-ful. No core or delta areas were present. Ann had measured the bruises on the victim's neck, and the size indicated a male perp with large hands.

The hyoid bone was broken. She shook her head sadly as surgical instruments clattered and clinked and danced in the silence of the death-wrapped room. Ann made an incision in the scalp on the back of the head and carefully peeled the skin forward over the face to expose the skull. Jeff made an odd noise and put his hand over his mouth. Ann turned.

"Use one of the sinks, officer. Don't mess up my floor unless you're going to stay to mop it up.

"Surprised he made it this far," Ann said to Hyde as Jeff vomited forcefully in a metal sink. "Breaking in a new one?"

Hyde yanked the tab off a can of diet Coke and took a swig. He wasn't wearing a white mask over his mouth; he'd rubbed wintergreen oil under his nose. "Gotta break 'em in right," he barked. "No easy way, is there?"

Ann didn't answer. Using the high-speed oscillating power saw, she opened up the skull and used a chisel to pry off the skullcap. Ann lifted the brain out, examined it, and weighed it. Tissue samples were taken to be sent to the lab for further analysis. She returned the stomach and heart and brain, organs that needed to be preserved for the investigation, to the body cavity. In New York, Ann had had an assistant to reassemble the body, replacing viscera and organs and putting the triangular piece of rib cage back in place. The assistant would also stitch up the y-shaped incision from pubis to mid-chest, wash and sponge the body, cover it with a black rubber sheet, and return it to its mortuary compartment. But Ann didn't have an assistant, it wasn't in the budget, so she did those tasks herself. Studying the heart, she'd thought of one of her grandmother's proverbs. Nai Nai was always reciting them. *When the ear will not listen, the heart escapes sorrow.* Nai Nai had raised Ann after her mother had died, had taught her to listen, taught her to protect herself from lies. Ann wondered whose lies Beverly had listened to.

She switched on the recorder. Ann's words had a shallow, chalky feel as they floated across the room. "It is my opinion that Beverly Wilcox, a 58-year-old female, died as a result of a seizure and cardiac arrest due to strangulation. The cause of death was cardiac arrest. It is not yet evident what caused the seizure. The manner of death was homicide. It is my opinion, based on body temperature, postmortem lividity to the right side of Beverly Wilcox's body, and the marks and loose skin around the victim's wrists, indicating she'd been dragged after her death, that she died some time between noon and 6:30 pm on June 3, 2004.

3

Ann dialed the phone.

"Cole," a gruff voice said on the other line.

"Tony," Ann said, "good to hear your voice."

"I would say the same, except whenever you call me, it's usually bad news. Tell me I'm wrong. You know, I'm retired now…"

"Sorry," Ann said. "Wish I could. I need your help with a case."

"When I first retired, I asked Daneen, 'Now what am I going to worry about?' I shouldn't have asked. Whadda ya got?"

"I knew I could count on you. A woman was strangled and left in a field behind a museum. Killer left a button beneath her tongue."

"Anything unusual about the button?"

"Union infantry. Genuine article."

"So, the guy's obvious. Daring."

"Not a one-time killer or a professional. No defense wounds under the fingernails. No scratches. I'm waiting for the lab results. But there's something else, Tony. It's almost like…I know this is going to sound weird."

"Nothing surprises me anymore, Ann. I've seen it all, remember?"

"I don't know. I can't explain it. Something beyond the normal is bothering me here but I can't put my finger on it."

"Shit, Ann."

Ann thought of her aunt, the one she would never meet, the one who was brutally murdered in 1961. The one she dreamt about all the time. Her father had told her about the execution of the killer in a Texas state prison three years later. It was something she'd never forget. The guy had been a parolee named Ivey.

"I may just be dredging up old ghosts, but it's Ivey. I know he's dead…but there's something about the killing that reminds me of him."

"You mean the douche-bag who killed your aunt? They gave him a ride in the chair, didn't they?"

"That's the one."

"Trust your gut. You want me to look over his file? I know field agents in Texas and can probably pull a few strings."

"OK. Couldn't hurt."

Ann thought of the stories she'd heard as a child about hopping ghosts. Could killers be reborn? Could their ghosts come back? A hopping ghost was a corpse that hadn't decayed, whose main soul, the *po*, had not yet left for the other world. The *po* is watched over by friends and family and is helped back into the cycle of reincarnation, fed with offerings in the hopes that it will have its fill of food and wine and leave contented and cause no trouble.

"You want me to work up a profile?"

"While the trail is hot," Ann said. "One more thing."

"What is it?"

"Something I've kept from the public, something that might be valuable when interrogating suspects. And another thing—there's a detective on the case who wants to shove dirt in the public's nose, so taxpayers will know what he has to deal with every day. Selfish bastard. He could really screw up the investigation. He hates me because I have ovaries."

"Tell me everything you know."

After she'd filled Tony in, they made arrangements for Tony to travel to Doylestown. "I'll shoot you over some preliminary teletypes," he said, "then we'll nail down the profile."

Ann hung up, thinking about Ivey, thinking that her aunt would've been 63 this year. She couldn't fight the chill, the irrationality of her thoughts. *Ivey's dead and gone*, she told herself. *Dead and gone. People saw him die.*

◆   ◆   ◆

After looking at the crime scene photos and police reports he received from Ann, Tony made some notes.

White male, aged 30–45, robust, neat appearance. May have known the victim on a casual basis, well enough so that he may have been able to approach her and lure her into a vehicle. Possibility of attempted sexual assault on victim, and when victim resisted, she'd been killed? No defense wounds. Didn't leave full fingerprints. Binding and rope tying suggests individual works well with his hands. Uses his hands in some sort of craft or hobby. Probably has a regular job. College level schooling. Suffers from some sort of paranoid psychosis. Acting out some sort of ritual. Probably suffered childhood trauma, most likely of a sexual nature. No sexual penetration. Perp has some sort of chronic sexual problem? Probably an avid reader of porn mags. Potentially divided personality. Multiple? Committed homicide in a predominantly white residential area. Not a transient. Lives in area. May try to inject himself into the investigation somehow. May try to be 'helpful.' Has sufficient strength; moved body from wooded area to field. Unknown suspect familiar with area and probably traversed it many times. Based on crime scene photos and police reports, perp is organized, logical, picked his victim and then stalked her. For now, he has some control over his mental illness. If he loses that control, his crimes will become more random, less organized, probably more violent and sexual in nature.

Tony paused, chewed pencil mid-air. He knew most sexual killers were below the age of 35, but he felt in his gut that this guy was older. Somehow, the guy had found a way to control his paranoia through his twenties and early thirties until it became so overwhelming that it had resulted in the recent killings. How? How had he managed that? And what had triggered it? *Or, perhaps victim wasn't the first.*

Tony also knew that some men with slight body types tended toward schizophrenia. Outdated thinking among many of his colleagues, but something that tended to be true. But this guy was built. He was strong. He'd carried the body from wherever he'd killed the victim and left it in the open. Introverted schizos didn't eat well, didn't think in terms of nourishment or appearances, so this guy was extroverted. Plus, the brazen nature of the killings. Introverts were usually slobs; no one wanted to live with them so they lived alone.

Tony started writing again.

Neat. Probably lives or has lived with someone. A girlfriend? A wife? Makes a good salary. Car will be neat and stylish—no leftover food wrappers or cigarette butts or empty soda cans—and an extension of his sexuality? Or lack of it?

He may have spent time in psychiatric facilities, either as a patient or a volunteer.

He dropped his pencil on his desk and took a sip of lukewarm coffee. Shit. It <u>did</u> sound like another Ivey. Except for the schooling. Maybe.

4

Ann stood in her backyard, watching a silver stream of water arc from the hose she was holding. She'd discovered she liked to garden, when she had the time, and she was determined to fix up the ramshackle yard, do some planting, make something take root. Gardening brought a sense of life and beauty, helped to keep her sane.

When she'd bought the house, the backyard was a tangle of weeds, wild flowers, and scraggly bushes. Her eyes fell on Nathan's cottage. Funny, it was *her* cottage, but she always thought of it as his—her tenant's, a recently divorced flight medic. It was 9 o'clock in the morning, and she didn't see his black Volvo in the graveled drive. A fresh breeze cooled her skin, and she reveled in the warmth of the sun. She wondered how he managed the trauma of being a flight paramedic, of seeing the broken bodies, the broken spirits. Did he do volunteer work? Go on late evening runs until his mind was emptied?

She handled the stresses of her own job by volunteering in women's shelters when she could. There were always the telltale bruises on the women's arms, the dark black circles of violence under their eyes. And the lies too—women so scared and so empty that they lied to themselves, even when there own children's safety was at stake.

There was the solid physical evidence they'd been abused—bruises in the shape of fingers, hands that had squeezed them so hard they left marks. And then the unpleasant chain of events would start—a child taken from the home for its own protection and placed in foster care. A child who loved its mother more than anything despite the physical abuse, the fearful environment, the trips to the emergency room. But often, her help at the shelter freed these women and gave them their dignity and safety back.

Sometimes, Ann wondered how she did what she did as medical examiner, exposed to violence and rage and death. But her need to help someone was greater than her need to look away. Helping the living took away some of the horror of helping the dead to speak.

Maybe that's how Nathan felt too. There was something mysterious and intense about him. Once upon a time, she would've thought that was a sexy quality in a man. Now, she thought sadly, that very same quality unnerved her.

Would she ever trust anybody again, after Peter, her soon-to-be ex-husband? She didn't want to be that kind of person, someone who didn't believe in love and happy endings anymore. She was determined that when it came to dating, all roads would not lead back to Peter. Truth be told, they weren't all bad experiences.

At first, Peter had been courteous, polite, a bit reserved and aloof. She'd turned him down the first few times he'd asked her out, not wanting to date a lawyer. And with his fast cars, fancy suits, and dimpled, sun-kissed smile, he was everything she thought she didn't want in a man. It all came back to a weak moment. Too much champagne, a handsome lawyer who said all the right things, the romantic skyline of New York, the panache of colorful lights on Broadway. And the fact that at age 32, she was tired of being alone, having to hold herself to different standards because she was a woman in a man's world. Tired of having people think she was a cold, hard-hearted bitch who threw herself into her work.

Her heart ached with the sorrow of it all, the betrayal. Things came back to her now, things she had subtly closed her eyes to while they were together. She had wanted so desperately to believe in their perfect lives, in the beauty and magic of his promises. But whenever they'd grabbed lunch together at a popular café or bistro, there were the knowing looks from attractive waitresses; the way he'd talked to them, casually flashing a quick smile and lowering his voice. And while Peter always wanted to go to glamorous parties and hobknob with high society, she preferred to stay home, slip on a pair of comfy sweats and a T-shirt, and curl up with a good book.

Maybe she was simply a conquest to him, and once she was caught in the snare of his charm, the game was over. But her best friend Beth and Peter, *together*? That was what caused her stomach to tighten into an ugly knot, the thought of them…of that other woman with the tattoos on her ankles…of what they were doing when she'd arrived home unexpectedly early from a conference. The images of naked limbs, hungry mouths and eager hands playing on the television in the bedroom and playing out on their <u>bed</u>.

Oh, there was the magical night he had proposed to her…they'd been dining at Alva, a Mom-and-Pop restaurant with a contemporary New York vibe and a sign that glowed softly with warm blue neon letters. It was between Broadway and Park Avenue, nestled in Manhattan's trendy Flatiron district. She'd had the Caesar salad while he'd had the duck.

An attractive young waitress with wheat-blonde hair down to her waist had waited on them. She remembered the appraising look the girl had given Peter, dressed in tan khakis and a black, short-sleeved shirt that showed off his tan to perfection, his finely sculpted arms. "Hi Peter," she'd said. "The usual tonight?" At the time, Ann hadn't thought anything of it; Peter moved in wide circles and knew a lot of people in different walks of life. He was easygoing and charming to them all, and earned people's trust quickly. The waitress had winked, looking at Ann. "So you're the lucky girl tonight," she'd said. Ann thought it was just something people said, just small talk. But now…it had a whole different meaning. *An intimate meaning. There were others.* And she'd thought Peter had taken her to a spot that was special, just for them.

He'd smiled crookedly at the waitress and, after she left, slid the little black velvet box across the table to Ann. He hadn't gone down on one knee to propose, hadn't said anything at first. Just smiled at her and took her breath away. What a fool she'd been. Then there'd been the hand-in-hand walks through Central Park, the mornings he'd wake her up by nuzzling her neck and saying erotic things to her…the bed sheets kicked eagerly to the floor in their haste to taste each other, feel each other; a leisurely cup of coffee afterward as the sun had streamed in their Upper East Side apartment window, glinting off her slender, gold wedding ring. Shaking herself free from her thoughts, Ann concentrated on the flowers, on making something neglected beautiful again.

A moment later, the silence was shattered by the ring of her cell phone. She clicked it on. "Ann Yang."

"Hi Ann, are you ready to be with me yet?"

Ann's body tensed. "You have the wrong number. You've reached the Medical Examiner."

"It's taken me a long time to find you. You have no idea. But we'll be together soon, I promise."

"Who is this? How did you get this number?"

"It wasn't hard. I know a lot of things about you. Like the way you smile, the way you flick your hair over your shoulder, the way you wear pain and fear in your eyes. Like when you read my letter."

A chill raced up her spine. The anonymous letter. The anonymous, threatening letter she'd found in her mailbox last week, before she started working the murder case. A note that read:

WE'RE WALKING THE SAME PATH. YOU WON'T SLIP AWAY FROM ME THIS TIME. YOU DON'T HAVE MUCH TIME FOR DREAMING.

Who would leave her a note like that? She remembered the creepy calls she used to get at her apartment in college. The caller always asked her what she was wearing, or *not* wearing. Probably just a frat boy. She told the caller once that she was recording him, and the calls had stopped.

There were people who resented her presence at work. Then there was her impending divorce. Maybe this was Peter's way of getting even with her. He couldn't have her back, so he was going to make sure she wasn't happy without him. He'd told her that himself, outside the courtroom, venom in the voice that had once caressed her with sweet words. As if he had any right to be angry!

"I could make it all better for you, Ann."

Did Peter put one of his friends up to this? First the letter, now the phone calls too?

"Do I know you?"

"We know some of the same people. Women who weren't who they pretended to be. Women who weren't you."

"Get lost, creep."

Disgusted, and shaking slightly, Ann cut the call off. Boy, she had been <u>really</u> wrong about Peter. If he had put someone up to crank-calling her now, and writing that letter, she hadn't known him *at all*.

As she was turning the dripping spigot off, she heard someone calling her from the front of the house. "Back here," she said, seeing Mark coming down the stone path carrying sketches under one arm, tools under the other. He was wearing faded jeans and a dark green T-shirt, a pencil stuck behind his ear, every inch the carpenter/artist type. Mark Russler did renovations and remodeling and came highly recommended through a friend of her sister's who worked in the ER at Doylestown Hospital. Ann had found a picture of the dining room of her home from the early 1900s and wanted to make it look like it did then, when Nell Schaffer and her family had lived there. Nell was a beautiful girl who disappeared without a trace in 1903; Ann had done some research on the house after buying it.

Ann's sister Bo had told her that Mark did volunteer nursing work with mentally ill patients. She had immediately felt a connection with him, having spent a lot of time counseling battered women who possessed similarly fragile mental states. Sometimes people weren't bad, they were just sick.

Mark was attractive in a non-threatening way, with medium brown hair and hazel eyes, a nice build. There seemed to be no arrogance about him at all—a refreshing change. She sensed he had wanted to ask her out, to dinner or something, but he didn't seem like the kind of guy who rushed things. He seemed more like the kind of guy who waited for the right moment.

He looked at the hose in her hand. "Sorry, didn't mean to intrude on your Monet moment." Ann smiled. She and Mark were both interested in art, and had discussed Monet in detail once while he worked in her dining room sawing and hammering and she worked in the living room, studying lab reports. In college, she had taken time off from her medical studies and spent a summer at Giverny, dabbling in her first love, writing, and photographing Claude Monet's gardens and his beloved French village. She had been taught that observation should be the key that unlocks the creative imagination, not the cage that traps it. It was something that had stuck with her; it was something Peter had never understood, her desire to create something beautiful with words, or with the flash of a camera, from what she saw around her.

Peter's keenest desires, she'd quickly learned, involved money, expensive play things like flashy boats and cars, tailored clothes, and being the best at absolutely everything he did.

At Giverny, before she'd met Peter, she'd stayed in the historic little village in a quaint stone cottage with terraced gardens on the side of the narrow, 1-mile-long rue Claude Monet. She'd photographed the historic Hotel Baudy, where Cezanne, Pissarro, and many of the famous American Impressionists had stayed. It was now a museum with a charming courtyard and an immense rose garden. In fact, several of her photos were framed and now adorned the walls of the house, including her favorite, a black-and-white photo of Monet's famous lily pond.

Mark looked at the pale blue morning sky, the white clumps of clouds shouldered together like a caucus. "Insanity. To be working inside on a day like today."

"If you don't have time today…"

Mark smiled. "For you, Ann, anything. Besides, the weather can change in an instant. They're calling for rain later this afternoon."

"If you're sure. If you have something more important, it can wait until next week."

"No way. Once I start something, I get obsessed with it, and I have to finish it. I don't feel satisfied until the last nail is hammered, the last wood shaving swept away. This is one of the most interesting projects I've had in a long time." His eyes lingered on her face and she felt a blush rising on her skin. Indeed, her dining room, with tools, wood, wires, and paint cans everywhere looked like a demolition derby had been run there. But Ann knew that was the sign of a true artist—you had to make a mess before you could clean it up.

"OK then. Hammer away. Can I get you a drink or something?"

He shook his head. "No thanks. I'll just get started."

His hands were full, so Ann held open the screen door for him and he went inside. Her eyes strayed to the agreeable width of his shoulders, the leanness of his waist; she'd noticed he hadn't shaved that morning, the dark whiskers that grazed his rugged jaw giving him an earthy appearance. She hadn't wanted to notice these things, but she did; she missed the feel of a man's rough cheek against her own, the feel of a man's lips exploring her own, the feel and taste of being with a man. *Fingers gliding over skin, forehead to collarbone to toes. Skin remembers every stroke, every abrasion.*

With determination, she hunkered down and began yanking large fistfuls of weeds out of the flowerbed, tossing them over her shoulder. She reveled in the feel of digging her fingers into the earth, of the warmth of the sun, of the cobweb-like patterns of the clouds, which had started to unravel. The way the sky was shifting, it made her think of her favorite painting with the melting clocks, *The Persistence of Memory*, by Salvador Dali. Soon, she'd lost herself in the physical exertion of gardening. As she heard Mark's hammer striking a nail, the bite of his saw in wood, she was glad she was a long way from the taxi-cluttered streets of New York, from the apartment they'd shared, a long way from Peter and the person she had been just a few short months ago. In fact, Ann realized, she didn't really know who she was anymore.

5

He sat outside at Starbucks, sipping a black coffee and watching. Watching and waiting. He felt friendless today, abandoned, adrift, restless. When he prayed, he no longer heard his mother's soft, pendent voice. What scared him even more was that he didn't hear his father's voice very much now either. Because *his voice*, that other voice, was getting stronger. His voice had risen above the others. And his voice was telling him to watch for her. His next victim.

He took a sip of coffee, feeling its bitter warmth reach deep down inside him, searching in vain for a quiet place in his head. It was Saturday. A woman pushed a child in a stroller. Teenagers with pierced noses and bellies roamed the streets. Couples in shorts, T-shirts, and sandals walked their dogs through town. *You know we're looking for her.*

The voice was like a hammer in his head.

Leave me alone.

He concentrated on watching the street signs change. *Walk. Don't Walk. Walk.* Green and red thoughts flashing in his mind.

"Hey man, can we use this chair?"

Startled, he nodded to the goth teenagers at the next table. It took two of them to drag the heavy black wrought-iron chair over to their table. Scrawny arms, pale skin, dyed black hair.

No, we want someone pure, the voice said.

I don't have to listen to you, he thought. *I* don't.

Her.

He focused on the girl on the corner, waiting to cross the intersection. She was slender, pretty, alone. She wore a pink T-shirt, khaki shorts, and sandals. Her black hair was roped into a ponytail.

Ann.

For a moment, he was very still as he watched her walk across the street. *No way.* He closed his eyes, sipped his coffee, hoping she would be gone when he opened them. The divergent thoughts in his mind created a spectacular fender-bender.

Go away!

The voice laughed.

So, you know her. You like her. Maybe even more than like her. She's the one.

He got up so quickly he nearly knocked his coffee cup over. There was one place he could go where the voices grew quiet. The church with the stained glass windows. He'd taken to calling it the church of the butterfly, because he felt enclosed in colorful wings whenever he went there. He liked the soft plushness of the pale blue carpets in the sanctuary, the way the sunlight streamed through the windows and fell on him in waves of consonance. He got up, ducked around the corner so Ann wouldn't see him, and started walking toward the church. But he had a funny feeling in the pit of his stomach. The voice knew about Ann.

He'd thought he'd tricked the voice into forgetting about her, forgetting about the first letter that voice had made him write to Ann, made him slip into her mailbox. He didn't *want* to write another one.

As he walked, he felt imperfect, like a piece of glass cut at the wrong angle, a sanctuary emptied of voices, a sharp convex of polluted thought. He rubbed his temple. Everything was familiar but out of place, out of focus. Ann did feel like truth in his soul. And no one else had ever come close to feeling like truth in his soul. But she didn't know who he really was.

Give it up, pony boy. She's milk and honey, the Promised Land, and you're starving. He walked faster.

It would be so easy. I've seen the way she looks at you. She wants you. You know what I mean. She wants you to touch her, everywhere, but she doesn't know it yet.

The thought should've been a warm one, but it was raw and biting, like he'd been physically cut by something sharp. Now he was in a flat-out run, careening alongside the black wrought-iron fences curling their tongues around a large cemetery. He thought he heard the voices of the dead whispering to him from the cracked, charcoal veins of the stones.

Stop. Stop! But he couldn't make them stop. By the time he reached the end of the gated cemetery, he was Kevin. He slowed to a leisurely walk, not sure why sweat glistened on the back of his neck and his arms.

He passed a church with colorful stained glass windows, windows that made him think of blood and baby soft sky. Kevin never prayed. He hated to pray. A smile slid to one side of his pale face. A fresh breeze seemed to propel him. He felt preternaturally confident he would find her today, the one who would wear the uniform.

He also felt dirty, sullied by the naïve thoughts of the other one who sometimes took over his mind. He thought of the mirror, the antique mirror into which he often gazed. It was in the back bedroom. It showed him things. It didn't judge him. It loved him back.

He couldn't fight it. He was dirty. He was bad. The wind came as a teasing caress on his back. He headed home. He knew where he was going and what he'd do next. He knew where to look for his next victim. *The clinic.*

6

Ann drove around for a while, not really sure where she was going. She drove through town, streetlights burning pleasantly, couples walking to a movie or a quiet dinner, traffic crawling through the small streets. A half-warm cup of coffee sat snugly in the cup holder; a half-eaten veggie sub, still in its wrapper, sat on the passenger seat. Turn the clock back, Ann. Why was Beverly Wilcox dead, and why had the killer left her body in such a public place, knowing she would be found? Humiliation? To taunt the investigators? At the very least, she knew it was a game to whoever had killed Beverly. A deadly game.

She kept driving; passed the courthouse. Shops were shutting down; chic little restaurants and cafes would be closing soon too.

Her stomach grumbled but she ignored it. The part of the sandwich she'd eaten sat in her stomach like a rock. She was feeling restless, edgy. The Jeep seemed to glide down Main Street in slow motion. Flashes of the murdered woman's face flickered in her mind. She approached Route 313 and turned right, suddenly knowing where she was going. Soon she found her car driving slowly down the tree-shadowed lane and stopping beside the huge, brawling outline of Fonthill Museum, the bark of the trees rough and pockmarked, reminding her of GI Joe in fatigues. The parking lot was dark; in the distance, at the bottom of the sloping field, she could see the yellow police tape twirling in the ghostlike breeze like a drunken ballerina. She trudged across the darkened field, aware of the monstrously huge curved blocks of cement at her back.

"Slow night, doc?" asked Jeremy Ganes, an old-school cop.

Ann nodded, slipping under the crisscrossed tape, lost in thought. She'd missed something, she was sure. The whole crime scene was so staged, so arrogant. She was sure it was here.

What was it?

The position of the body was still clearly marked. She scanned the dark woods, the canopy of leaves stretched like fabric over a head. Had the killer returned to the scene? Was he watching them now? She walked around the site, looking at where the body had been, from different angles. She hadn't died here, that much she knew.

Beverly, who killed you?

She closed her eyes and listened. A breeze waffled over her. It would've been nighttime when the killer dragged the body out of the clearing. She turned her back and scanned the dark woods again, still as a deer in headlights, then turned back and looked at the shadowy walls of the medieval-looking, concrete castle with its rounded corners and crevices. The museum had closed at 5 pm the day before Beverly's body had been found. She walked down the muddied path flanked by towering ivy-covered trees that seemed to glimmer and shed light until she reached the old stone building that had been part of the original grounds. The walls were inked with graffiti; rusted iron bars covered the window. There was some mystery as to the original purpose of the building, and standing there alone, looking up at it—WHO LEARNS WILL LOVE AND NOT DESTROY THE EARTH THE FLOWERS AND THE JOY—Ann shivered. Behind the wooded building, one would eventually reach East Street and the Acme supermarket. Peering through the iron bars, Ann could just make out some of the graffiti: *This place sucks Harm's balls; 4 Gangs; Blow Me.* Typical teenager stuff. There was an empty paper coffee cup on the floor and shards of broken glass. Ann turned and walked back up the small path to the edge of the field. It was a deliberate staging of the body. Ann had been taught to look in the opposite direction from the one the perpetrator wanted you to look in.

She thought about the museum. There were eleven different ways to enter and exit Fonthill; she knew because she had toured it on several occasions. Walking through it, she had seen how its rooms literally sweep into each other with a surprise at every turn; Mercer's use of natural light throughout the castle was a marvel. Popular tours at Fonthill include the "Behind the Scenes" tour, in which you get to climb up Fonthill's tower and explore back passageways. The kitchen, servants' quarters, crypt, and terrace pavilion are open for the guided tour. You had to pre-register for the tours. She made a note to get a hold of that list, although he could've signed any name to it.

She imagined a few scenarios, including the killer dumping the body in the woods, then seeing the façade of the museum. He decides to casually tour it right before it closes, excited by the fact that Beverly's body lay in the woods nearby. He probably took his time, blended in, and then when the tour was over, slipped out one of the exits to the woods. Where he waited.

Mercer lived like a hermit, didn't like to be photographed, took a couple of naps each day, and preferred riding his bicycle instead of driving a car. The early 1900s. Simpler times.

The killer had then hauled the body to the edge of the field, relinquishing his prize to the world. Was he somebody she knew? The killer wasn't a professional.

She was certain of it. Yet, there had been no fingerprints other than the victim's. What was she missing? She stepped over where the body had been; saw in her mind Beverly's bulging eyes as dark and empty as the night sky. It had appeared that he hadn't taken anything as a souvenir. Her diamond ring had sparkled on her lifeless finger. Matching earrings glittered untouched in her earlobes. Was it Shakespeare who wrote, "Yet hath my night of life some memory, my wasting lamps some fading glimmer left?"

Leaves rustled above her. The wind picked up. Ann went back to her car for a flashlight and headed back into the woods. She lined up a spot based on one of the windows of the museum, a window that faced the woods. After about 15 minutes, she grew frustrated. She changed direction, fanning out to the right side of the field. She nearly tripped over something and swore.

Jesus. It couldn't be.

She called to Jeremy. "Get your ass over here."

The burly, middle-aged cop came lumbering in, looking annoyed. The look turned incredulous and a blush washed up his pimpled throat and ruddy cheeks. On the opposite edge of the muddy field near the parking lot were tire tracks. "Shit, how'd we miss those?"

Ann then pointed to the base of a tree at pieces of broken taillight. "Could be teenagers were out here necking. Or it could be something else. Call the crime scene unit and get them out here."

7

Touching, embracing, biting. Stroke her labia. Locate her G
Spot by inserting your middle finger into the vagina, placing it against
the anterior wall, and making a tickling gesture.

Ann sat down and took a sip of coffee. It was late. The wind jounced the branches of trees outside her house; she heard its low moan and curl against the windowpanes. A storm was coming. After an exhausting day, and another late-night phone conversation with her divorce lawyer, Ann wanted nothing more than to sink into the contours of the plush white sofa in the living room, snuggled under her favorite tattered blanket. The sofa was her only piece of lush furniture—an extravagance in an otherwise conservative and pleasant room. She so desperately needed sleep.

Instead, she had changed into sweats, made coffee, donned slippers, and grabbed a box of things she'd found in the attic, leftover from some previous tenant. She was still cleaning out the attic bit by bit, when she had the time.

Through the window, she could see the little cottage at the end of the drive and wondered what Nathan was doing. Was he home, or had he been called to the scene of another accident? She thought about Mark. She wondered if he was attracted to her.

She also wondered why she was surrounded by divorced men—Nathan and Mark were both divorced. Nathan had offered up all the details of his; she'd heard about Mark's divorce from her sister Bo. No one knew anything about Mark's wife. He never talked about her.

There was a light on in the upstairs window of the cottage, but maybe Nathan had left it on and gone out. It was really dark at the back of the property. She felt comforted having a male close by, though she didn't like to admit it. She resisted a strong urge to pick up the phone and invite him to join her for coffee. Distracted from the box by the newspaper, she opened it and started to read. Her eyes fell immediately on the article about Beverly Wilcox; she hadn't wanted to speak with the reporter. Bare facts. That's what she'd given him.

Woman Found Near Fonthill Woods was Murdered

The woman whose body was found in the field behind the Fonthill Museum Wednesday was murdered, the county medical examiner ruled yesterday. An autopsy showed that she had been strangled and had several broken ribs. The woman was identified by police yesterday as Beverly Wilcox, 58, of Main Street, Doylestown, who had been missing since early on May 31. Police said the body had been lying near the woods behind the museum for several hours before it was discovered by a man walking his dog.

Friends who knew her said yesterday that the wealthy, recent divorcee had been very active in supporting hospitals specializing in the treatment of men and women suffering from addiction to alcohol and drugs and from mental conditions like schizophrenia. Wilcox had donated $15,000 to a local treatment facility. Friends also stated that she herself had been in drug rehab as recently as last Christmas. "Like other chronic diseases, treatment is effective, but there is no 'cure,'" Wilcox stated in an Intelligencer *article last fall. "Addiction is a chronic disease caused by the interaction of biological, psychosocial, and environmental factors. You are always at risk for relapse and recovering individuals need to understand that total abstinence from all psychoactive substances is essential to maintain sobriety. Hospitals and help groups are really, really important."*

Wilcox's body was found in the green country behind Fonthill, the former home of industrialist Henry Mercer. She was fully clothed and a brass button with an eagle, presumably Union from the Civil War, was found beneath her tongue.

Fuck. How had the reporter gotten that information? Ann hadn't wanted anyone to make the button public. Someone did. She threw the paper down and began to dig through the box she'd found in the attic. It was labeled "miscellaneous/cottage." She'd been going through boxes, getting the place cleaned up and organized. She'd gone through the box yesterday but hadn't really had the time to look at everything. She pulled a few things out and saw what appeared to be an old cigar box tacked shut. Gingerly, she removed the tacks and opened it. It contained a small, leather-bound diary. Gold-lettered initials were scratched in the lower right-hand corner. *FN.* And the year *1902.* Ann shivered. One hundred years ago, a beautiful girl named Nell had disappeared from the house without a trace. A teenager named Farrell Neff had been blamed and executed. Had Farrell kept a diary about Nell before she disappeared? Before he died? *FN.* But why would it be in the house?

She opened it, half afraid to read the dead boy's thoughts. It was sewn together with thread and was falling apart, the first few pages containing ink that had run in jagged fingers of time and regret—hard blue streaks that became faint at the bottom of the pages. Touching the pages she began to read and felt the house almost vibrate with unseen energy.

April 2, 1902

Did you ever want something so much it hurt? I know it's wrong, but I can't help it. The first time I saw her, standing in a circle of her friends, books in hand, her blonde hair dampened slightly from the rain, I was enthralled. She didn't notice me at first. I watched her like a crow watches a shiny piece of ribbon, noting the slant and angle of her green eyes, the soft curl of her upper lip when she laughed. Watched her like other boys watch her. I think it was the cigarette I was smoking that caught her attention. I can smoke in public and people don't think it's out of character. My father, after all, is a low-life who used to shuttle people back and forth underneath the ashtray-silver skies in his coaches. That was before he became interested in farming. It doesn't matter. I'm still trash, low-class, wrong side of the tracks. I've been smoking since I was 15; my father doesn't care. Not every day, because I think it's a disgusting habit, but selectively. More than anything, I just like the sound of the match striking into flame, the tip of the cigarette glowing angry red.

We are both 16 and go to the same school. People watch her all the time; I drift in and out of the classrooms and hallways like a shapeless shadow. I scratch my letters out and add my sums and find it all so engineered. There has been nothing in this place for me—until now.

It started to rain harder and her friends scattered to the safety and warmth of their gingerbread homes like pins coming loose from thick hair. I stood in the rain, smoking and staring at her. Slowly, she crossed the street, attracted by the bright glow of the cigarette.

"Hi, I'm Nell."

I looked at her clothes, the snow-white pearls clasped delicately about her neck, her smooth skin. She was tall and slender, her waist cinched in beneath a pleated pale blue skirt with a single ruffle at the hem. She wore a matching tailored blouse and expensive shoes with dainty buttons on the sides. She looked around furtively, then at my cigarette. "May I?"

I nodded my head and watched, fascinated, as her pink lips closed around the cigarette, trying to coax the smoke into her rebellious, virginal lungs. She coughed, daintily covering her mouth and handing back the cigarette. "I've seen you in school. Are you going to tell me your name?"

I did. We walked along the street for a while, both of us silent but somehow knowing that by breathing the same air, we had changed something. We started a friendship that day. I think she knew from the very beginning that I would understand things about her that her rich and polite friends never would.

I want her all to myself. She is cool composure while I am practiced vapidness, milk-and-water trying to be wine. I wonder if she knows I watch her all the time.

April 9, 1902

It's been a week since we spoke. I've lived in each and every word as if it were one of her hand-me-down sweaters. What did I expect? She didn't notice me in school. It was as if the moment we shared curled to the edge of her memory and evaporated like the smoke of the cigarette we exchanged.

It's an experiment. It's not over yet. I know that. She'll grow bored of her rich friends, of the people who try to find a polite way into her thoughts. I know something about her that she doesn't know. Not yet.

I stare at her back as she moves righteously down the hall. She is used to admiring glances, used to attention. She barely notices it. I wonder how she would feel if people suddenly stopped staring at her glorious hair, her perfect face, her deep green eyes?

She doesn't realize we're all experiments. My father used to drive dusty stagecoaches. Then it was trolleys hammering down the tracks. Now he's a farmer who can't grow a potato or a turnip to save his life. I was 7 when I realized that's what I was to my parents—an experiment. My father keeps things in glass jars in the basement. Odd things like bugs and liquids and parts of machinery, all neatly labeled and dated. My mother rarely speaks—she walks around mechanically folding towels and linens, cooking dinners, washing dishes, always scrubbing. She gets packets of something from The Saint James Society, and when she gets one of her headaches, she takes the packets and disappears into her room for days.

When I was little, I went into my father's basement one day and took a jar off one of the lower shelves. I smashed it on the cold concrete floor. I had 5 more smashed before they both came running, looking like scared animals. I had cuts on my fingers and my arms. I urinated, the amber liquid dousing my trousers and puddling around my bare feet, curling around shards of glass.

My mother's brown eyes floated in a skull of incomprehension. She rubbed her temples. 'Why did we ever have a child?' she asked my father. Then she turned and went to her bedroom, experiencing one of her headaches that lasted three days. My father looked at me and I could see him mentally taking notes, probably thinking about all the different angles at which the glass had shattered and counting how many new jars he would have to buy and what to put in them. He took me upstairs and bandaged my cuts, then went back downstairs. He didn't say anything. I heard his broom sweeping up the glass that I had burst and shattered, and I knew then that here were two people who should not have had a child. I watched from the top of the stairs as he swept, knowing that he was neatly sweeping pieces of me into that corner. Nell's father is a doctor. She has sisters. They laugh and talk with each other. I wonder, which is more beautiful? A piece of splintered glass hit by an unexpected prism of sunlight, or a whole jar sitting in the darkness, never knowing it could be shattered in an instant by a small hand?

April 13, 1902

The most amazing thing happened today. Friday the Thirteenth. Is that significant? I'm not usually superstitious. Nell was heading to class when she must have seen me slip out a side door. I am good at cutting class—my teachers have given up on me. They don't see any reason to contact my parents about my absences anymore. What's the use? I'll never make anything of myself.

I walked, lighting a cigarette, and watched the gold-bronze of the afternoon shift into ruby smoke, portending a storm. That's when I heard footfalls behind me. I turned, startled, to see her. Watching me. I turned and walked across the field, framed by the stickly bones of trees coiling high into the air, until I came to my favorite spot. A wide fallen log at the edge of nowhere where I can sit and look out over my empty domain. I sat down. She did too.

I took a drag and handed her the cigarette. She took a puff, then coughing, handed it back, looking out at the field, trying to see what I was seeing.

"You shouldn't smoke. It's a bad habit," she said.

"Don't you have any bad habits?" I asked.

"I…yes, I guess so." She was silent for a moment. "Why do you come here?" she asked.

"Why shouldn't I?"

"There's nothing here."

"I see everything here," I responded.

"People think you are strange," she said.

I laughed, the sound rattling up through my throat like it was an unused rusty cage.

"People think you're beautiful."

Though the day was chilly, I was beginning to sweat. My hands felt damp. I stared at her profile as she looked out across the fields. I ground out my cigarette with the heel of my boot.

I placed my hand over hers. She was startled, but she didn't move away, as I thought she would. She just kept staring at our fingers. I laced them together. She met my gaze and I saw in her green eyes all the decorated Christmas trees I had never had, the backyards green with summer I would never play in, the sweeping, lawn-lined streets where I would never live.

"Why did you do that?" she asked.

"I don't know," I replied. "I just wanted to touch you."

We sat there holding hands, me a study in fawning humility, she a stone statue.

Then she broke free like a spark jumping from a fire and I watched her walk haughtily away until she disappeared into the square structure that was our school. Was she starting to splinter? Did she feel what I felt the moment our skin touched?

April 14, 1902

I don't bother her in school. It's not that I'm ashamed of myself. It's just not the thing to do. I have no desire to step into a shallow pool; I've grown accustomed to the reckless, deep walls of my own poisoned well.

What a glorious Saturday. I found myself on the trolley today, heading to Willow Grove Park. I was surprised when she sat down next to me, alone, not saying a word. Eventually we reached Philadelphia. I enjoyed her nearness; I was excited by the proud way people stared at her. Soon we were north of Philadelphia in a crowd of well-dressed ladies and men departing the trolleys, descending the stairs, and walking through the tunnels that had been dug under Easton Road. There's an inscription above the door to one of the two tunnels:

For myriad souls this is the shrine—The temple of the art divine.

Emerging from the tunnels, we walked by lakes to the park entrance, bulwarked by a giant clown sign, and were greeted by the sights and sounds of the amusements and the massive Music Pavilion—atop which colorful flags whipped and snapped in the breeze. I couldn't help but think as we came out of the darkness into the light, that some things begin where they end.

It was warm and a band was playing. "Do you want to see the fountain?"

She nodded. "I've never been here before." I looked at her in amazement.

"Come on. I'll show you around." We raced to the electric fountain. It was next to the lake and the Music Pavilion. As notes squirted out of trumpets and trombones, water sprayed in multicolor magic from the fountain—creating rainbow claws that grabbed at air and shadow and shimmering strains of floating, bobbing sound—a band of color, a curved prism of joy. In that moment, she was pure acoustics, bouncing off my paper-thin walls.

After the fountain, I have two favorite things in the park, one of which isn't even considered an attraction. The old weeping willow with its branches drooping about it like a giant grass mantle—a crabgrass turtle. It looks like a nosey old man bent down with age. The other is the giant boat shaped like a white swan. It holds about 10 people as it glides across the silvery waters.

The crowds were thickening, so we took a ride in the big swan. As I sat absorbing the plated reflections of the water and watching her, I remembered something I'd read once. Swans can be shape-shifters, creatures of water, earth, and air. They can also take human form but can always be recognized by having a gold or silver chain around the neck. I read something about Hinduism, that the Ham Sa, "that pair of swans," depict perfect union—they are breath and spirit. As my father says, I know a lot of useless, trivial things. I couldn't help but feel, as the light breeze leaned on the waters and the sun caught her beauty at every angle, that I was breath and she was spirit.

We rode several more rides, then sat in a gazebo and talked for a little while. To tell you the truth, I don't really remember what we talked about. It was inconsequential compared to what came next.

I know the names of lots of trees. Isn't that strange? I've always liked trees because they're old and sturdy and sprout up everywhere—the edges of vacant lots, the middle of yards, the tops of mountains and hills. They are born on the wind and have no boundaries. But I wasn't thinking about the multitude of oak, beech, ash, dogwood, Oriental plane, tulip, poplar, or Japanese maples scalloping the park as we sat in the car that would take us through the Unique Coal Mine. The ride is an exact reproduction of the St. Nicholas Mine, and St. Nicholas, Pennsylvania. A view of the Mahony Plane is painted on the outside, showing the other big breakers, the culm banks, the miners' homes in the foreground and the mountains in the distance.

Nell and I sat close as the coal car rattled through the breaker. There weren't many people on it. I watched mechanical figures, miners, with burning lamps in their caps, digging coal. Several stopped to glance at us. Others worked away obliviously. Farther on we saw a mine mule stable, then a realistic scene of a mine explosion. It is all staged mechanically, but looks so real.

I still don't know why I did it. In the darkness, in the fake explosion of the mine, I leaned over and kissed her. My lips were sloppy and groping at first, hers rigid and surprised. She pulled away, as I expected, but I could feel her energy, her shock, her curiosity. Before she could ask me why, I did it again, this time coaxing her lips to relax into mine, the coal car vibrating our bodies into an acute awareness of each other. It was over too quickly; the ride was coming to an end. As we exited, we both breathed erratically, as if we had been through an explosion ourselves. Neither of us spoke as we made our way back to the park entrance. I couldn't resist popping into the Mirror Maze, and wondered if she would follow me or abandon me. She followed.

As we bounced and lengthened, thickened and then stretched like taffy in the glass, I wondered if she liked what she saw. Did she realize the old Nell was gone forever? The mirrors joined us together so that you could not tell where one began and the other ended. For one brief, fantastic moment, I saw myself reflected in her eyes. For one brief, arrogant moment, I was an object of affection, loved by someone beautiful; I was Nell.

As we were leaving the park, it was nearly dark. We could see the electric fountain. At night, it's even more magnificent—the concealed electric lamps jettisoning sprays of tinted rainbows into clouds of dancing iridescent mist. I can't write anymore just now. I'm afraid she will turn away from what she experienced, turn away from something beautiful as if it were ugly, tight behavior…turn it out as if it were a leftover square of fabric for which there is no use except to patch up something that's coming apart.

8

He hung up the phone and smiled. The old man had been an easy pushover. It hadn't taken long to find a buyer for the car, a 1978 two-tone edition of the Eldorado Custom Biarritz Classic with a flashy paint scheme of Arizona Beige and Demitasse Brown and dark brown accent striping. He wasn't surprised the old man wanted to buy it. You could learn so much about people without really even trying.

He'd advertised the car on eBay, the man freely chatting with him by e-mail, telling him about his son, how much he missed him, and how he would love to have the car because his son had driven one like it. His son had died years ago and the man's memory was fading. He didn't want to forget him.

He made calls like this one from Jeannie's phone. Or from pay phones. It was safer. The buyer was two states away. He'd enjoy one last ride in it, remembering how the woman from Doylestown had looked when she'd realized they weren't going to a fancy restaurant for dinner and drinks, when she'd started to get really scared. Then he'd hand it over to the old man with no worries.

He sat down on the frayed toast-colored couch. Well, at least her kid wasn't home from school yet. A tattered pink teddy bear and a wool blanket lay rumpled at one end of the couch. A fashion magazine lay open on the Formica end table. Dirty dishes were piled in the sink in the kitchenette; an opened jar of instant coffee sat on the counter. Jeannie's half-filled mug sat by the small microwave. She was a regular fucking Martha Stewart. He felt one of his headaches coming on and bellowed for her. "Bring me some goddamn aspirin, will you?"

He didn't care that she was sleeping after working a 14-hour shift at the mini-mart. "And bring me a beer while you're at it."

Several moments later a short, thin woman with circles beneath her large dark eyes emerged from the bedroom. It was a tiny, two-room basement apartment; he dropped in whenever he liked and always unannounced. Her daffodil-blonde hair was mussed, the dark roots beginning to show; her cotton nightgown was faded and worn. She carried a half-empty bottle of aspirin in one hand and a can of Miller Lite in the other.

She handed them to him. "That piss again?" He cracked open the can of beer, grabbed a few aspirin, and popped them into his mouth. He swallowed the pills with his beer.

She'd retrieved the can from the small refrigerator in the bedroom. She didn't drink, so she always bought the cheapest beer for him. And always cans, never bottles. That left more room in the fridge.

He put the bottle of aspirin down.

"You look like shit, Jeannie. Why don't you buy yourself a new nightgown or something?"

"Because I spent my paycheck on your beer."

He stood up and she took a step back.

"Are you talking back? You don't want me to make you wear the uniform, do you?"

Silently, she shook her head. The bruises he had left on her arms and legs last week were now a blue-brown-yellow braid of ugliness across her skin. "You know what happens when you talk back."

"I'm sorry," she whimpered. She knew what she had to do—what she always had to do to make it up to him.

Sometimes he would disappear for days, and she found herself hoping he would never come back, that he'd forgotten about her. When she'd first met him, she'd thought she'd hit the jackpot as far as men go. He was attractive, well dressed, and, she'd thought, way out of her league. He had money. She'd thought that if they fell in love, they could have a nice place uptown, with a real dining room and a fenced-in yard and pretty wallpaper on the walls. That was months ago. She'd been depressed, and he'd taken her out to a few fancy places for dinner. He'd bought her a fancy outfit or two. Money and friends had been in short supply since she'd left her family on the West coast more than twelve years ago, and she wouldn't go crawling back to them. She lived in a basement that was always cold and she was lucky if she got to enjoy a decent meal once in a while. But she'd actually had it good then—before she'd met *him*. Before he made her wear that uniform, the one she wasn't supposed to tell anybody about. It was hot and it made her itch. And when she put it on, he got an odd light in his eyes. It was old, from some war or something, missing a button or two, and it gave her the creeps.

Maybe someday she'd have the courage to move out, to leave. But for now, she just didn't have the strength. As she turned and walked silently into the bedroom, she imagined she was some place else. She didn't think about what was going to happen. Sometimes she thought he would kill her. And now there was Katy to think about. Her world was closing in on her.

He followed her in, shutting the door behind him. The space heater in the tiny room glowed red beside a pile of dirty laundry. Even in the summer she had it on because it was so damp and chilly. He looked at the walls. She'd done more drawings. Mostly simple stuff—butterflies, horses, puppy dogs, the Pisces sign. The stupid shit fancied herself an artist.

Jeannie braced herself as he took a swig from the can and began to undo his pants. Silently, she said a prayer, and thanked God Katy wouldn't be home from school for a few hours. Hopefully, he would be gone by then. She drew her nightgown over her head, discarding it on the pile of clothes, removed her panties, and kneeled naked on the carpet in front of him, careful to avoid the frayed patches where the concrete poked through.

"No, jack me off first."

She was so tired. She had to be back at work in a few hours. She thought back to a time when she was a little girl, when her mother still smiled and called her Ethel Jean. Nobody called her Ethel Jean anymore. The world was like a big, shiny diamond then, a glittering jewel to be slipped onto her finger and enjoyed, beautiful and full of promise. Now she saw it for what it was—a crumpled paper bag, an empty wrapper thrown in the trash—a thin brown dream in the dirt. And it tasted bad.

9

Katy sat on the hard black plastic chair in the ER waiting room, her arms crossed over her chest, her head bent low. She hugged herself as she rocked back and forth. Her mother was going to be all right, she was going to be fine! She had to be because Katy had no one else.

Occasionally, a nurse came over and said something kind or asked her if she wanted a cup of water or a soda. Katy just shook her head and kept rocking. A mother, father, and crying infant came through the doors, the mother and father looking flushed and worried. A man with a bloody towel wrapped around his hand sat in one of the chairs waiting to see a surgeon. She'd heard him matter-of-factly explaining to the nurse that he'd been working under a car and somehow the jack had come loose and the car fell, smashing one of his thumbs to a pulp. Same thing happened two years ago, he'd said.

Squares of greasy yellow light and fractious shadow danced feverishly on the walls; her mind didn't seem to want to work. She'd come home to their apartment after walking into town to get an ice cream cone. Her mother sometimes left her some pocket change on the counter. It was right under the cabinet where her mother kept all her pills, the same pills that made her sleep like a rock, made her eyes look sad and far away. Pills with funny names that began with "P" or "D". It made her so mad. Her mother was young and pretty. Sometimes, she just wanted to take all the prescription bottles and toss the blue and white and pink pills in the trash, or flush them down the toilet, watch the colors make cotton candy streaks in the water.

She had looked in on her mother first, who was in bed, watching TV. "I'm going to get an ice cream," she said. "You want to come? You want anything?"

"No thanks honey."

Those had been her mother's last words to her, before…

Vaguely, Katy became aware of someone speaking to her. She tilted her big blue eyes up to the face and watched the nurse's mouth moving, but it was so hard to concentrate, so hard when she kept seeing it all, over and over again, in her mind.

"Dear, are you sure you don't have an aunt, a cousin, a friend, someone we can call, someone who can be with you here?"

No one, no one. And if her mother…No, she wouldn't think about it.

She pointed to the policeman they'd sent to her house after she dialed 9-1-1. He was getting a drink of water from the water cooler. He was tall and had a big red mustache. After her father had died last year, and she'd come to live with her mother, a mother she hardly knew, things had gone from bad to worse. They lived in a basement apartment where it was always cold and smelled like cigarettes. She didn't even have her own bed but slept on the couch. Her mother served her things like Pop-tarts and crackers with Cheese-wiz for dinner, *when* she served it. Sometimes it was a candy bar and a diet Dr. Pepper. She couldn't count on breakfast when she got up, not even milk or orange juice. She and her dad had lived close to the beach. She missed the feel of the sand in her toes, the symphonic sound of sea hitting beach, the cool ocean breezes tugging on her long hair, the warm feel of her dad's hand in hers as they walked the beach looking for shells and tiny crabs. Her dad had always taken such good care of her; he always made her favorite things for dinner, made sure she had healthy snacks like fruit and didn't watch too much TV. He'd said he'd always be there for her but he'd died. When she was eleven.

"Can I talk to <u>him</u>?" she asked the nurse.

"Sure, honey." She patted Katy's arm and went to speak with Tim. Soon, he was sitting next to Katy.

"You're a very brave little girl," he said. "You probably saved your mother's life dialing 9-1-1."

Katy felt hope stir in her breast. "You mean…she'll live?"

Tim always hated these questions, especially when they came from a child. He didn't want to lie; he wanted there to be some truth in the answer. "Well, she's not out of the woods yet, but I think she'll live."

Katy lowered her head, a mass of shiny blonde curls. Then she wiped at a tear. "Why did she have to take all those pills? I mean, didn't she know they could kill her?"

Tim gently pushed one of her long, blonde curls off of her forehead. His heart was aching for the little girl. He had a daughter himself.

"Sometimes people make mistakes. She might have forgotten how many pills she'd already taken."

"That must be it, because she wouldn't *really* want to…I mean, why would she…"

Tim grasped her slender hands in his. "Listen, they're taking good care of your mom. And we're going to take good care of you, too. If you want to, you can visit with my family for awhile. My daughter Crystal is about your age. She doesn't have any brothers or sisters and I know she'd enjoy your company. We'll have to go to the station first and straighten it out though." He didn't say, *at least until Child Welfare or Protective Services figured it out.*

Katy felt a dam break inside her. She missed her dad so much. She yanked her hands away and started sobbing uncontrollably. "Don't lie to me! She wanted to die! She wanted to die because…of me!"

Tim looked startled. "Katy, I'm sure that's not…"

Katy pulled a crumpled piece of lined notebook paper out of her jeans pocket. Oh God, the paper had come from one of *her own* school notebooks. "It is," she said quietly. "I found this by her bed. I forgot about it when…when the ambulance came and took her away."

Absently, she wiped her dripping nose on her sleeve and handed him the piece of paper. "Nobody wants me. Not even my own mother. She would rather be dead than keep living with me."

Carefully, Tim put his arm around her, tender yet affectionate. He smoothed the paper out. "You said you found this beside her bed?"

"It was on the floor, like she wrote it and then let it slip out of her hand or something. Ever since…ever since I came to live with her she's been sad. The counselor at school told me she was depressed."

"You know how people get sick sometimes?"

Katy nodded.

"Well, sometimes people can get sick mentally. They can get confused, do things they don't mean to do," he said gently.

"I think she did mean to do it. And it was because of *him.*"

"Who, honey?"

Katy just hugged herself tighter, rocking again. *No, she shouldn't say anything more. He would know. Somehow he would know. And then he would come after her.*

Tim stroked Katy's back softly while he read the note.

Dear Katy,

I'm sorry. This will be yucky for you but then I'll be gone and you'll forget all about me. I'm no good. There is something wrong with me that can't be fixed. I wasn't meant to be a mother. I wasn't meant to be a wife. I wasn't meant to be loved. But I hope you will find love. You're a beautiful girl. A beautiful secret I kept for so long. I never thought I would see you again. I'm not a strong person. I'm weak. I'm sure it was a shock for you to find out who your mother was, to see how I live. Don't ever think I don't love you. I do. It's just not enough. I'm beat up, bent, damaged as a doornail. All my love, Jeannie

God, such things for a child to read. She hadn't signed the note "Mom." Just "Jeannie."

"Oh Katy, I'm sorry," Tim said. "Sometimes people get so sad and they think there's no hope, no one to help them. But I promise I'm going to help you and your mom." Katy looked up at him, a tangled shadow of fear and tears brimming in her eyes. "Was your mother afraid of someone?" he asked.

But Katy had retreated into her own world again. She thought of the butter-flies, horses, and puppies, the colorful drawings in her mom's bedroom. "Will you take me home?"

Tim had been patrolling nearby when the call had come over the radio. "Possible overdose," the dispatcher said. "Twenty-nine-year-old female." Possible overdose didn't tell you much. Not what was taken, the level of consciousness, the respiratory status. Officers often accompanied paramedics to overdose calls for adults because of the likelihood of an unpredictable situation. Mike, another officer with broad shoulders and bushy, black hair, was waiting at the front door to the apartment building when he arrived.

"Little girl called 9-1-1," he said. "Her mom wasn't moving and she couldn't wake her up."

Inside, as the paramedics worked over the woman and then loaded her into the ambulance, Tim tried to distract the girl. He learned she had just turned twelve. She had gone downtown for ice cream, then stopped at the book shop, lost track of time skimming through a Harry Potter book and *The Last of the Really Great Wangdoodles*, and came home to find her mother unconscious. She squeezed the ears of a tattered pink teddy bear her father had given her as she talked, the bright pink nail polish on her fingers chipped. She loved books, she told Tim, but her mother didn't have a lot of money, so she went to the book-store and read them in chapters, sitting in the aisles. She'd had shelves of her own books at her dad's house, all sitting neatly on bookshelves her dad had painted himself the color of eggshell.

She'd gone with Tim in the police cruiser to the hospital. Now, looking around at the apartment again, Tim was struck by the shadows, the sadness, the sour smells of despair and hopelessness. It was sparse—not much furniture. A couch, an end table. Dirty dishes. The bedroom contained a lumpy mattress, a space heater, and piles of dirty laundry. Several thick art pencils lay on the floor beneath the wall with the drawings. Empty beer cans littered the bedside. Empty prescription bottles. Empty *life*.

"Where's your cat?" he asked Katy.

"She's not a cat. Patches is a kitten. She's probably hiding in the closet. I'll see if I can coax her out. Kevin kicked her once. That's why she hides in the closet."

"Who's Kevin?"

"He's sort of my mom's boyfriend. He makes her buy him beer and he…hits her sometimes."

She went into the back bedroom and he heard her rummaging in the closet. She came out with Patches, a tiny calico kitten with white paws, clinging to her arm. She rubbed Patches' head.

"I'm sorry," Tim said. "You know, your mother can register a complaint against him, get an order for protection from the police."

Katy's eyes brightened. "She can?"

"Yes. When she's better, I'll talk to her about it personally." He looked at the small girl whose only companion from her previous life seemed to be a pink, stuffed bear. "You know, Katy, we don't live in this world by ourselves. You can count on me." She brushed a tear from her cheek and nodded her head.

He folded the suicide note and put it in his pocket for the time being.

After they'd put Patches' food and litter box in the backseat of the cruiser, they drove off. Tim thought of the girl's mother, lying unresponsive on the mattress, her dark, unkempt hair obscuring her face. When did people stop living? When did they lose the ability to cope? When the heartache turned to shadows? Some died long before their hearts or livers or lungs gave out, he thought sadly.

He called his wife to tell her they might be having a dinner guest, knowing she would understand, and to make sure they had ingredients on hand to make extra cheesy lasagna for dinner and chocolate chip muffins, Crystal's favorite. That was something Crystal and Katy could do together. And it would keep Katy's mind occupied with other things, if only for a short while.

Tim felt angry at Jeannie for the destruction she'd caused, the terrible damage she'd done, the hurting of her small child. Like a pebble tossed into still waters, rippling outward, he wondered how far her mother's act would reach into Katy's soul. And then he felt guilty for being angry with someone who was so sad she just wanted to die. The paramedics carried many different drugs in their med boxes and Tim knew that the drug Narcan had pulled Jeannie out of a respiratory depression caused by the overdose. But who would pull her soul out of the pool of despair it was swimming in?

10

Students warming up on the stadium track in the early fog-shrouded morning had found her. They stood around awkwardly in their tattered sweatshirts, shorts, and sneakers, their gym class now a gawking session.

The killer was telling them—telling her—it was all a game. And he'd decided the best way to get his point across was to leave the body in a high school football stadium.

The body of the graceful twenty-one-year-old was draped over the bleachers, fifth row up, home team's side. For some reason, Ann was reminded of ballerinas and bleached white cinematography. A feeling of raw hopelessness and anger settled in the pit of her stomach. She knew already what she was going to find. Another public place. The wallet close by. It was a weekday, and there were 800 or so high school students in the building, going to classes, catching up on gossip, sneaking cigarettes in the bathroom, getting ready for their next classes.

The killer was getting bolder. Yellow police tape swathed the bleachers and part of the track. Cops and crime scene technicians crawled about like hungry ants marching toward crumbs. Cameras flashed silver light in gray fists of fog. Ann felt the sweat glistening on her neck.

She felt sick as she looked at the young body, clad only in a T-shirt and underpants. Sandals on her tanned feet. Tiny silver earrings in the shape of stars dangled from her ears. Friends remembered she had been dressed in a white T-shirt, a tie-dyed skirt, and sandals. The police had found her car a few miles further down Route 202 beyond the bypass exit, abandoned along the side of the road, out of gas and smelling like marijuana. It was certainly staged to look like she had run out of gas and had been picked up by her murderer. But Ann had a feeling that things weren't as they looked.

She felt like she was in an Escher painting. No matter how many steps she took, she always ended up back at the same place.

While she worked, Hyde filled her in. Two days ago, Dorothy Peterson had called the police to report her daughter missing. On her last day alive, Laura had spent the afternoon with her younger sister. She shopped at a store on Main Street, where she'd bought a black T-shirt and a pair of shorts. She was supposed to meet her boyfriend Paul for a beer at Kelly's bar. Her sister overheard her calling her boyfriend, telling him she would pick him up around 9 pm at the restaurant where he worked. That night she drove her Saturn to Del Val College, where she was taking a summer course in psychology. The class had ended at 8:45. She never arrived at Kelly's.

At about 9:30, Paul called Dottie to tell her that Laura hadn't shown up. He drank a bottle of beer in the bar of the restaurant, waited some more, and finally went home at 10:45, feeling uncharacteristically concerned. He called Dottie again and finally went to sleep after 2:00 a.m. Laura didn't come home that night.

The Phys Ed teacher had called the police. Laura's wallet and car registration papers were scattered on the track in front of the bleachers. Ann had pulled the white Jeep into the parking lot next to the stadium, passing the sign Announcing "Doylestown, Home of CB West Football, AAAA State Champs." She'd grabbed her kit, pulled on gloves, and walked through the stadium gates of War Memorial Field not expecting to find this.

The police had wanted to arrest the boyfriend, but his alibi was solid. He'd worked until about 8:55 at the restaurant the night of her disappearance and his manager confirmed it. The manager also verified that he'd been sitting at the restaurant's bar until about 10:45. The police found cannabis, razor blades, and cocaine in Laura's car, but her friends and her family insisted she never did drugs, wouldn't touch them. She was in therapy to overcome addiction. The kid was brokenhearted; he'd been sitting at the bar with an engagement ring. He was going to propose to her; he had just been waiting for the right moment. Now that moment would never come.

She knelt beside the body with a sickening feeling, knowing she would find a fractured hyoid bone. Kids cradling books and carrying knapsacks were being let out of school early. They spilled out of classrooms, flowed down concrete steps. Cops patrolled the sidewalks, trying to keep them away from the stadium, helping to redirect them to the buses. A few boys tried to scale the chain-link fence but were quickly hauled down and removed by extra cops on duty. The gates to the field were locked at night. How had he gotten in?

In her mind, Ann could see the stadium filled with cheering fans as it would be in the fall, hear the deep beat of the drums as the band played, see the kids circling the track in jittery, look-at-me packs, the parents watching the football game intently under the bright lights of the bleachers. The stadium would have to be off-limits to the public, the school, until they were done investigating the crime scene.

Finally, she looked beneath the girl's tongue. They'd since determined the first button was genuine Union infantry. Ann was afraid the murderer was changing his methods. She felt sure she would find evidence of sexual assault this time. This was an anger-driven crime. Killers changed methods mid-stream if they had a good reason to. Ann just had to find out what that reason was. Another button. And this time, he'd taken a souvenir.

11

Kevin closed the door behind him. He stood for a moment, soaking in the darkness. He walked to the table—he knew exactly where everything was, even in the dark. Striking a match, he lit two small votive candles and placed them beside the tall mirror. The mirror was painted with high-gloss black paint.

The candle spread warm, ghostly shadows about the room. He liked the butterscotch swirl of blackness. He stood in front of the mirror and began to chant. At first it was a monosyllabic whisper. He continued to chant, over and over, his voice growing louder. He didn't look at the mirror, but through the surface of it. He gazed into its blackness. At first he only saw an image of his six-foot-four frame, his newly dyed black hair (when had he done that?), his large hands. He knew what the mirror wanted. Before he could see the colors, before the mirror would present its visions, it wanted something from him. The force of it was so strong. Kevin liked that. Slowly, very slowly, he began to remove his clothing. He continued to chant, the words sliding through the inky darkness of the room, moving through the marshy, splattered light.

The mirror spoke to him. "Touch me."

His hand gently brushed the bristly mass of hair between his legs. He began to stroke himself. The mirror talked to him. "That's it," it said. "Yeah. Fuck yourself with your hands. I like that. I like to watch you fucking yourself. I want to see you come."

Soon, his head bent low, he leaned against the wall, watching liquid threads of himself slide slowly down the mirror. Then he saw another image. One he hadn't seen before. His breathing ragged, his veins thumping, he studied the woman. She was wearing an old-fashioned nightgown, the fabric opaque, the neckline high, the sleeves long.

She moved slowly up a set of stairs, looking at him provocatively. He couldn't see her face. Just a mass of honey-colored hair that fell down her shoulders and her back in wide curls. She turned away from him and suddenly he was staring at the brawny outline of a man. A man with sweaty, callused fists. The red flannel shirt. The room suddenly smelled of cheap wine and cigarettes. "No!" he said, spilling his naked form backward onto the carpet.

"You're a dirty, wicked boy," the mirror said. "You killed that girl."

Kevin reached for a candle and blew it out. He closed his eyes. "Fuck you!" he yelled. "Fuck you!"

He dressed hurriedly, then shattered the mirror with his fist. He knew what was happening but he didn't feel any pain. He didn't feel anything. He didn't notice the blood dripping down his palm onto the carpet, mixing with black, glittery, jagged edges of painted glass. Lyrics from a Stones song flickered in his head. *I see a red door and I want it painted black. No color anymore I want them to turn black. I see the girls walk by dressed in their summer clothes. I have to turn my head until my darkness goes.* He opened the window, inhaling the smell of raw earth and approaching rain. A dark shape unflattened itself from the wall of the room and moved away. He knew who it was. It was that other part of him, the good part, the one who tried to keep him quiet. He laughed, a harsh, gloating sound in the hollowness of the room. *I won.* He knew the good part of him was never coming back.

He walked to the bathroom, washed his hands and bandaged his cuts, then dressed. He removed all the things that belonged to that other voice. His clothes, his pictures, his stupid books. He kept his own books—Freud, de sade, von Sacher-Masoch. He put the others in a bag and dumped them in the trash.

Goodbye loser.

As he did it, he felt the brush of a new erection like a kiss. He would not miss the other one. The other one felt too much. The other one cried. Kevin could not cry. The other one had talked while under hypnosis about killing a woman during the Civil War. Idiot. What if he'd talked about Beverly too? About the other girl? Now he would have to get the copies of his taped hypnosis sessions and destroy them.

He looked at the jagged scratches and cuts on his hands and arms, the small flecks of black paint where the glass had dug into his skin. Only an artist could admire the truth behind his creation. Admire and *fear*.

12

Bruce pushed his glasses up. They had a habit of inching down the bridge of his nose while he made notes about his patients' sessions. He took a sip of lukewarm coffee and pressed the rewind button on his tape recorder. The click and whir of buttons was a familiar late night sound in his downtown Doylestown office, an attractive three-story brick building that had been restored in the early 1900s. Once the site of newspaper offices, it now housed his psychiatry practice, a private law firm, and a dating service. The joke around the office was that the first floor screwed with your mind, the second with your wallet, and the third with your heart.

It was funny how many people from his past he'd run into in the thriving, eclectic township—it really was a small world. There was a saying among those who lived there; all roads converged in Doylestown.

He hit play and continued to scribble. He preferred the act of writing things out versus using a computer; he remembered things if he wrote them down, and that method usually triggered something important later.

Subject regressed easily. He stated he'd practiced the prescribed relaxation techniques during the past weeks. Possible subjects to explore: relationships with women and authority figures, chronic, unexplainable pain in left elbow. Unusual session. Regressed immediately to traumatic event in past life as medieval foot soldier then skipped around to several past lives in first session. Unresolved anger/violence? Note: research clothing/weapons of foot soldiers in Middle Ages; Civil War uniforms; Civil War battles, 1864 or 1865?

He stopped the tape and thought about the sessions. The things the subject had recalled were things he could have been exposed to in school, a book, or on the History Channel. He made notes about other things too—things he wouldn't be able to verify that could turn out to be significant or to have no relative meaning.

Civil War timeframe: The name 'Lavinia.' At next session, ask subject more about the 'box.' Subject clearly agitated by the box.

Bruce adjusted his glasses again, then annoyed, took them off and laid them on his desk. It was nearly 9 pm. The window of his first-floor office was slightly ajar; occasionally he caught the sound of couples talking, walking by on their way to a late night dinner or a movie at the County Theater. It smelled like rain. He tapped his pencil on the desk. Something was eluding him about the past session.

"Gerdie," he called out to the waiting room area, "Can you listen to this?" Though it was late, he knew Gerdie would still be at her desk, and with her German background, he knew she would know what the words on the tape meant. He often heard her switch to German when she was on the telephone and didn't want anyone to know what she was saying. At 57, she was a handsome, efficient woman. She couldn't type worth a shit, but she was organized and excellent with the clients. Even after hours of psychotherapy with his clients, she probably knew more about them than <u>he</u> did. People opened up to her. She was warm, talkative, sincere, and put them at ease the moment they walked through the front door.

When he'd moved his practice from Plainsville, New Jersey, to Doylestown 10 years ago, he had convinced her to come with him. That his business was thriving was in no small part due to her skillful handling of his clients. That personal touch was critical to his business, especially now that one of the services he offered was past-life regression—a controversial subject in America. He'd been skeptical of it until two years ago, when he began to see results in some of his patients who'd been refractory to traditional methods of psychotherapy.

Belief in reincarnation was well established in the older European countries, but relatively new to the United States. He still wasn't sure what he believed, but usually when he researched historic details his patients related under hypnosis, they turned out to be accurate. Gerda sometimes helped him with his research.

He'd made sure to read the findings of other scientists practicing past-life regression therapy and found that their results were strikingly similar to his. They too were finding this therapy extremely helpful to patients with emotional and psychosomatic disorders. People thought their fears were based in the future, but the theory was that they were often based in the <u>past</u>. People always worried about things that *might* happen, not realizing that the things they feared may have *already* happened in a previous lifetime—things they'd forgotten, or only dimly remembered in another consciousness.

Gerdie appeared in his office doorway, her pleasingly plump frame adorned with a flattering dark brown pantsuit—probably her latest purchase from Talbot's. She had good taste in clothing, but her lipstick was too dark and she wore too much chunky gold jewelry. Still, on her, the effect wasn't unpleasant. She was a warm, confident person and that's what he liked about her. She wore what she liked. She ate what she liked. She never made excuses when she went downtown for lunch and returned with a sandwich, coffee that was practically white from all the cream she'd used, and a thick slice of chocolate cheesecake. She never talked about how much weight she wanted to lose, how she should be exercising, or her private life.

He rewound the tape and pressed play. The thick voice thumped across the air. "*Ich werde Sie wieder, meines süßes finden.*"

She looked puzzled for a moment and then smiled. "Oh, I think…I'm pretty sure that means *I'll find you again my sweet.*"

Bruce bent his silver head over his notes and wrote it down. He rewound the tape again, ejected it, and slipped it into an envelope. He handed it to her. "Please make copies tomorrow for the subject and the files."

She frowned. "No problem. I'll be sure to make a copy for the files and for *him.*" Gerdie never failed to find some subtle way to remind him that patients were people, not subjects.

Bruce scratched his square chin, a shadow of silver stubble beginning to make its appearance. "What's on tap for tomorrow?"

"Two appointments before 10 am. I scheduled a half-hour break for you, then one more, starting at 11:30. After that, lunch and three more sessions. One at 1:30, one at 2:30, and one at 3:30. Afterward, you may be able to catch up on some of your research."

"Do you have dinner plans, Gerdie?" Their relationship was both natural and professional, so Bruce had no qualms about asking her to join him.

She planted her hands on her hips. "I have a German appetite. Do you think I could ever wait until 9 pm to eat dinner? You were on the phone."

Bruce retrieved his glasses. "Your loss. I was going to head downtown for a big plate of spicy pasta and clams."

"I'll take a rain check."

"Suit yourself. Don't stay late and don't tidy up my desk. I know where everything is and I need to look through my notes first thing in the morning. And for God's sake, make sure you lock the office door after I leave. You're too trusting." He didn't like her staying late by herself after he left.

She shook her head. "I don't know how you function like this." Papers were strewn wildly across his desk, books were haphazardly piled on shelves, and a ringed coffee stain was beginning to take up permanent residence on his desk.

Bruce winked, his clear blue eyes shadowed with amusement. "Some day you and I are going to get to the bottom of this obsession with neatness, Gerdy."

"I don't need to be psychoanalyzed," she huffed. "I'm neat. That's all. Sometimes things are just what they are, doctor. There. I just saved myself thousands of dollars of therapy." She walked away, mumbling something about how he thought too much and worked too hard.

Bruce sighed. He was in the mood for friendly companionship. Last year, he'd finally removed the picture of his late wife from his office. He wasn't dating yet. Gerdy was just a friend, but he really enjoyed talking to her. She was interesting and full of life and attractive in a down-to-earth, sultry sort of way. He took his notes and put them in a top drawer, knowing Gerdy would straighten up anyway. She was protective of him and didn't want his patients getting the impression he was absent-minded or disorganized. He wasn't either of those things; his office just gave people that impression. "If you can't keep your desk happy, how are you going to help someone through an emotional crisis?" she'd asked him once. He'd spread his arms wide and told her the mess was a sign of genius. She'd looked doubtful.

He'd removed a lot of personal things once he'd started regressions; souvenirs from the safaris he and his wife had taken, the Lion Bell, the bronze sculptures, the ceremonial masks. He didn't want to implant any impressions.

He put down his pencil. *I'll find you again my sweet.* It was a strange thing to recall. Why was it bothering him? He'd think about it tomorrow. Those clams were calling his name.

13

Gerdie finished filing, stuffing the last tape into the metal file drawer. She tidied her desk, grabbed her purse, and switched off her desk light. Shrugging her shoulders into her hip-length black leather coat, she switched off the main lights and stepped outside. She'd never felt uncomfortable being the last to leave the office, but tonight, for some reason, she felt a tinge of apprehension. The entrance to the office was on the side of the building and not well lit, though she had enough light to find the key she needed to lock the door.

The green-gray glossy bushes that usually looked so cheery in the daytime now looked like strange scratchy lumps in the muffled dark. It was oddly quiet. Maybe it was just the strange words that she'd listened to on the tape recorder in Bruce's office. *I'll find you again my sweet.* All Gerdie knew was that she would never want to be a psychiatrist, and she was pretty sure she wouldn't want to date one. Pretty sure. I mean, how could you ever really know if a patient made things up or was telling the truth? If you were dealing with someone who just wanted attention or was a psychotic, homicidal madman? Someone who'd watched *Friday the 13th* and *Three on a Meat Hook* too many times?

For example, the man who had come to the office for the first time today, and who had undergone hypnosis in Bruce's office, was pleasant looking, well dressed, and polite. Classy even. And he knew some German, so he was educated. But lots of people who walked into the office looked normal, not necessarily in need of psychotherapy. She thought about past life regressions. Something she'd read once popped into her mind. *He who does not know his past may have to relive it.* Strange, why would she think of that now?

Locking the door, Gerdie turned to thread her way down the neatly manicured path to where her tan Ford Taurus was parked. She usually left the office by 9 pm, but she guessed it was about 10:15 now. There were some things she had wanted to finish up and had lost track of time. Though the walk to her car was short, it seemed like a country mile. It was an unusually dark night and cool.

She found herself wishing she had taken up Bruce's invitation to dinner. He was an attractive, athletically fit man with a full head of silvery hair and intense blue eyes. His hands were large and sturdy, and he always smelled pleasantly of aftershave—nothing overwhelming. But he still pined after his wife, and he <u>was</u> a psychiatrist. Gerdie had sensed his interest, the spark of chemistry between them that could be fanned into flame, but something held her back. She'd never married and she liked her single life. Maybe she'd gotten too used to it. Maybe they were too good of friends. A physical relationship, love? That would complicate things. And she didn't want to be second place to a ghost.

Indeed, they'd had a lot of interesting late-night conversations—everything from psychological and psychiatric assessment to the brain's organic composition and the attempt to link biology and genetics to violence. She remembered how excited he'd been once about a federal program in the early 90s that attempted to treat violence as a public health issue, identifying youths at risk for becoming violent and creating appropriate interventions. Bruce did a lot of work with disturbed youths and was extremely intelligent. She found herself fascinated by his views about biological markers, nutritional deficiencies, brain-chemistry abnormalities, and genetics. But Bruce had never fully grieved over the loss of his wife. In fact, he seemed to avoid the subject of her death completely. He never talked about it. Physician, heal thyself, she thought.

"Verflucht es," she mumbled, dropping her keys and bending down to pick them up. As she grabbed them, she froze. She found herself staring at a pair of dark sneakers, which belonged to a pair of legs not five feet away. Repositioning one of the keys between her index and middle finger, she stood, trying to remain calm. Glancing up and quickly away, she saw that the still figure was hidden by a thick tangle of tall buddleias—the arching branches draped with panicles of flowers.

Taking off, she ran as fast as she could to her car and screamed as loudly as she could. Looking back, she saw nothing but swaying branches—purple-blue and white flower petals shaken loose, broken, floating silently to the ground—as a couple on the nearby street came to her aid.

"Are you all right?" the woman asked.

As she caught her breath, she nodded her head. "Yes, I think so. There was someone in the bushes. I think it may have been a prowler. I'm pretty sure I scared him away."

The man, appearing to be in his early forties with brown hair that curled at his shirt collar, pulled a black cell phone out of his jacket pocket. "We should call the police."

Gerdie shook her head. "I don't think it would do any good. I only got a look at his sneakers anyway, not his face." She glanced back at the bushes, a sick feeling in the pit of her stomach. "He's gone now."

Who was he? How long had he been hiding there, watching her through the glass of the unlocked office door? Did he know she was the only person in the office? For the first time, she felt violated. Someone had shattered her feelings of security and she knew she would need to change her late-night habits. Her brain chose that moment to recall the article about the Doylestown woman who had recently been murdered.

"We should really call the police." The woman, wearing a low-cut blouse, and possibly ten years younger than the man, her full lips painted a gaudy red and her hair dyed platinum blonde, agreed with her date.

"Thank you, but I just want to go home," Gerdie said. "I'll tell my boss in the morning."

Reluctantly, the man put his phone back in his pocket. "Are you sure there's nothing we can do?"

"I'm fine, really. Thanks for asking." Gerdie was tired. The last thing she wanted to do was wait around for the police and talk about a prowler who was long gone by now.

The couple walked away toward the center of town as Gerdie climbed into her car, locking her doors and practically peeling out of the parking lot. Rounding the corner, her purse toppled over and spilled out onto the seat and the floor on the passenger side. In a shaft of light from a streetlight, she saw the white plastic tape from the session lying there. Now that was strange; she thought she'd filed the tape.

14

Ann gave her sister Bo a look, then answered Greg's question. Her sister wasn't supposed to tell anyone, especially not the cute cop she was dating, about the stupid letter she'd received.

"C'mon, I had to tell him. It's creepy, Ann." Her sister was a nurse in the emergency room at Doylestown Hospital, and Ann was glad Bo's apartment was only minutes from her house.

Ann sat down on her sister's green leather sectional, slipping her hands beneath her knees. "It's no big deal. It's probably just Peter, up to his sick tricks."

"But what if it's not? I mean…I hate to think this way, but what if it's the nut running around this town who killed those women?"

"You mean the one I'm going to catch and nail to the wall?"

"Yeah, that one."

Ann shook her head. "Listen, it's Peter. I know how he thinks. At least I do now."

Greg twisted open a Corona and took a swig. He smiled, and Ann could see why her sister had broken her own rule about dating cops. "Better safe than sorry," he said. "Do you have more than one letter?"

"I've only received one from psycho-stalker."

"Have you ever had a stalker?"

"Nope. Just some creep who used to crank call me in college. Ask me what kind of panties I was wearing. I told him I was recording the calls and they stopped."

"What kind *were* you wearing?" Greg asked.

Bo hit him and they all laughed.

Greg scratched at the dark stubble growing on his square chin. "Probably just some sex-starved freshman. Why don't you trike-test the letter?"

Ann arched a delicate brow. "Someone's been studying their forensics."

"Greg, she's a medical examiner, you know, a *forensics* expert?" Bo said. "She's already thought of that."

"Actually," Ann said, "I haven't thought about doing much of anything with the letter. It's just a stupid letter. Can we all just forget about it? Anyway, they'd float the letter in ninhydrin, rock it like a baby, and Peter's print would come up."

"What if they find a print and it's not Peter's?" Greg asked.

"Greggie here doesn't know when to stop," Bo said. She curled her pink lips softly around his earlobe. "Sometimes, that's a good thing." Greg didn't blush. He earned points for that with Ann, who had always been in awe of her sister's sensual nature and lack of shame. If he'd blushed, Ann knew this would be their last date.

Ann popped her Corona open and raised it high. "Cheers. Here's to not getting another creepy letter from the jerk. But if I do, you'll be the first to know." The three of them took their beers out on the deck and sipped them as they watched dusk turn to night and a million glittering stars appear. To Ann, they looked like spilled shards of glass. Greg put his arm around Bo's small shoulders and tangled his long fingers in her glossy black hair. Ann felt a twinge of envy. It was a beautiful night to share with someone. She stood, grabbed her jacket off the deck chair, and said her goodbyes amidst feeble protests.

15

Bruce walked up the short path to his office, his mind on the day's appointments. He was surprised to find the office locked and dark. He was trying to find his key when he heard Gerdie pull up in the adjacent parking lot. She was always in before he was. This was the first time in all their years working together that she'd been late.

He watched her walking up the path, her hair mussed, her clothing wrinkled, tired shadows dancing under her eyes. She wasn't wearing her signature red-chocolate lipstick either. In fact, she looked like she hadn't slept at all.

"Gerdie, you OK?"

"I'm so sorry, Bruce. I didn't mean to be late, I…"

"C'mon Gerdie, you don't need to apologize. You've never once been late. Do you want to talk about it over morning coffee?"

Gerdie frowned. She looked at him, her dark eyes filled with indecision. "Do you have any…enemies, Bruce? I mean, any dissatisfied clients or anyone like that?"

"Not that I know of," Bruce said, opening the door and holding it for her.

She switched on the lights, taking a quick glance around the office, and threw her purse underneath her desk. Nothing looked askew.

Bruce watched her curiously. "OK, out with it. You are not your usual self." He put his hands in the pockets of his gray dress pants and waited. She couldn't help it, but she liked the strong slant of his shoulders, the easy long leanness of him.

She pretended to shuffle some papers on her desk and stared at the painting of Echo and Narcissus on the front wall. It was an interesting choice for the office. In Ovid's retelling of the myth, Narcissus is the son of the river god Cephissus and the nymph Liriope. A seer told the parents that the child would live to an old age if he did not look at himself. Girls and nymphs fell in love with him, including a nymph named Echo. She was so distraught at his rejection that she withdrew to a lonely spot and faded away until she was only a plaintive whisper. The goddess Nemesis heard her prayers for vengeance and arranged for Narcissus to fall in love with himself. He stayed watching his reflection and let himself die.

A few of the more prudish parents had asked him to remove it, since it contained a nude female, but Bruce refused. It was art and it suited. Gerdie was suddenly disturbed by the painting.

"Gerdie, are you listening to me?"

"Sorry. Last night, when I was leaving, I was locking up and there was someone in the bushes."

"What?" Bruce said.

"I dropped the office key and was bending down to get it when I noticed a pair of black sneakers in the bushes. I ran and screamed as loud as I could. A couple was walking by and they stopped to see if I needed any help."

"Why didn't you call me right away?" he asked.

"It was late…" Gerdie hadn't meant to say that. She knew how Bruce felt about her working late.

"How late?"

"Well, maybe 10 pm or so. I had some stuff to do."

"I really wish you wouldn't work so hard, Gerdie," he said. "Did you get a look at him? What did the police say?"

"I only saw his shoes and pant legs. I, um, didn't call the police."

Bruce swore. "Why not? Between you, me, and the walls, do you know how fucked up some of my clients are?"

Gerdie felt like crying. She had never heard Bruce talk like that. He had never been angry with her before.

"Jesus, Gerdie. If anything would've happened to you…"

"Maybe it was just some kid or something…someone you treated before."

"Show me where you saw him." Gerdie took him outside and showed him. Bruce bent down, careful not to touch anything, and looked at the area she had pointed out. "I'm calling the police. They might be able to lift a footprint or something."

They went back inside and Gerdie sat down as Bruce dialed the police. "Let's forget the coffee. I'm giving you the day off. Your nerves are shot. And no more late nights."

"But…"

"No buts. After we talk with the police, you are going home, getting some rest, and working this out." He sighed. "Is there someone who can be with you, lend you some company?"

Gerdie nodded her head. "Sure, I can call my sister."

"Yeah, I need to speak with a detective about a prowler," Bruce said into the phone. Ten minutes later, an officer was walking up the path.

The officer asked them some questions then examined the area. "Lucky we had recent rain," he said, opening a small case, pulling out a brush, and bending down in the bushes. He gently applied powder to a surface, sweeping the brush back and forth. He coated the surface with two to three sweeps. Then he blew on the surface, using a small can of compressed air. "We don't want any air pockets or fish eye," he said. "Looks like we may have a partial print here. Fish eye hinders the tape from being smoothly applied over the surface."

"What happens to that print?" Gerdie asked.

"A latent print examiner will look at it, at the footprint friction skin ridges," he said as he continued to work carefully. "But it may take a while; they get hundreds of cases a month."

He placed tape across the surface in overlapping strips. Starting at one edge of the tape, he ran his index finger along the center of the tape as he applied it. Then he smoothed the tape from the center out to each edge. He ran a pencil along the seam of the overlapped sections of tape to fill in the gap. Then he removed the tape, pulling it up gently and placing it on a backing medium. He explained how it would be labeled and put it in a large glassine bag, sealing it with evidence tape.

"You know, normally, we don't do this every time someone sees a prowler. But we've had a few other calls. They may not be connected, but if we could get a print, we might have a lead."

Bruce thanked the officer and walked Gerdie to her car. She promised to call him if she needed him.

Gerdie wanted to believe it had just been some kid, but she had a bad feeling about it. Her German intuition was on high alert. When she got home, she pulled all the shades down, checked that every window and door was locked, and resorted to the much-needed oblivion of sleep before calling her sister.

16

Phone. Ringing. Ann squinted at the alarm clock. Four am. Wearily, she picked up the receiver. "Hello."

She held it out from her ear as Chinese swear words rang through the bedroom air like tiny darts. She should be used to hearing Nai Nai swearing at four in the morning. This time, she was upset about the way men were handling the investigation of the recent deaths, and the criticism of Ann in some of the newspaper articles. Criticism just came with the job. Ann had learned long ago that you couldn't please everybody.

"Nai Nai," Ann said softly. "It's four in the morning."

"I read newspaper. These men doing bad job with investigation."

"I can handle them." Having been born in China and raised and educated in the United States, Ann had a mix of eastern and western values, but saw herself as more and more American. Nai Nai on the other hand, was more of a traditionalist though she fully supported Ann's independence. At sixty-nine years old, she was still a tiger, full of energy. Nai Nai had practically raised her and her older sister Bo.

"I have dream," Nai Nai continued. Ann lay back on her pillows and closed her eyes. Nai Nai's China dreams, that's what Ann called them. Strange visions as fragile as china. Nai Nai did have a gift for interpreting them.

"You are taking trip."

"Nai Nai, I am not taking a trip."

"You make trip. I have dream. To place of colors and great noise. You see. I burn prayer for you. What you look for, not there. I see empty hills. Be wary. You cannot negotiate with tiger for its skin."

"Nai Nai, go back to sleep. I can take care of myself. You taught me well." As Nai Nai ranted, Ann listened to rain licking the ceiling. As a child she had hated the rains in China. Now she missed them. Nai Nai's voice rustled like green bamboo leaves in the wind. The sound of *home*. Nai Nai and Bo were the only ones to whom Ann could speak Cantonese, the only ones from whom ancient sounds of the past rolled off the tongue—reminding her of calligraphic figures scratched on ancient tortoise shell or the whitened bones of an ox, connecting them like a string of blue pearls across years, water, earth, sky.

It was Nai Nai who had made her little dresses with gold thread and colorful beads when she was small; it was Nai Nai who had told her stories of her mother, who had died giving birth to Ann. Bo wasn't so interested in hearing those stories. She couldn't remember their mother. She'd moved on. It was just Bo's nature.

Ann had always regretted that her body had not shaped her mother's; that she'd never had the chance to curl against her mother's body in sleep, clutch at her face with her baby hands, hear her soft voice singing as Ann hugged her back. Bo had but she couldn't remember.

And it was Nai Nai who had cleaned the sand and mud from their little brown sandals, gave them their first lessons from Chinese books, taught Ann, especially, a love of language and words. In them Ann could taste salted fish, day-old rice, singed linen, dried herbs and bark. Long-ago lace sewn firmly to the edges of her childhood.

Ann heard Nai Nai sigh on the other end of the phone. "I am old woman, ancient she-dragon. What Americans call stupid bitch? I will speak. Remember, woman hold up half the sky."

Ann laughed. She was required to respect and listen, but it had never been something she hadn't wanted to do where Nai Nai was concerned. She loved Nai Nai dearly. "Nai Nai, it's not 'stupid bitch;' it's '*she*-bitch'. There's a big difference." Laughing, she asked, "And how many times do I have to tell you? Woman hold up *whole* sky with one hand because she's too busy to spare two."

17

Mark felt like a tapestry cut apart by a blade. Some of the cuts he'd been aware of. He didn't know when the others had been made, only became aware of them at odd times in his life, when he *felt* the missing pieces of himself. Maybe that was why he liked to tear things down and rebuild them. He had some of his father's old tools and liked how they felt in his hands. Especially since his father had died before they'd had a chance to patch things up.

A light rain was falling, making darkness the color of muddy, wet socks. The cadence of the windshield wipers, the soft *thud, thud*, calmed him, made him feel disconnected from time and space. His thoughts drifted to Ann Yang.

It was strange, but when he was working on her house, discreetly glancing at her from time to time as she pored over lab and crime reports in her living room, he felt he had come home. She was strangely familiar to him. It wasn't just the unusual restoration of the charming Victorian house that intrigued him. It was something else. A strange, powerful feeling that during these moments, he was putting something right, that *they*—not just pieces of house—were coming together somehow.

Why hadn't he told her this? She'd probably think he was crazy. He had secrets. Would she understand if she knew?

He turned right and headed out past town on his daily errand, wondering, how do we manage with broken hearts? When dreams become skinny splinters of light that still sparkle but cut and scratch? Somehow. *Somehow.* The wind picked up; strange weather for the time of year. As he continued to drive, he tried not to feel Ann in every cell and nerve of his body. He tried not to think of her. Maybe it wasn't fair. But the feeling, the *knowing* was too strong.

Later, in the dark hospital room, he sipped a cup of coffee that tasted like cigarette ashes. He looked at the girl sleeping peacefully in the hospital bed, long, dark hair the color of cherry bark spilling over a thin pillow. Her eyelids fluttered lightly. She was dreaming. He couldn't imagine what she was dreaming about. We all look like angels in our sleep, he thought sadly. Liked fleeced things, soft and silky and untrue.

18

It was late, but Ann didn't feel like sleeping. She logged onto the Internet and found the unofficial website about the murders in Doylestown. The board was thoughtlessly called "Dead in Doylestown." There was a lot of chatter about the murders—theories, speculation, and outright lies about the victims. People were scared. Ann wasn't sure why she was interested; she knew these kinds of sites were usually garbage. Still, she scanned the message threads from the past two days. They were talking about Beverly. "Husband a loser." "She did drugs." "She was really a prostitute." Ann was enraged. It was bad enough what had happened to the woman. Now people were posting rumors about her, insisting she had brought this trouble on herself. Disgusted, she was about to disconnect when she noticed a thread toward the bottom of the screen.

I think I know who killed Beverly Wilcox.

Ignoring her practical mind—the one urging her to shut down the slow hunk of metal and plastic occupying her desk—she clicked on it and read. The thread name was "butterfly."

I think I know the killer. This is not a joke. I started dating a man and he was really charming at first. Now I am afraid of him. I think he's going to kill me. I think he kidnapped that woman who disappeared and turned up dead, and I think he killed her. I don't have proof, but he talks about that woman; he knows things about her. Things not everybody would know. Things I didn't see in the paper. I can't say more right now. Please, please, someone help me. I don't know what to do.

Ann couldn't ignore the woman's pleas—she'd often come to the aid of battered and abused women through her volunteer work. She knew they often felt trapped, helpless, immobilized by fear. She clicked a button and posted a reply.

If you are afraid for your own safety, go to the police. There are also plenty of women's shelters. If you feel threatened in any way, get help now! Trust your intuition, butterfly.

19

In the morning, Ann had been hoping to see a reply from "butterfly" on the website she'd visited, but nothing else appeared in the threads. She made herself a fresh pot of coffee and while it was brewing, opened her personal mailbox. As she scanned the message titles, she thought of the killer. Was he some sort of sex freak? Power freak? Why wasn't he leaving palpable clues if he was new to this sick game of his? Her eyes caught on a single message: *I've Been Watching YOU Ann.*

Double-clicking the message, she opened it. No other choice. It was from someone who called himself "Chaos."

Not my real name, of course. But fitting. I'm creating lots of chaos, aren't I? I have to admit, it's fun. You don't need to give poor, little butterfly any more advice, Ann. She's taken care of herself. Are you sitting in front of your computer now, reading this? I like to watch you, Ann, that gloriously shiny black hair, those inquisitive eyes. You're smart, aren't you? Got your degree from good old Harvard. Impressive. But not as smart as Chaos. Then you got married, stopped working for a while. Is it true that Chinese women are, by nature, submissive? But you wouldn't be, would you? You know those women I killed? They were just practice. I'm working my way up to you. They were too naïve, too trusting, too pathetic. You would fight me, wouldn't you?

PS: I won't be ignored. PPS: Do you notice when the rain tastes like blood?

He'd typed "Goodbye for now, Chaos" in Chinese. Ann made a mental note to have software installed on her machine to traceroute threatening messages. She forwarded the message to homicide and to Tony and then saved it. Soon she'd have the IP address of the system the e-mail originated from, even the country/region of the e-mail source, showing the location on a world map. It could be just some loser impersonating the killer. Could be the real thing. Could be Peter. Ann was exhausted. Stirring extra cream into her coffee, she reached for a familiar yellow-lined pad and wrote the date, the exact time the message had been sent, and the name "Chaos."

She thought of Nai Nai, who had given her huge jars full of oil and cooking fat and alcohol when she was at Harvard to be used to burn and smoke out ghosts. She wondered if someone *had* been watching her in the tree-lined shadows of the streets at night, at the crime scenes. Was she being haunted? Ann had no doubt that the ghost who was watching her was no ghost at all but flesh and blood.

She wondered about his hands, his fingerprints. Were they mainly arched, tented, whorled? For some reason, she suspected he had beautiful hands. His fingernails would be neat, trimmed. Would he get careless and leave a print on the next victim? She was certain he was only getting started.

One thought kept going through Ann's head. *You can't reason with Chaos.*

20

Ann threw her purse and papers on the table and checked her phone messages. She'd had a great therapist in New York but she'd heard about hypnotherapy and had been wanting to give it a try for a long time. She hoped the blinking light meant someone had called her back.

Hi Ann, this is Dr. Kenneth Baldwin from the Swan Center of Clinical Hypnotherapy. Wanted to get back to you. It's unfortunate that I must report that at the clinic we don't currently work with past-life regression. That in no way is a statement as to belief or disbelief, it's just we deal more with known psychiatric or psychological disorders, and any regressions that we do are within a person's known lifetime.

The man laughed then continued on.
But I do wish you the best. In fact I can give you a number of one of my colleagues. He's done past-life regression. If he can't help you, he'll know someone who can. His name is Bruce Miller, and his office is in town.

Ann wrote down the number on a scrap of paper, mildly annoyed that the man thought past-life regression amusing, and looked at her watch. Eight-thirty pm. She'd call and leave a message anyway. After two rings, a man answered. "Center for Healing and Peace. This is Bruce."

"Oh, I wasn't expecting anyone to be there this time of night," Ann said. "This is Ann Yang. I was hoping to leave a message about making an appointment for a past-life regression but now I can ask in person. I got your name from Kenneth Baldwin. Do you always work this late?"

He laughed. "Not all the time. Aren't you the county medical examiner?"

"Yes. Listen Bruce, I want to try hypnotherapy to deal with the trauma associated with my job. Also, I have chronic anxiety. I recently moved here from New York and I'm looking for a good therapist. I'd like to be regressed, but I don't know if I can be hypnotized."

"Sure, OK. You know, that's a common myth that certain people can't be hypnotized. The only people who can't be hypnotized, who can't bypass the critical part of the mind, are people of diminished intelligence, people who've been in serious accidents, in a coma, that sort of thing. People go into a trance state all the time. Have you ever driven somewhere, and then realized when you got there, that you had no recollection of driving?"

"I do it all the time."

"You were in a trance state. Let me tell you something about anxiety, Ann. I'd be happy to see you. We could do an intake session first, and then you can decide how you want to do this. But you don't need regression in 90 to 95 percent of anxiety cases. Direct suggestion works fine. Only about 5 to 10 percent of people need to go back to that moment in time where the fear took root. When you're hypnotized, your subconscious takes you where you need to go—that's how it works. But it's just as durable if you work with direct regression, or this lifetime."

"Well, I think I'd really like to do a past-life regression. I've had counseling before, and it works for a while, but then I find myself slipping back into my old patterns. And there's something else...it's really strange, but I feel like I've lived before and that...something terrible happened to me." She didn't tell him she felt it was going to happen again.

"That's not strange at all. I've hypnotized people who swore they didn't believe in past lives and under hypnosis they've told me things I've later been able to verify—things that supposedly happened to them lifetimes ago."

Bruce filled her in on fees and she set up an appointment for Friday morning. Between the divorce, the threatening letters, and the murders, Ann was feeling a little like a Fruit Loop in a bowl of Grape Nuts. But, uh, she would keep that to herself for the time being.

21

The initial intake sessions had gone well, Ann liked Bruce, *and* the office was catty-cornered to Starbucks. She crossed the street and approached his office, noting the green- and gold-lettered sign hanging outside, fresh mocha latte in her hand. Bruce had agreed that given her profession and her odd feelings of being chased through time by a malevolent soul, she could probably benefit from a past-life regression.

She found him easy to talk to as she'd related things from her past, talked about her mother's death, her father, who lived in California now, her sister, and her anxiety. It seemed she always burdened herself by abnormal fears despite her wonderful childhood. They talked about medicines, which Ann had had some success with in the past, but she agreed with Bruce: no medicine can reach the real roots of the problem.

He had commented on her coffee; of course she knew the caffeine contributed to anxiety, but it was one thing she wasn't ready to give up. And she usually didn't drink more than two to four cups a day.

She breezed into the office. "Hi Gerdie. How are you?"

Gerdie, wearing a raspberry blouse that was exquisite with her coloring, looked up and smiled. She had a gold angel pin on the lapel. "Well, hello Ann. It's nice to see you again. How are you?"

"Good, thanks. And you?"

"Hanging in there, you know, the usual. You can go on back."

Ann walked down the narrow, carpeted hallway to Bruce's office.

"Hi Bruce. I guess I'm your first basket case of the day?"

He laughed. "Hardly. Let's talk a little about what we're going to do today and then we'll get started." Bruce went over the process so she would know exactly what was happening. "When you're ready, lie on the couch with your eyes slightly closed and rest your head on the pillow. You know this is a safe environment."

Ann reclined and they focused on her breathing first. With each exhalation, she released stored-up tension and anxiety; with each inhalation, Bruce instructed her to relax even more. After several minutes, Bruce told her to visualize her muscles relaxing, beginning with her facial muscles and jaw, her neck and shoulders, her arms, her back and stomach muscles, and finally, her legs. Ann felt her body sinking deeper and deeper into the couch. She felt sleepier and sleepier, more and more calm. Bruce counted backward slowly from 10 to one. Ann was able to concentrate on his voice. By the count of one, she was already in a moderately deep state of hypnosis.

Bruce began to regress her, asking her to recall progressively earlier memories of her life. Ann answered his questions, speaking in a slow and deliberate whisper. While he taped the session, Bruce also took notes. Then he took her back past her current lifetime.

"I want you to look around. Can you tell me where you are, what time you are in?" he asked.

"Time? This is...before history. I mean, before the history we read about in textbooks. It's an island. I'm on some sort of wooden ship. It's moving from the island," Ann said.

"How do you feel?"

"Like someone is pulling my heart out. The farther the ship moves from the shore, the more desolate I am." Ann's body had visibly tensed.

"Look at your feet, your body. What are you wearing?"

"There's nothing on my feet. I'm barefoot. I don't know what I'm wearing. It's shapeless and very coarse. It *doesn't* matter. The people on the ship made me wear it."

Ann's body shook. "I want to die. Someone standing in front of me is gripping my shoulders, trying to calm me. He's speaking, but his voice sounds far away. I don't really hear him. I don't really feel him. All I see is the shore getting farther and farther away as I struggle...I can't understand why he is holding me back, why he won't let me jump over the side. I see a band of dark natives with something like spears, paint or something, smattered on their dark faces. They're standing in a circle, getting smaller and smaller, clutching him, clutching him, and there's nothing I can do!"

"Are you a prisoner, a slave of some sort?"

Ann sobbed. She tried to push at the imaginary arms holding her. Her breathing became erratic. She was crying and trying to pull air into her lungs at the same time.

"They've taken him...they've taken some of the other children too. How did this happen? How? My son...my little son...I can't help him..."

"I want you to go ahead a little bit. Tell me what's happening now."

"The people, my son, I can't see them anymore. I am sure they will kill him. I am sure I will never see him again. I don't want to live. The ship is slowly passing a very tall cliff, its crimson-black edges saturine and glaring-wet. Some of them tried to escape…"

"Some of your family, your friends?"

"My people. The nearest word I would use is clan, though it wasn't really that. I look up to the top of the cliff. I can't look away. There are horrible things up there…something like cross trees? The people who tried to fight, to escape, to help the others, they're dead. They are hanging from their necks, swinging lifelessly in the darkening sky. It's…gruesome. I bury my head into the chest of the man holding my arms; his feet are shackled like mine. They *wanted* us to see it…to see what they've done to our people. They are horribly cruel."

"Can you look into this man's eyes? Do you know who he is?" Bruce asked softly.

"Yes," Ann whispered. "He is my mate."

"Look into his eyes. Do you know this man today, in your present lifetime?"

"I don't think so."

"What can you tell me about him?"

"He is the father of my son. He is very strong. I sense something in him, like I've known him for a long time, or…before. I know that in this life I am never the same again, but this man who also lost his son, he will teach me how to live and love again, how to go on. I never see my son again. Please…I don't want to stay here anymore."

"OK. You don't have to stay. You are done with that lifetime. Jump ahead to the moment of your death in that life. What do you see?"

"I don't know where I am, how old I am, or what happened. I'm just floating above my body, looking down. I'm confused. I hear a voice, thin but resolute, like wind moving down a corridor without walls. I am glad to leave the earth. I am glad not to be afraid anymore."

"Listen to the voice again. Can you hear it now? What is it saying?"

Ann mumbled something in a language Bruce had never heard.

"What is the voice saying?" he asked again.

Ann gasped. "It's my son!" She sobbed, this time with happiness. "His spirit is with me. We are not human, we are not bodily forms, but we *are*. It's like…he is putting his small hands on the scars of my heart, his small form drawing out all the pain I've carried with me my whole life. There are no words, but I know what he's thinking. He's telling me he's OK, that he knows I'm sorry. He doesn't want me to be sad anymore."

"He's safe. They killed his body, but not his spirit. He's telling me we will be together again, that we've been together many times."

Bruce watched his patient and took notes. Ann looked more peaceful now. Occasionally she moved her lips but said nothing. She cried. She smiled. Her body trembled. Bruce let her revel in whatever moment she seemed to be experiencing with her son.

"Ann, I'm going to take you back to the present now. When you awake, you will remember much of what you saw and experienced today. Your son is in a safe place. You don't have to live that life anymore. You can move on. Do you understand?" She nodded.

Slowly, Bruce counted backwards from ten. Ann opened her eyes.

22

Clifton Barks stared out the window of Doug Grover's executive office on the fourth floor. Sunshine sparkled on the shiny hoods of BMWs and Mercedes below as he sat down in an oversized leather chair.

"Cliff," Doug said. "We have a situation."

Clifton had never liked Doug, with his dark blue suits, his crisp white shirts, his buffed and polished smile. Doug was a 41-year-old, on-the-way-up, "yes" man. He'd known it the first time he'd met him.

Clifton was originally from Pakistan. Doug's dark eyes studied him, and Clifton had the feeling Doug was trying to unnerve him. Doug was freshly shaved and smelled of brisk cologne, a salt water fish trying to cover up his true smell. His office was immaculate. Numerous framed awards hung behind him on the wall, and a framed picture of Doug with his arm around a beautiful, young, tanned blonde woman was propped on his desk, facing outward, so everyone could see the happy couple in love. More likely so everyone could see her ample endowments.

<u>Flavor of the month</u>, Clifton thought. He'd worked in medical research a long time. He'd seen Doug's kind many times. The kind that took off on weekend jaunts to Paris with exotic women and returned with French wine for all the secretaries. Doug didn't have children; he couldn't know the pain of losing one. Doug lived in a superficial world of sales meetings, numbers, hot sales reps who no doubt furthered their careers in his satin-sheet—covered bed and black, leather-interiored BMW.

"The toxicity issue with Lucinate X," Clifton said.

"Bingo," Doug said.

"It's disappointing after such spectacular efficacy results," Clifton said. "The number of patients with manic schizophrenia who experienced toxicity and seizures. It's too high. We'll have to extend the studies, adjust the dosage. But it has so much potential." The drug also treated myriad forms of depression—it was kind of like a super selective serotonin re-uptake inhibitor with amazing neurological properties.

Doug stood and walked over to the window, lacing his quarterback hands behind his back. The gold ring he wore on his thumb glinted in the sun. "Well,

Cliff, you, of all people, are familiar with the drug's excellent results in treating the condition. The drug significantly quiets the voices these people hear in their heads. It's going to be the first NNK with this kind of potential. You know that means this could be the first drug to significantly impact these patients' lives, give them a shot at living normal lives."

Clifton couldn't believe his ears. *Yeah, and the company stood to rake in millions.* He knew what was coming. "My name is Clifton," he gritted out between his teeth. Since he'd lost one son to a motorcycle accident and the other had been struck with lightning and now lived with a neurological condition the doctors couldn't understand, he'd changed. He didn't fear vice presidents in slick Armani suits.

"C'mon Cliff, no need to get formal on me," he said. "You're our top researcher. I know your history. You've seen a number of outstanding compounds discovered and brought to pharmacy shelves. I respect that. I feel as if I know you…intimately…after reading your corporate profile, seeing you in action."

Clifton detested arrogance in weasels. The VP had only been with InnoPharm two years.

"We're a small organization. We will be in a better position to survive if we keep to schedule with Lucinate X."

Clifton cocked an eyebrow. "Just what *are* you suggesting, Doug?"

Doug returned to his desk and sat down. "We can't always have things the way we want them," he said. "These patients need this drug. We can't risk losing millions of dollars that the delay in research would surely cause. Plus, we just don't have the funding for that."

"Bullshit. This *isn't* about sales dollars," Clifton said. "It's about *safety*. This drug could *kill* in the wrong dosage. How would that look for InnoPharm, Doug?"

It was as if Doug hadn't heard a word he'd said. He looked Clifton in the eye. "Well, Cliff, I don't think you understand the importance of the situation. I've already weighed the issues." He tapped a sleek, gold-handled pen on his desktop.

Clifton's anger grew. He knew increased competition, more blockbuster products coming off patent, and a decrease in the number of new drug applications were leading to difficult times ahead for the pharmaceutical industry. More and more mergers were the answer to supporting languishing pipelines. But the truth was he was getting tired of it all. He was getting tired of being so full of hope after bringing a promising new compound to the final testing stages and seeing it botched by some idiot in a suit crunching numbers. Bringing a new drug to market was sort of like raising a child. He became so attached to the compounds. They had to be brought to market with a gentle hand, a caring hand, before sales guys like Doug did their damage. He actually thought of the compounds as people, which was what good marketing executives were *supposed* to do.

"Sometimes communications can get in the way of achieving sales, Clifton."

Clifton stood up, ready to storm out of Doug's office, barely keeping a leash on his fury.

Doug smiled, a smile that didn't quite reach his wooden, depthless eyes. "Don't go just yet, Cliff. Our merger with BioX didn't create the synergies we first envisioned. But funding has already been earmarked for our targeted projects."

Clifton balled his hands into fists. The so-called merger had already diverted the focus on innovation for at least a year. He'd had an inkling about the toxicity issues, and he'd wanted to do the titration studies last year, but the funding wasn't there. He knew both companies would now need to focus on filling the gaps, so R&D would take the hit again—because of people like Doug. "We stand to lose one to three years of productivity," Doug said.

"So you fucked up royally with your merger," Clifton said. "I'm not going to put patients' lives at risk to save your sorry ass."

"We have to keep the investors happy and meet investor demand for double-digit earnings growth. That's not going to happen without Lucinate X launching fourth quarter. You and I both know it's critical now to be aggressive in educating key stakeholders on the benefits to society of an innovative pharmaceutical industry driven by private capital markets. How can we do that without bringing innovative products to market quickly?"

"I don't give a shit about your earnings growth. My job is to ensure the drug's safety. Right now, it's not safe. Did you *read* the clinical reports, Doug? Patients with no underlying or apparent CNS disorders are having seizures—life-threatening seizures. Some have died as a result. Their hearts stop beating; they stop breathing. They die. Yes, it's a drug with a lot of potential, but we need to do titration studies *now*. In fact, I know the FDA will question the safety results. They aren't going to approve it for use when they see the numbers."

"Your son, the one struck by lightning?" Doug said. "I understand he has pretty high medical bills. Good thing you work here. Good thing you have those health benefits. Not to mention life insurance."

A chill danced up Clifton's spine. "Is that a threat, Doug?"

Doug sat down, swiveled around in his chair, and pulled up his electronic calendar for the day, dismissing Clifton. "Not a threat, just giving you something to think about. You might want to reexamine the toxicity results."

He could walk away now, get a job somewhere else, but Doug would make it difficult for him. He thought about an article he'd read recently in the newspaper, where Doug was quoted as saying, "We will always search to help more patients rather than garnish the most dollars." It made him feel sick. Then there was the other feeling, the horrible feeling he'd failed his younger son. *He could still help his older son.* How would he do that if he was unemployed? Or…worse?

"It might be hard for a man of your age to find a new job, Cliff, even with your stellar track record."

Clifton knew he'd exaggerated the safety concerns to Doug a little bit, that some individuals in the organization would see the numbers as on the line. He also knew, with the intuition of an experienced medical research director, that he was right. There were a lot of talented, dedicated, sane people in marketing. Their voices could easily get crushed by people like Doug, people whose argument was that time will tell. Perhaps patients would die. Perhaps there would be lawsuits. Perhaps the company would hire the right lawyers and win the lawsuits. That was years, and millions of dollars, away. They would rather launch the drug and take the risk.

"Bastard," was all Clifton said as he left Doug's oversized office. He had a lot to think about. Including whether or not he had the balls to be a whistle-blower.

Two days later, he was in Doug's office. "I've thought about what you said. I went back and ran the calculations a few times. Turns out it wasn't as bad as I thought." He was lying through his teeth, and he hoped Doug wasn't suspicious. Smoke and mirrors. Two could play at that game.

◆   ◆   ◆

Clifton Barks was sitting on a promotion to VP of drug discovery. As current VP of chemistry, he had oversight of all of InnoPharm's drug-discovery efforts as well as directing the exploration of new neurological disease targets and identifying important new drug candidates to add to InnoPharm's clinical development pipeline.

Before he joined InnoPharm, he was the associate director of lead discovery and early discovery chemistry at BioPharm, where he managed the identification of new clinical compounds to treat infectious and neurological diseases. Before that, he'd held a faculty position at Hopkins, where he conducted his research.

He received his PhD in organic chemistry from Ohio University, following his undergraduate education in England. Leafing through stacks of mail, he found a manila envelope with his name neatly lettered on the front.

When he opened it, he was surprised. He started to sweat. He was playing by *their* rules. At least, that's what he wanted them to think. So who doubted him? Who hadn't he fooled? The photo he'd extracted from the envelope shook in his hand, every black-and-white grainy detail jumping out at him. There was no note. None was needed because whoever had sent the photo knew what it meant, and knew Clifton would understand. Everything he had worked so hard for, everything he thought he was, crumbled. Disappeared. He'd thought he'd buried his past long ago. After all, he'd been a professor when the photo was taken, a photo he had not known existed until now.

In it, he was naked, fully erect, and kneeling behind the buttocks of an exotic-skinned woman. She was not his wife. She was on her knees in front of him, her buttocks in the air. Dark, soft flesh pressed against the tip of his penis. A wave of shiny, lustrous black hair fell over her shoulder in waves; her ruby red lips (that's how he remembered them) were parted in ecstasy. She'd been one of his students.

A costly temptation and a mistake. One he was ashamed of and one no one else knew about, or so he'd thought. Someone obviously wanted to remind him to be careful. She had been silk and fire in his arms, an unexpected, guilty pleasure. His sons had been small then, his wife exhausted from her new duties as a mother. It wasn't fair, but the romance of their relationship had disappeared. And for a brief time, he'd turned to Najanai to console himself.

He looked at the photo again. His ruby ruin. As he'd sunk his flesh, his frustrations, and his insecurities into her, she'd moaned, the sound as delicious as the first breeze of autumn, the first turning of a red-gold leaf in the fall darkness. That he felt guilty was probably a result of acculturation. Had he stayed in his native country, he could have several wives and mistresses, no guilt. Though he'd never admit it to anyone, he thought he felt guilt because he had grown as a person, as a man. Still, his wife would probably divorce him. He hated to think of losing her, of the pain, the gouge, this would cause her. He had to find out who was responsible and get his hands on that photograph.

Maybe Najanai was behind it. Najanai. He hadn't thought of her for years. He hadn't seen her in years. He was at the zenith of his career, making a six-figure salary. A good target for blackmail. He and his wife had been through enough. *Doug.* Everything had just gone from bad to worse in one hell of a hand basket. Would Najanai be surprised to hear from him?

23

Mark was still working when Ann got home. She'd let him in that morning. She greeted him, raced upstairs to change into shorts and an oversized T-shirt, made a cup of herbal tea, and curled up on the couch in the living room, comforted by the musical sounds of Mark's hammer. She hadn't eaten much lunch, and now her head ached. It was after 7 pm. Her mind felt fuzzy and her body felt overwhelmingly tired. Tomorrow she would get a call from her lawyer about whether or not Peter had accepted the latest terms of the divorce. They'd been going back and forth for months. She'd been the one wronged; yet she was the one making compromises.

He didn't seem to want to give an inch, whereas she just wanted to move on. She'd seen a bulletin hanging in the grocery store and she almost took it down to make a copy and send to Peter. It was for a seminar. "The Positive Side of Divorce. Using your divorce to springboard into a happier life. Recognizing the gifts of your marriage." She'd love to see his face when he opened it, with a note suggesting he attend.

Ann didn't like being alone. She'd always known that. Despite her independence and strength, she didn't like the sound of silence. She always noticed when it was too quiet.

For a moment, she'd thought Mark had left. He was standing between the dining room and the living room, a pencil behind his ear, watching her.

"You look tired. Everything OK?" he said, his full lips curling into a friendly smile. She was struck again by the quiet strength of his body, his deep hazel eyes, the way his jeans hugged his muscled thighs. He had strong hands. It was one of the first things she noticed about a man.

She looked at her teacup, swirling the amber liquid around. "I'm fine. Just the usual bullshit. But thanks for asking."

He looked at the stereo. "What's in the CD player?"

Ann rubbed her temple. "Stan Getz. Playing the Burt Bacharach soundtrack. You know, 'What the World Needs Now.'"

He leaned down and turned it on. He took the pencil from his ear and laid it on the coffee table. Then he grabbed her hand. "C'mon," he said. "I don't know what the world needs now, but I know what you need."

His touch was warm and solid and she let herself be pulled out into the back-yard. It was dark, the sky a drizzle of uncut diamonds shimmering on black felt. He pulled her against him and she stood motionless for a few moments, just let-ting herself feel his arms around her, the solid wall of his chest, his breath on her neck.

Finally, she spoke, her voice a quiet whisper. "What do I need, Mark?"

"This." Slowly, he moved her body with his. As soft jazz floated out through the kitchen window, they danced. Ann trembled ever so slightly. It felt like they were the only two people on the planet. The leaves on the trees trembled too, caressed by a soft night breeze. Mark didn't speak, just pressed her body softly to his as they moved. He was a good foot taller than she was. In the middle of the yard, he stopped. All around them was the quiet, inky darkness, the strong arch of tree limbs. He took her hand and placed it on his chest, over his heart. She felt its strong thudding. "Ann…"

Headlights of a black Volvo cut across the drive, scattering through bushes that partially concealed the yard. Mark didn't finish whatever it was he was going to say. "Looks like your tenant's back."

Ann stepped away, dropping her hand. She'd almost let herself get swept away. Wasn't that how it had all started with Peter? She wasn't ready to confront her feelings for Mark. "Maybe I…we…should go back inside." She hugged her arms about herself, missing the presence of those strong arms. He didn't move. He just stood there and looked at her. "You know, your soon-to-be ex-husband is an idiot."

Ann laughed. "No, I'm the idiot for marrying him. I'm the idiot for believing in things that were never meant to be."

Just then they heard footsteps. "Ann…" It was Nathan. "Oh, sorry. I didn't realize you had company."

"Oh, it's just Mark…" After the words were out of her mouth, she regretted them. He wasn't just Mark, just the guy working on her house, but she wasn't ready to admit that to herself.

"I'll come back later."

"No, that's OK. We were just heading inside. Can I get you a beer or some-thing? Is everything OK with the cottage?"

"Actually, if Mark doesn't mind…"

"Not at all."

"I had a really rough day," Nathan continued. "I know you'd understand, Ann. I just need someone to listen."

"Sure," she said, feeling oddly disappointed. Mark was staring at her like that was the last thing she needed. To listen to someone else's troubles. She hoped she wasn't that transparent.

"I've got some Coronas in the fridge."

They headed inside, and as Nathan poured his heart out about the horrible accident scene he'd been called to on Route 309 and sipped his beer, Ann was thinking about Mark. He went about his business as if nothing had happened, as if they hadn't just danced together in the privacy of her moonlit backyard. Nathan seemed agitated that she wasn't alone.

"Kinda late to be workin, huh?" he said to Mark.

"Carpenters have deadlines too," he said, continuing to pound a nail steadily into the wall.

Ann was tired. After Nathan finished his beer, he sensed it and got up to leave. Sometime later, Mark left too. Quietly. She didn't even know he was gone until she came downstairs to look for the diary after changing into her pajamas. The music was still playing. She stopped and listened to it for a while, closing her eyes and remembering the feel of his heart, strong and steady, beneath her hands. Was that how she made him feel? How did he know she needed to be held, when she didn't even know it herself? She was getting into dangerous territory.

Switching the music off, she made an omelet with baby spinach leaves and mushrooms and afterward headed back upstairs with Farrell's diary, her head filling up with thoughts of phone calls and more rounds with Peter. *Time to Feng Shui the old brain*, she thought. *There's no room in here for Peter anymore.*

24

A weekend in New Orleans. Just what the shrink ordered. Or would've, if he'd gone to see him. But he wasn't seeing his usual shrink, and he wasn't taking his medicines. Ativan, Depakote, Valium. Or the experimental stuff he got from the hospital ward where he worked part-time. He was freeing himself from everything—from all the rules. But his rage was building; he was as jittery as a spark on a wire and needed to take the edge off.

In one of the local coffeehouses he got a cup of coffee as dark as Mississippi River water. Doubling back into the Quarter from the Esplanade, he walked three blocks along Chartres to the city's oldest site, a creaky old building that began as a convent in 1745.

He felt an erection rise in his pants as he thought of the young, virgin nuns who had arrived in 1727; he imagined their pert, little breasts, dusky nipples, long slim legs that had never been spread by a man. *So* pious.

He passed the iron cross in the landscaped courtyard, passed the trees. For some reason, he thought of his older brother, the star, the brains of the family, the one who counted.

You were the star, and I was the stump, even after you died, he thought. *But not anymore.*

Once inside the main building, he stared at the hand-hewn spiral cypress stairs. He took a tour of the compound that included the Our Lady of Victory Church, in which gilt fleurs-de-lis decorated the pine-and-cypress ceiling. Overlooking the impressive altar was a statue of Mother Cabrini, whose aged presence once walked the halls of the convent.

Where are your virgins now?

He stood in the light straining through handpainted windows. On one of the windows was the scene of Our Lady of Prompt Succor, and beneath that a small scene of the Battle of New Orleans.

The battle is only beginning. I'm just getting started.

Later, he found himself behind the St. Louis Cathedral, in St. Anthony's Gardens, with no recollection of how he'd gotten there or how he'd spent the past few hours. He inhaled the smell of damp earth, took the soft, ice-cream colors of the stucco houses inside him. He stood beneath the sycamore, oak, and magnolia trees near a small white obelisk paying tribute to the thirty French sailors who died near New Orleans after an outbreak of yellow fever in Mexico. He didn't care about them.

Twin flagstone alleys lazed alongside the cathedral and the garden. A young girl with long blonde hair stepped into view carrying a bag from Faulkner's House of Books and holding a book open while she walked.

She didn't seem to be aware of anything but the words on the pages. Her face was unusually pretty—round, smooth cheeks, eyes the color of robin's eggs.

He stepped closer; she still wasn't aware of his presence. He caught the faint smell of perfume squaring off her pink, freshly scrubbed teenage skin.

She looked to be about seventeen, not more. She wore short dark blue shorts, a white tank top, and flip-flops. No bra. That's what he loved about the women of New Orleans. Uninhibited. Her toenails were painted bubble-gum purple, a color only a teenager or a woman in mid-life crisis would choose. From her ears dangled colorful homemade, Picasso-like earrings. She was a little more slender than he usually liked them. He felt his blood pumping, sounding like crunching in his ears.

It wasn't supposed to happen here.

Still, he was glad he'd brought a button along.

He had on a pinstriped suit, dress shirt, and tie. He carried a leather briefcase and looked respectable enough. Just another successful businessman. He pulled the map out of his pocket and pretended to study it as he bumped into her. "Oh, sorry," he said, shaking his head. "I'm lost. Wasn't watching where I was going." He adjusted the stylish silver-rimmed eyeglasses he wore for effect.

She looked up at him and smiled with her lip-glossed mouth. "No problem. I wasn't watching either." She blew a bubble that popped loudly and slipped her book into her bag. "My mama told me never to read and walk at the same time." She laughed sweetly.

The book she was reading was something by James Patterson. "You like his thrillers?" he asked.

"Yeah. You read his stuff?"

"Yes, but I don't have a lot of time to read. I'm a reporter. I write true-crime novels in my spare time; that's why I'm here in New Orleans." His lies—she licked them up like ice cream.

"Really? I love to read true crime, especially Ann Rule."

"Really. Ann's a good friend of mine. Listen, I'm trying to find my way to a book signing but I can't make any sense of this map. Maybe you can help me."

"Sure, mister." She had a southern drawl, a feminine lilt in her voice. He liked it. His eyes brushed over her young breasts then back to his map of New Jersey. Acting exasperated, he stuffed the map back into his pocket. "My Porsche is parked over there; would you mind being a navigator? I have a book signing in less than an hour, and I really need to find this place. I'll even give you an autographed copy of my book."

Her eyes slid over the sleek black car. He'd rented it two days ago and spray-painted it with black water-soluble paint.

"Where's your signing? What's your name?"

"It's Kevin. I'm not sure where the book shop is, I think I follow I-10 and then, oh, I don't know."

"I just came out of Faulkner's. It's not Faulkner's?"

"No."

She hesitated but then agreed to go with him, settling into the soft leather of the passenger seat, cracking her gum loudly. He switched on the ignition, his eyes admiring the soft skin of her calves, her trim ankles.

New Orleans. The Big Easy.

Soon they were heading east on I-10. "Where's your book signing? What's your name?" He smiled, but said nothing. The girl was starting to get nervous but trying not to show it, trying to tell herself she wasn't really in this situation. "You shy?" she asked again. He just smiled, eventually pulling off the main road into a secluded wooded spot he'd scouted out earlier.

"I need to get home. It's getting late."

He relished the fear in her eyes. He pulled an ornate ice pick out of his coat. He'd actually read a scene like this one in one of those thriller books. "Do you believe things happen for a reason?" he asked as he brought it to her throat before she could grab the door handle. He was hard as a rock now.

"Please don't hurt me," she whimpered.

"Oh, I wouldn't dream of *hurting* you," he said. "I think things happen for a reason." He yanked her onto his lap and shoved some pills down her throat. "This will make things easier.

"Don't struggle. The best formed ego-defense is denial." Gagging, she finally swallowed them. He waited until she became still, her eyes glazed, her arms limp at her sides. He hauled her outside, into a thick tangle of oaks. He laid her down and brushed a finger along her cheek. "*Il est temps de mourir mon bonbon.* It's time to die, my sweet." A short while later, he jabbed the ice pick into soft flesh.

♦   ♦   ♦

Later, he sucked on a gin fizz in a chichi New Orleans bar listening to the pinball sounds of jazz and watching drunken people chank-a-chank. He sampled the complimentary cheese. He thought of how her blood, the blood of a virgin, had spilled onto the crocodile green grass beneath her. He felt relaxed. At the corner, the sounds of Al Hirt, the Dukes of Dixieland, the Cajun Cabin, and Chris Owens rolled out and thunked in the humid night air. He was looking forward to retiring to his room, Room 5, the one with the big bed you could get lost in and the oversized shower converted from a coal bin. He was going to take another nice hot shower later.

The door of the bar was flung wide open; outside, men ambled about, dressed in stark white clown makeup, baggy trousers, and red fright wigs. Funny, what some people thought was spooky.

In his room, he thought of the final touch, of sliding the brass button beneath the girl's warm, wet tongue. His third victim. He hoped they'd figure it out. But cops were stupid. They took a long time about things.

He slid his clothes off his sweaty body and stepped into the shower.

I'm the star now, the only *star.*

He was also the only one who knew the secret about his brother. He was disappointed that his stepfather was dead; a shame he wouldn't be able to enlighten Pops about what'd really happened. His brother hadn't accidentally drowned in that lake on the family vacation.

After he showered, he lay naked on the wide bed beneath the tattered mosquito nets. A Stones song pounded through his head. *Pride and joy and greed and sex…that's what makes our town the best. Pride and joy and dirty dreams and still surviving on the street…and look at me, I'm in tatters, yeah…I've been battered, what does it matter…*

He thought of his dead wife. Then he closed his eyes and slept like a baby.

25

"What did you think of the note?" Ann asked Tony over the phone.

"Odd. I think he wants us to believe there's more than one person acting out these sick fantasies. But I don't buy it."

"Neither do I. Maybe it's a clue to where we'll find his next victim, although I hope not." Ann thought of the note that had been left on Laurie's body in the stadium. It was a stanza from Herman Melville's Civil War poem *The Scout Toward Aldie:*

The cavalry-camp lies on the slope
Of what was late a vernal hill,
But now like a pavement bare—
An outpost in the perilous wilds
Which ever are lone and still;
But Mosby's men are there—
Of Mosby best beware.

At least the *note* had been kept out of the press.

"Maybe the guy thinks he's some kind of guerrilla fighter. I did some research on Civil War sites," Ann said. "Including Bucks County. Nothing much struck me. Except that the ground that shaped our nation is quickly being paved over for shopping malls, housing tracts, McDonald's and Wal-Mart's. Nearly 20 percent of America's Civil War battlefields have already been destroyed. Only 15 percent are protected by the Federal government. God, I have a headache."

"Sounds like you need a beer. Meet me at Blue Star in twenty minutes? We can hash it all out."

"Sounds good. See you there."

Ann hung up, thinking about the things that connected her with Tony. A former FBI agent and six-foot-four lean black man who reminded her of Morgan Freeman, Tony had taught cultural diversity, among other subjects, to classes of mostly white males at the academy. He was highly respected by his peers and supervisors. Ann had done some innovative research on ethnic discrimination that had somehow found its way into Tony's hands. That's how they'd met.

They both liked solving puzzles, getting arrests, getting the bad guy. They both experienced discrimination every day. They both had blue-collar parents who were hard-working and had made sacrifices for their children. Tony's father lost an arm in a conveyor belt accident in New Jersey. His clothes got caught in the belt of a machine that separated clams and oysters, cutting his arm off near the shoulder. The arm couldn't be saved, but Tony's father had survived.

Ann changed into tan khakis and a black T, ran a brush through her hair, and headed off to Roosevelt's Blue Star on foot. The little restaurant was tucked away down a quaint alleyway from the main street. Historic, patriotic artifacts hung on the walls; jazz from the bar across the alleyway thumped loudly into the humid night air. It was one of Ann's favorite haunts—not just for the atmosphere, but also for the American cuisine. They served great chops and burgers.

She quickly spotted Tony at a table near the back and joined him. He had two beers in front of him and he pushed one toward her. "Guinness Stout. Just waiting for your sweet lips."

"You're such a gentleman," Ann said. "And they say you're such a hard ass."

They both took a few sips of beer and let the music, the floating sounds of people mingling and relaxing and living a *normal* life, wash over them. "I had a thought on the way over here," Tony said. "The guy may be a re-enactor. Maybe he had an ancestor who fought in the war. Maybe he's a Civil War buff."

Ann pushed a tendril of glossy black hair behind her ear. "I did look into that. The 104th Pennsylvania does reenactments. They begin in March and end in November. They take part in a reenactment each month around Philadelphia, and in Jersey, Delaware, Maryland, or Virginia."

"Living history," Tony said. "Always kind of gave me the creeps, people wanting to relive all that blood and gore."

"They set up encampments to demonstrate and interpret the Civil War era for visitors and students. Could be something there. Maybe that's how our guy picks his targets. If it is, he'd have to be somewhat wealthy; the clothing, leather goods, fees for events, transportation and food all adds up. Clothing alone can run a grand." Ann rubbed her temples. "Maybe it doesn't mean anything, but there's something else."

Tony took another swig of Guinness. "Spill it."

"A guy who fought in the Mexican-American War and the Civil War, Davis I think his name was, raised a regiment of infantry and a six-gun battery—the 104th Pennsylvania volunteers. He took the men and boys and set up a camp of instruction just outside town, on the site of the present-day Central Bucks West

High School. There could be a connection, somehow, with Laurie's body. Maybe that's why he chose to leave her there, in the stadium."

Tony shook his head. It was always harder to catch this kind of criminal—an intelligent, brazen guy who had taken his fantasies to a higher level, who had probably, up until the time he killed, lived a normal, even upstanding life. But even the intelligent ones eventually screwed up.

"So, we have victims who vary in age, occupation, education. What could tie them together? We have buttons popping up beneath their tongues. And from the autopsy reports we know the victims had an experimental drug called Lucinate X in the bloodstream. And a psycho quoting Herman Melville. What does it all mean?"

Ann drummed her fingers on the table. "I've been thinking about something else. It's really weird."

"I live 'weird' on a daily basis, remember? Let's hear it."

"I've been seeing a hypnotist, undergoing past-life regressions to deal with the trauma of my job and my recent divorce."

Tony didn't interrupt—didn't judge. That's what she liked about him.

"The thing about PLR is that you don't have to believe in it for it to work."

"PLR? Don't go all 'acronym' on me now, sweetie."

"Sorry. Past-life regression."

"So, does it work? Do you have memories of past lives?"

"I didn't think I could be hypnotized, but yes, I did. And some were very disturbing. In one, I was in Virginia, meeting a friend who had come home from the war, telling him I was getting married, and then...

"Then I felt his hands on my neck, strangling me. I remembered *being killed*. Not once, but a few times. *By the same soul*."

Tony whistled. "Heavy duty."

"I don't know if I believe in past lives. Maybe it's just possible that you can inherit fears and memories like you inherit curly hair or blue eyes. I don't know how it would work, but it could explain why people suddenly develop irrational fears or have 'memories' of past lives."

"It's not such a strange theory," Tony commented.

"It gets weirder. What if people are reincarnated and this guy is tracking me down <u>again</u>, in *this lifetime*?"

"You have an open mind. Who's to say what's possible? Cases have been solved by psychics, why not by hypnosis?"

"You are so chipper tonight. And I was hoping to shock you."

Tony kept smiling. "Nothing could ruin my mood tonight. *Nothing.* Now, about Peter. 'Bout time you took out the trash. Never liked him."

"Care to tell me why you're so chipper?"

Tony leaned back against his chair and stretched. "I'm going to be a dad."

"Shit!"

"That was my reaction too," he said, "along with unbelievable joy. Imagine, me, a dad, after all these years!"

Ann jumped up and hugged him. "This calls for a celebration." She sat down and motioned the waiter. "We need something a little more classy than beer. My friend here is going to be a dad! Surprise us!" The waiter, a young man with tanning-bed skin and tousled tawny hair, congratulated him.

"And we'll need cheeseburgers with the works, and fries. Make his bloody and mine well-done."

"You got it," the waiter said and headed off to the kitchens.

"I can't believe it!" Ann said.

"I know. Jesus, I mean, I'm *retired.* When he goes to college, I'll be 73."

"He? You seem pretty certain it's going to be a boy."

"It doesn't really matter whether it's a boy or girl. It's fuckin' great!"

"Is Daneen happy about it? Does she want to…keep it?" Daneen was 42, thirteen years younger than Tony, and his second wife.

"Yeah, absolutely. We both know, given her age, it will be a high-risk pregnancy, but we're willing to experience the difficult days ahead if it means we can hold our baby in our arms, hear his or her first cries."

"I'm so happy for you both," Ann said, thinking of her first marriage, her hopes for children, and how it all seemed so far away now. "Wait until I tell Nai Nai. She'll be knitting you socks and sweaters and baby blankets tomorrow."

Tony scratched his head. "I don't know how we'll do it. Maybe it's not fair, given my age."

"Fair has nothing to do with it. It just is. And it's wonderful."

"Yeah. I don't have to schlepp into a basement at the academy and track down psychos every day of the week. I figure I can spend a lot of time with my kid."

The burgers and fries arrived and the waiter had managed to rustle up two glasses of champagne. "Here's to Baby Cole," Ann said. "And to the happy parents. You and Daneen will find a way."

They were quiet for a while as they enjoyed their food. "There's another reason I wanted to see you," Tony said. "We may have a break in the case. A friend of mine at VCAP did some cross-checking and came up with something interesting. How do you feel about New Orleans?"

Ann finished chewing slowly. *VCAP. The Violent Criminal Apprehension Program. The computerized program that allowed for nationwide cross-checking of cases and matching of similar unsolved cases on the basis of MO and signature analysis.* "I don't think I want to know why you asked me that."

"Body of a young woman was found outside the city. Button under her tongue."

"You waited until now to tell me?"

"I'm a little distracted tonight, sorry." He took out a fine Cuban cigar, lit it, and sucked on it like it was candy.

Nai Nai's dream warning echoed in Ann's head. *You take trip. To place of great color and noise.* "Bring on the Turbo Ale and the po'boys," Ann said.

26

Ann had spent the flight to New Orleans sitting between Tony and an obese man who was constantly throwing up into the little white barf bags supplied by the airline or getting up to go to the bathroom. He was sweating profusely, and by the end of the flight, she had heard his whole life story, interested or not.

Tony and Ann had agreed to meet the NOP, the New Orleans Police, at 2:45 pm at the crime scene that day. After their plane touched down at the New Orleans International Airport, they shuffled through the airport, grabbed a few hot dogs and Cokes, and got a dull grey Century Buick rental car that smelled like stale cigarettes, cheap air fresheners, and body odor.

It was 85 degrees outside, the humidity close to 90 percent. With the radio honking jazz sounds, Tony drove them through the city, across the Mississippi bridge, out onto I-10E.

"I haven't been to Murder City for years," he said. He was wearing a dark blue T-shirt and jeans and sweat was beading on his brown neck. "Forgot how much I fuckin' hate the humidity." Ann carried an envelope full of crime scene photos on her lap. She pulled them out and studied them.

"Guess the killer didn't know the forensics and autopsy units here are top-notch." She would have preferred to have a live crime scene to investigate, to mingle with the homicide detectives and crime scene technicians and medical examiner's assistants in the hang-happy air. She wanted to investigate the tall houses sleeping under the pale shadows of wrought-iron balconies, to drink dark coffee and listen to the soft slur of business being conducted in a myriad of languages.

The pair was silent as the New Orleans highway whittled by.

"Daneen is worried about you. I know some good guys; I could you fix you up. You know, Peter was a bad apple, but that don't mean the whole damn tree is rotten."

Ann rolled her eyes. "I don't need any help in the dating department, all right?"

Tony shrugged his shoulders. "You know why you should listen to jazz when you're in New Orleans?"

"Because I like it?"

"You've never heard about the Orleans Axeman?"

Ann shook her head, munching on an overdone hotdog and popping a tab off a can of Coke.

"Some nutcase went around hacking people up in 1919, mostly Italian grocers, and leaving bloody axes at the scenes. Wrote a note to a newspaper, and they printed it, telling everyone he would kill again, fifteen minutes after midnight, on St. Joseph's Night, March 19, but would spare the occupants of any place where a jazz band was playing. Some say there has never been a louder night in Big Easy history—no one was killed that night."

"Did they ever catch him?" Ann asked.

"No one knows for sure who he—or she—was."

"Why do you say 'he or she'?"

"Had to be small. Maybe a boy. Cut open panels in back doors and squeezed through them with an axe."

Ann sifted through manila dividers stapled with papers and five-by-seven photos. "Says here our ten-seven is the daughter of a well-respected businessman." Ann liked to talk jargon with Tony; it always amused him. Ten-seven was police communication code for "out-of-service." Kind of heartless. "She spent time in Charity's detox unit only to come face-to-face with a psycho. No defense wounds. Whoever he is, she trusted him enough to get in a car with him and drive away."

"Drug deal? Temptation? Wrong place, wrong time?" Tony said, rubbing his unshaven chin. "Have I said how much I fuckin' hate the humidity?" They had now chosen to roll down the windows and blast the AC.

"Yeah. I get the picture. New Orleans isn't your streetcar of desire."

"Oh no, baby, I *love* New Orleans. I just hate the fuckin' humidity."

Forty-five minutes later, they pulled off a highway, down a sallow, rutted dirt road, into a circle of bald cypress trees and long-leaf pines. The scene was stale but still yellowed off by tape and two suited-up NOPs stood talking in the shade. Despite the heaviness of the air and the distance separating them, both Tony and Ann caught the younger officer's remarks. "Lookee here. It's salt 'n pepper from the press."

Ann didn't even *look* at Tony. Tony was not someone you wanted to antagonize, and how he would react to the racial slur was anyone's guess. Ann was hoping he wouldn't pop their heads off with his meaty fists.

The younger-looking uniform, twenty at most, had dark red hair, thin circles under his watery blue eyes, and a drawn look about his face. He was smoking a cigarette. "Creds," he said, blowing trails of smoke from his thin lips. "You're a little late for the scoop," he added, cackling like a hyena.

Tony cracked his knuckles loudly and took his time about flashing his FBI badge. "I'm just a po' black boy trying to make my way in the world." When the uniform's mouth gaped open, Tony reached over, pulled the cigarette out of the man's mouth, and crushed it out with his sneaker. "Not only can this wreck a crime scene but it can be hazardous to your health. Remember, only you can prevent forest fires."

The officer's face turned glad-red and his lips squared together, but he held himself in check. He'd seen the tattoo on Tony's bulging bicep. Tony was a former marine. Saw the ass-end of the Vietnam War. Combat photographer too. Tony rarely, if ever, showboated, and Ann was enjoying it.

"And the broad here is Ann Yang, medical examiner from Bucks County, PA. No need to present your creds, fellas. I already know who you are. Sylvan and Wheatley. Both bucking to get into homicide. District Seven. Tired of writing traffic tickets and cleaning commodes? Well, booooooyyyys, this might not be a holy-shit case for the NOP, but it is for us. Possible serial with wide hunting grounds. Channel 11 ain't on line 2 and the mayor doesn't want to be briefed, but I need some information pronto."

The other uniform, an older man with a protruding beer gut, brown hair sprinkled liberally with grey, and a sagging chin and belly, stood a little taller. He reminded Ann of a mushroom in a frying pan. You could tell they were the kind of cops who handed over their paychecks directly to Budweiser.

"You do understand this case has been upgraded to red ball?" Tony asked.

"Yes Sir," Wheatley gulped. "Didn't expect nobody but the press. Nobody said nothing about the Feds."

Ann felt admiration for Tony even as sweat trickled down her leg, inside her jeans, which covered the ankle holster of her Glock. How did he always know the things he knew?

Pencil and sketchpad in hand, Ann examined the flattened copse where the body of the young girl had lain, half of her body covered by the brush, half exposed—another journey ended much too soon, now just a memory of broken dreams—while Tony pulled together the raw material for the death investigation.

She stared at the spot from every conceivable angle, sketching, looking at the crime scene photos. Her eyes scanned blood spatters and trails, weeds, brush, blades of grass, memorizing textures and patterns. Why was the body here? What did the 'artist' want them to see?

Tony continued to interview the officers. Obviously, the city didn't think the murdered girl warranted anything more than two junior officers from Mayberry guarding the crime scene, certainly not typical of the accolades for the rest of the department. Maybe if it had happened in a different city, one with less crime, filth, and despair, it would've been higher priority. Tony wouldn't be giving a press conference that day or assisting the NOPD or any FBI special agents-in-charge, the US attorney, or the Governor in urging women to take measures to protect themselves. No, they'd wait until more bodies turned up. Until they determined that it may be the same serial killer crossing state lines, Tony probably wouldn't be able to marshal FBI resources to help track down the serial.

On the way back into town, Ann and Tony discussed the medical examiner's report. "This case should be a slam dunk," Tony said. "Burn marks on the ground two feet from the body. Cause of death—seizure, cardiac arrest; strangulation."

"The killer tried to burn off the victim's fingers, probably after she was dead," Ann said. "Oh, and thirty-three postmortem stab wounds from a sharp object, probably an ice pick. Medical examiner believes the stabbing lasted more than a minute. A fucking minute. And the killer didn't leave his knife or ice pick behind. They usually do in cases like these, don't they?"

"That's what I was thinking," Tony said.

Ann knew the medical examiner had fingerprinted the corpse, fingerprinted himself. He was experienced and exceptional at what he did and like Ann, didn't wear gloves at certain crime scenes when gloves made handling evidence awkward. Gloves could very easily smudge a fingerprint.

Ann knew that he'd also carefully run a razor-sharp penknife under each fingernail of the corpse and placed the residue in evidence envelopes. But the victim hadn't scratched the murderer; there was no blood in the scrapings to cross match to the killer's blood.

"Yeah, the two fuck-ups I interviewed told me that two detectives did some canvassing near the bookshop, but nobody has talked with neighbors, ex-boyfriends, etc., yet. Whadda ya think of the burn marks?"

"Blow torch. He was probably freebasing after he killed her and got the idea to try to burn off the pads of her fingers. Which explains why he didn't succeed. And maybe why he didn't leave her wallet behind for us to find, like he did with the others. Impaired judgment. If it wasn't for the button, there wouldn't be much to link this case to the others. I need to find out if Lucinate X was present in her system."

"Good thing you wore your sneakers. We have a lot of sidewalks to stomp, doors to knock on. But don't worry," Tony said. "We'll top it off with Swamp Water, fresh oysters, and some Cajun music."

The dead girl was now a name in red ink on some detective's dry-erase board in the precinct's coffee room, Ann thought sadly. Just then the sheep-like bleating of Tony's cell phone interrupted her thoughts. He flipped his phone out of his T-shirt pocket.

"Yeah," Tony said. He nodded a few times, said "OK. On it," and hung up.

"We might have a lead. Young kid recently moved back home after a stint in detox called the tip line. Says he remembers seeing a pretty young girl who looked like Tiffany getting in a dark-colored Porsche near Faulkner's and driving away. He described the driver as a tall man with unnaturally black hair and cherubic features. That's the word he used. *Cherubic.* We're gonna have to talk to the guy. Could be all bullshit too."

Ann was silent, staring out the window. "You know what people think I keep in my desk drawers?"

Tony looked at her.

"Earrings, tubes of lipstick, perfumed scarves, Kotex, sushi. They think I'm a secretary with a gun."

"Just your average GFUs, Annie," Tony said, finally pulling into the hotel parking lot and then punching up a number on his cell. "That's slang for General Fuck-Ups."

"I got that," she replied.

"How you feelin' today, baby?" Tony spoke into his phone. Daneen jawed his ear off for a while and then Tony said, "OK Sugar Lips. Talk to you soon. I have a surprise for you and baby Cole." He hung up and grinned like a kid who'd just found a twenty dollar bill on the ground. "Baby Cole. Ain't it sweet?"

"Sure is, Sugar Lips," Ann said.

27

When Tony and Ann arrived at the NOPD homicide unit offices at 7:45 am the next day, they both felt their enthusiasm waning. No motive. No suspect description to broadcast.

They were shown to the homicide room, a big room with depressing gray walls, metal chairs, old desks shoved up against each other, wadded-up greasy napkins on the floor, and posters hanging on wall with slogans like DON'T LIKE MY ATTITUDE? Call 1-540-EAT-SHIT and SERIAL KILLERS BELIEVE IN POPULATION CONTROL.

They were joined by John Harding, who worked plainclothes follow-up investigations, two detectives, and the head of the Homicide Unit, Payne Grist. After introductions, Payne offered them coffee in Styrofoam cups, which they eagerly accepted. "Noxious brew, but it'll wake you up," he said.

He quickly brought them up to speed on the facts. He had called First District, which handled the French Quarter, and asked for a record review, specifically noting anyone arrested in the last week carrying a concealed knife-like weapon. The detectives had since covered the Quarter thoroughly then branched out into the city. Payne showed Tony and Ann the short report on the Tiffany Sly murder, alerting other detectives to keep their eyes peeled for anything that might assist. Then Ann and Tony brought them up to speed on the murders in Doylestown, the profile Tony had worked up, their theories. They thanked the officers, promised to share any new leads, and left.

As they stepped out into the hot sunshine, Tony slipped his shades on. Ann could tell he was stoked. He would tackle some of the more difficult interviews; Ann would walk the block and a half to the medical examiner's office.

"What do you think?" she said.

"Killer's a friend or someone who's not immediately suspicious. Or a fucking nut job taking a little vacation from his normal stomping grounds."

"Good luck," Ann said.

A fucking nut job. The option they both feared the most.

Assistant Medical Examiner Jason Bloom was working the shift. After she'd slipped on bright yellow plastic pants and a jacket, Ann stood next to him in the morgue as he worked over a body. She wanted more information about what the autopsy showed. Jason was young, had thick black hair and eyes the color of pool water. He was soft spoken and Ann had to strain to catch his words, even in the cavernous vault of a room. His supervisor headed the pathology department at Charity Hospital, which handled autopsies for the entire state.

Jason padded softly from refrigerated box to refrigerated box, where bodies cooled.

"The Tiffany Sly case. Truly disturbing," Ann said.

"Yeah. What in the world happened?" he said. It was normal for medical examiners to be curious; like any citizen, they wanted to know who could do a thing like stab a young girl thirty-three times with an ice pick.

"Anyone could have done it," Ann said.

Jason handed some papers to Ann.

He pursed his lips. "The majority of wounds weren't fatal. The ones I saw on her arms, hands, and face anyway. She was already dead of cardiac arrest when he severed her carotid and jugular."

"You think it was an ice pick?"

"Yeah." He adjusted his silver wire-rimmed glasses and his eyes looked huge.

"The wounds are small, point four centimeters in diameter. Too small to be a knife and consistent with the circular design of a pick."

The killer brought the weapon with him. Premeditated.

"What was in her stomach?"

"Something strange. Some sort of hallucinogenic drug maybe? I'm trying to identify it…"

"It may be an experimental drug used to treat severe schizophrenia. We have two similar cases. Victims had something called Lucinate X in their system. It's an experimental drug for schizophrenics. Can cause seizures."

He looked visibly paler. "We're really in the shit here, huh?"

"Yeah. I'll have my office fax the reports over to you."

"Thanks." He scratched his chin, which was covered sparsely with tiny black hairs; he looked like a thirteen-year-old boy who was trying to grow a beard but who wasn't blessed with lumber-jack genes.

"What about time of death?" Ann asked.

"She was last seen around 1:15 pm in front of the bookstore on Tuesday. Based on the state of the body, the insect bites on her breasts, and fact that the stiffening disappeared, probably maximum 48 hours before they found the body."

That meant, at the outside, that she had died shortly after leaving the bookstore. Within hours.

"This guy was definitely paying attention in Sex Crimes 101; she was vaginally raped and sodomized. Acute anal and vaginal injuries. Her vagina was lacerated and her hymen torn. But no seminal fluid."

◆   ◆   ◆

Tony paused before a heavy door set flush with the sidewalk in the high façade of an old house. He raised the iron knocker and let it fall. He waited in the street. The houses on Orleans Street were crammed together, each one with balconies of ornate ironwork that reminded him of skeletal vertebrae.

The door swung open and a woman in stonewashed jeans and a faded peach T-shirt just stared at him. "Oh. You must be the FBI guy." She stood aside and Tony stepped in over the door sill. "Tony Cole. Retired FBI."

"Pauline Clemmens," she said. "Follow me."

The passage was long and paved with blue flagstones; the walls were the color of flesh. At the end of the passage was a large courtyard; palm trees waved in fractured sunlight. The court was surrounded by the walls of the house.

They sat down at a small breakfast table set in the open air. The sunlight shimmered on the silver coffee pot standing on white cloth. The woman lit a menthol cigarette. "You want some coffee?"

"Yeah, thanks. Never turn down the java."

Her hands shook as she poured it. She looked to be about fifty but Tony guessed she was only in her late thirties. Hard living.

"You want to talk to my son about the murder of that girl."

Tony nodded his head, taking a sip of the coffee.

"Well, if he saw something, if he can help, that would be the only good thing he done in a damn long time."

She blew a wide puff of smoke out the side of her mouth and combed her hand through her limp ash-blonde hair. Her roots were showing. An alcoholic, no doubt, judging by the ruddiness of her skin, the yellowish whites of her half-closed eyes. An alcoholic with a co-dependent alcoholic son. Why was it so hard for so many parents to simply love their children? Tony felt a burst of anger. He believed that one of the big reasons for crime was because children didn't have loving, capable, responsible adult parents to teach their children right from wrong. Children with self-respect. If the parent didn't have it, the kid wouldn't have it.

"I've been trying to get his lazy ass out of bed since 9 o'clock, but he just sleeps the days away since he come home from Charity, that detox center. He's been there a *few* times, you know?"

She called up to the balcony. Tony could see high over their heads the fan-shaped windows of the old house, open to catch the sunlight and morning breezes. While they waited, Tony marveled at the beauty of the home. "Nice place," he said.

"Yeah, *goddamn nice*, but it ain't mine. It's my father's."

A pale-faced skinny kid finally emerged and took a seat next to his mother. He was tall, with red-brown hair tucked into a ponytail. He rubbed his eyes, poured himself a coffee, and dumped half a bowl of sugar into it.

"You must be Paul. Thanks for agreeing to talk with me."

The kid nodded sleepily. "Don't know if I can help but I'll try."

"I appreciate that," Tony said. Odd, but something about the pair sitting before him reminded him of characters on Mardi Gras floats—caught in the trance between sleeping and waking. People who dulled the brilliance and beauty of life with drugs.

"Good coffee," Tony said. "I'd like to ask you a few questions, Paul."

Paul lit up one of his mom's cigarettes with his skinny fingers. "Shoot."

"You were in the bookstore last Tuesday during what time?"

"I went there to drink some coffee, you know, hang out, around 10:30 in the morning. I used to have a job there."

"Got his sorry ass fired too," Pauline said.

Faulkner House Books was on just about every walking tour of the French Quarter; Faulkner lived there while he penned his early novels *Mosquitos* and *Soldier's Pay*.

"You think you saw the victim getting in a car? What time was that?"

The kid blushed. "I actually saw her, the girl, inside the bookstore and thought she was kind of cute. I'm not a stalker or anything, but I was trying to work up the nerve to ask her for a date. So, I just sort of hung out and waited until she left the store and followed her out onto the sidewalk. I think it was like one o'clock or one-fifteen."

"I know this is all in the police reports, but I want to make sure they didn't miss anything. Maybe since that time you've remembered something else? The car..."

"A dark late-model Porsche. Something odd about it, like a bad paint job or something."

"And the guy driving it?"

"I was kind of hanging back, so I didn't see him real good. But he was tall, maybe 6'2", had black hair, a pin-striped business suit. Strange thing is he had a joint body. Seemed to be in real good shape. It happened fast. He just walked up to her, said something, pulled out a map, and she got in the car and drove away with him."

"Did you happen to notice what sort of a map it was?"

"Nope. I wasn't that close."

He blew a puff of smoke and watched it circle and billow in the wet-blanket air. "Clean-shaven too; no mustache. Looked like just another professional type, you know, briefcase up the ass."

"Did the girl look frightened? Like she was being forced into the car?

"She didn't look scared."

Tony glanced through the lower windows of the house, noting the large chandelier, stray pieces of heavy mahogany furniture, a table scattered with magazines and receipts, and large pots of flowering oleanders.

Paul looked at his mom. "Grandpap got any brew stashed around here?"

"You're not supposed to have any," she said. "But I could use one too. One won't hurt. You want one too?" Tony shook his head. She left to get her son the alcohol that so disabled him. It was hard for Tony to keep his mouth shut.

"I remembered the license plate this morning."

"What?"

"Yeah."

Tony scribbled it down on the pad he was taking notes on while they talked.

"You're pretty sure about the number?"

"Yeah. I feel pretty sure. I was thinking about the whole scene last night before I fell asleep and I dreamt about it, saw the numbers in my dream."

Pauline returned with two Miller Lites.

"That's all I remembered that I didn't tell the cops yet."

Tony stood up. "Thanks for the coffee and for the information."

Pauline slurped down half the bottle of piss in one gulp and wiped her mouth with a dainty white linen napkin. "Thanks, detective. Is it detective? What do you call an FBI guy?"

"Tony is fine."

"Well Tony, let us know if you find anything out."

"Thanks again Paul, Pauline. Everybody in your family have a name that starts with 'P'?"

Pauline snorted. 'Yeah, my dad, he's real fucked up. And not very imaginative. Rich, but fucked up. Had to name my son Paul so I wouldn't get cut outta his will. I wanted to name him Nimrod."

Back in the street, Tony called the precinct on his cell. The lieutenant answered. Tony gave him the plate number and asked that they call him right away after running it.

28

Candy was stoned already, swaying on her stocking-clad feet. He'd picked up the high-priced whore near the gaming casinos and promised he'd pay her fees if she indulged him a little bit. Now, two blocks from the casino, he'd paid cash in advance for one of the seven suites at the JW Marriott—10th floor—under a fake name, of course.

At the casino, the girl had looked beautiful, but on closer inspection, he could see her ash-blonde hair was dyed and there were tiny dart-lines of fatigue around her glassy blue eyes. She had expensive taste in clothing; now her white and turquoise paneled strapless corset and tailored black ball gown skirt lay in a heap on the floor with her stockings and black stilettos.

He followed her naked form from the large dressing area to the marbled tub. He was a little disappointed when he found what had been beneath the dress—ugly lines crisscrossed her waist from having sucked it in a good two to three inches; her breasts, though full, were starting to sag slightly. The girl was 22 at most; she'd probably been working the streets since she was 15.

He watched her wash herself provocatively in the tub but he wasn't getting hard. That made him angry. But then again, the game hadn't yet begun.

She seemed to be in her own little world. Funny, she was naked except for an expensive diamond watch.

He sat down and watched her for a while then stood and retrieved a crystal glass and a bottle. He walked through the plush living room and opened the door to the balcony overlooking a New Orleans skyline candy-coated with twinkling lights. Then he walked back to the bathroom. "Ever hear of the Green Fairy?"

"What'd ya say, sugar?" she asked.

His fingers tensed around the crystal glass then he relaxed them.

"You're not too smart, are you?"

She giggled and trailed her long, manicured fingernails over a breast dripping with water and soap suds. She had large, dark nipples. "Don't have to be."

"I asked if you'd ever heard of the Green Fairy."

"You're not going to make me dress up like one, are you?"

He smiled slowly. Then she noticed the gloves he was wearing.

"You <u>are</u> a strange one, aren't you? I don't have no diseases, if that's what you're worried about. I'm…selective. Plus, I go to the clinic once a year to get tested."

He ignored her ludicrous words. "The Green Fairy is a drink. It's called absinthe. It enjoyed its greatest popularity in *fin-de-siècle* Paris. Vincent Van Gogh, Paul Verlaine, Alfred Jarry and Oscar Wilde were among its most ardent imbibers. The real stuff can drive one toward madness and suicide."

The girl rolled her eyes. "Oh great, an *in-tel-lect-u-al.* Are we going to fuck or what? I have other customers, you know."

He was starting to get hard. "I have some of the real stuff right here, and I want you to drink it. And no, we're not going to fuck."

She stepped out of the tub, wobbling. "You're wasting my time. I'm not drinking that shit."

He struck her, forcefully. She fell to the tiled floor, her nose bleeding red onto the white tiles. "Hey, I don't let anyone beat me up mister. *Anyone.* That wasn't part of the deal."

He stood over her, his feet braced apart. "Get in the tub."

"I'm not getting…"

"Get in." He yanked her up off her feet and dropped her back into the water, which sloshed over the sides of the tub. She sucked in a mouthful of soapy water and coughed.

There was fear in her eyes now, fear as wide and rippling as the Indian Ocean at midnight.

She was too stoned to move, staring at the blood on her hands, the blood fanning out into the water, in confusion.

He brought the glass and the dark emerald liquid to her lips and forced it down. It hadn't been hard to find illegal, homemade absinthe in the city; everything had its price.

The girl gagged and choked on it as it went down.

"Some people believe absinthe stimulates creativity. Hemingway let his characters drink it all the time. There's one small problem, though."

Candy looked stunned. He unzipped his pants and dropped them to his knees while wrapping his tie around her neck.

"It's like having your brains smashed out with a brick."

Her arms and legs stiffened and he knew she was hallucinating. She started thrashing around the water like a mad animal, her face convulsing, her lips twisted and covered in foam. Before she could cry out, he tightened the tie around her throat. While the breath left her body, he came.

Afterward, he carried her gingerly to the balcony. He stroked her cheek. "No one's going to miss you. You're just a used-up whore spreading filth." He laid her down on the balcony and got a drink for himself, one with a lot less wormwood. He let it course through his body. Soon, his brain felt like it was floating.

He quickly changed into a jogging outfit and placed his glass on a discarded tray outside one of the doors further down the deserted hallway. He came back into the room, then slipped Candy's naked body over the side of the balcony and watched from the shadows as it fell to the street, a pile of broken bones, torn skin, and blood. Looking like someone headed to the hotel gym, he slipped from the room to catch his flight home, gloves in his pocket. Down there, she kind of looked like something out of Edvard Munch's painting the *Scream*. It was time to go home.

◆   ◆   ◆

Ann felt her sense of balance slowly returning when Tony told her the good news—not only had they run the plate of the rental car successfully, but two uni-forms patrolling the streets on foot found the abandoned rental car in an alley. It was in the process of being towed to the crime lab to be looked at by forensic pathologists and lab techies.

"Let's hope our guy got sloppy," Ann said. She felt a sudden burst of adrena-line, sure that if she were face to face with the killer right now she could kill him with her bare hands. Sometimes it was hard to remember that decent people made up most of the world.

While they were on their way to the crime lab, they got bottlenecked near the JW Marriott Hotel on Canal Street. Other people were sleeping. Sirens flashed and popped and a crowd had gathered. "Jeeeeesus," Tony said. "It never ends."

"It'll take them a good three hours to go over that Porsche; want to check it out?"

"Sure, what the heck."

Tony inched his way up to the entrance of the back parking lot and flashed his credentials out the car window. "What happened officer? I'm Tony Cole, retired FBI agent. We've been in town investigating a murder." The harried-looking uniform told them they'd had a jumper from the tenth floor and then waved them through.

Tony and Ann were let into the lobby and met up with house detective Rogers Davis. Tony quickly showed him his credentials and offered to assist the detec-tive.

"What happened?" Tony asked.

"Girl's dead. Looks like she jumped, or was pushed, from the balcony."

"Who reported it?"

"Guests next door phoned the switchboard to report an escalating and potentially dangerous argument around 3:20 am. Then, of course, after her body hit the pavement around 3:45 am, calls starting flooding in."

They rode the elevator to the tenth floor, searching the hallways first. The killer might still be there. But the hallways were deserted. It wasn't The Fairmont, but it was so committed to looking classy that it covered the electrical cords of its lamps with shirred designer fabric.

"We didn't find any weapons, but it was clear from what was left of her that she'd been strangled," Davis said. "The locks on the room are all functional; doesn't look like forced entry.

"A couple was sleeping next door. They said they heard what sounded like a man and a woman arguing in the bathroom.

"How long did they wait before calling the operator?"

"They said they waited a good twenty minutes."

"How did he get out?" Ann said. "Down the main elevator? Through the main lobby? How do you push someone from a balcony and then walk out of a hotel without anyone noticing?"

"That's a puzzle."

As detectives conducted a room-to-room search of the entire tenth floor, including the stairwell, Tony told him about the case they were investigating. "Do you know if the medical examiner happened to look under the girl's tongue yet?"

The detective looked puzzled. "I'll call him and find out. Why?"

"Our killer's been leaving buttons from a Union officer's jacket on his victims. One of them here in New Orleans." Tony scratched his chin. "Let's talk to the receptionist and get a copy of the hotel registration card. Get a description of who rented this room. If the person who stayed here is male, with dark black hair, we might have something."

Ann and Tony stood outside the room as crime scene technicians dusted the entire scene and took pictures. They lifted partials from the lone drinking glass. As Ann watched them spraying the Do Not Disturb sign with ninhydrin, she thought, *Too late. Already disturbed.* There was an almost astral, constellation-like way they connected their movements, searching in the silver arc of dust for elusive threads the killer may have left untied.

29

Celerity: swiftness; briskness; expedition; haste; quickness; velocity; vivacity.
Surprise: state of amazement; astonishment; attack; jolt; kick; revelation; shock.

Ann was glad to be back in Doylestown, but she felt that something had come back with her. Something she couldn't name. She and Mark made small talk over cheese steaks and Cokes at Chambers, a small restaurant on Main Street. She'd had to get out of her office for a little while.

The restaurant was dimly lit and candles flickered softly on the tables. It was a small place with an open kitchen, so you could see the chefs preparing the meals. It was one of Mark's favorites; that's why she'd suggested it.

"You know, this isn't necessary, treating me to lunch for working on your house," he said between bites.

Ann fingered the white linen napkin on her lap. She took a sip of Coke. "Well, lunch is my treat, I insist. But I didn't ask you here for that reason."

He leaned back and arched a dark sandy brow, stretching and resting his arms on the back of the booth. "Oh?"

Ann actually felt herself blush. "I just…needed a friendly face." She wanted to talk to someone about everything but she couldn't. Someone not associated with the case. So many leads. So many dead ends. The rental car in New Orleans hadn't turned up a single clue. It was probably rented under a false name and the guy had paid cash. Lately, she'd felt almost as if she couldn't fight the darkness anymore, couldn't look at one more senseless act of violence.

He smiled and she could feel her heart thumping in her chest. She stared at his arms and then caught herself. She had the odd feeling she could be *safe* in those arms.

"Well, whatever the reason, I'm glad you chose my friendly face."

They talked about food, music, old movies, and laughed a lot. They were waiting for coffee and dessert, a slice of key lime cheesecake, when Ann asked him if he thought things happened for a reason.

He slid a lean, tanned finger unconsciously up and down his glass of Coke. "I don't know. I've often wondered about that. I think I do."

"It sounds weird, but I've often wondered if we 'enroll' for life before we're born. Sign up. I mean, if we're like spirits, ether, something, that suddenly decides to be born to two people. And then born again to learn something else. Are our whole lives mapped out for us, or are we given choices?" Ann said. "Like my marriage, for instance. *That* was a very bad choice. I was so…stupid."

"No you weren't," he said quietly. "I think sometimes we want people to be who they're not. And when we discover their faults, we can't believe it. We've seen them 'through a glass darkly' for so long, that it's a shock to our system. Not to mention the heart. And think of all the things you go through in a marriage…all the responsibilities. Two people see each other at their worst. It's not like you're going to spend the rest of your lives necking in the back of your dad's Chevy with no responsibilities."

Ann felt a little uncomfortable with the astute remark. "What happened with your marriage?"

Now he had one arm slung over the back of the booth, the other resting on the table. Ann felt a sudden urge to jump in his lap and kiss him. She stared instead at the slice of cheesecake that had just arrived.

She took the first bite and he took the second. "This is divine," Ann said.

"We were young. She didn't…want me. She didn't want an unglamorous life, living paycheck to paycheck with a simple carpenter."

Ann almost dropped her fork. Was the woman insane? Mark was incredibly sexy, sensitive, a good listener…

"It's probably better that it worked out that way but it took me a long time to accept it." He leaned forward, reached across the table, and gently squeezed her hand, caressed her fingers. "I like you Ann. I *really* like you."

Ann squeezed his fingers back, laced her own through his. "I feel something too."

He withdrew his hand gently. "Truth is I haven't dated much these past few years. My father was sick; there was a lot of stuff going on. He died…" Mark was interrupted by his cell phone bleeping. "Damn. Should have muted it." He reached in his pocket. "Mark," he said.

Ann liked his name, the masculine way it rolled off his tongue. As he talked, she heard him promising to come over right away and fix a leaking dishwasher. She watched his lips move and wondered what it would be like to feel them touching her, to know what every inch of his skin felt like, to know his wildest dreams, his fears, all of his expressions, like how he looked when he watched a funny movie or when he was angry or passionate.

She'd had the same thoughts about Peter. No, maybe not quite the same thoughts. *These* were somehow different. Stronger. Like the man sitting across from her. Ann knew she was in trouble. *Deep* trouble. Mark apologized for having to leave so abruptly, explaining that Mrs. Denny was 87 years old and didn't have anyone else to help her. *That's OK. I was just about to vault over the table and jump your bones.*

"No problem," Ann said. "I understand. She's lucky to have someone like you." She watched him walk out of the restaurant, feeling empty after he left. She looked at her watch. *Shit.* It was 2:45 pm. She had to get back to the office. They'd talked for nearly three hours.

30

Ann woke up and stretched leisurely in the sun streaming through her bedroom window. She'd actually gotten a decent night's sleep. Probably because her 'date' with Mark had gone well. She turned on her side and froze. A bundle of withered-looking papers tied neatly with a blood-red ribbon sat on her bedside table. The papers looked like they had been ripped from a journal of sorts and someone had labeled them in black marker: FOR YOU, ANN. MORE OF OUR STORY. BUT IT DOESN'T END HERE, DARLING.

Fuck. He'd been in her room; he'd watched her *sleep*.

She grabbed the phone and dialed the police, then searched the house, holding her Glock in front of her. The police turned her bedroom into something from CSI, dusted for prints, and bagged the papers. *Pages from the diary.* "I want that back ASAP," Ann said. The officer nodded and promised he'd have it back within a day or two.

31

Bare moonlight struck the tips of Ann's toes as the curtains of her second-story bedroom window danced in a slight breeze. She was lying in bed, watching them sway. They were the curtains Ann's mother Ming Yue had patiently sewed during her second pregnancy, often staying up late into the evening to finish her stitches, or so her father had told her. They were yellowed with age but Ann had hung them in her bedroom in all the places she had lived. Funny, she thought, how far we travel from ourselves.

Ann couldn't sleep. After her house had been invaded by a French-fried fuck she'd had an alarm system installed. She'd even tied a string of bells to her door, just in case he found a way to come back. It was 2 o'clock in the morning.

Lately, Ann had been thinking a lot about her mother. It was almost as if her spirit was close by, protecting her. There were long periods in Ann's life when she hadn't thought of her mother. She wished she had memories of Ming Yue's face, her lavender smell; wished her mother would've lived to rock her for hours when she was teething and crying all night and the steady motion of another life close to hers was the only thing that would console her. Ming Yue would've done what the other young mothers did, wet a cheap washcloth with cold water and bunched it in her baby's mouth.

Ann thought of her more often now that she was older. Did Ming Yue dream about her life while she sewed, thinking of the future with each perfect stitch? A future bright with the happy laughter of her growing girls, the promise of maybe having a son one day, the silent strength of her husband's arms encircling her in this strange, new country?

A heavy rain hit the roof, making a sound like marbles slipping from a dress pocket to the floor. In the quiet darkness, Ann wondered if Ming Yue knew how close death was, if she felt it in the hours when everyone else was sleeping and she was preparing for the bright, new life she would bring into the world.

Ann's dreams for her life had always seemed short, shallow. She teetered on the edge of hope, not quite willing to step off the ledge and see if someone would catch her when she fell. She thought of all the people who had lived in the house before her. What had their dreams been like, their lives? Had any of them ever driven by the house after it was sold, wondering how it was possible that another family could live in the rooms that belonged to them? Did *houses* forget the struggles and joys played out inside them?

It seemed this house had long ago forgotten Nell, the girl who disappeared in 1903, and her family—forgotten the love of the large, close-knit family that had spilled into all the corners of its rooms. Ann was always aware of the fragile ties holding her to the earth; that they could be cut in an instant. She looked at the grainy black-and-white photo of her mother in the silver frame, sitting with her arm around her husband on a blanket of sand, smiling, her shiny black hair hanging over her shoulders to her waist. Her father and Nai Nai had told her that Ming Yue had always loved the salt-smell of the ocean. Ann had long ago lost the acclivous, sloping sounds of her native tongue. When she and her sister danced to their mother's 45 records of Elvis Presley, Bo would always correct Ann when she said his name as "Elbis Presby."

Her mother and father had immigrated to the US when they were young and found a brick wall of hatred, suspicion, and distrust before they finally found an apartment in a rundown gray stucco building with electric meters screwed to the sides of the building. They got a pair of lamps from the Goodwill with shades that had American eagles on them, an avocado-colored couch, a few chairs, a kitchenette, and not much else. When they first moved in, they had almost nothing, not even a bed. They slept on the bare, wooden floors, rolled in each other's arms. But Ann's mother was happy. And apparently, so was Ann's small, square-shouldered father. There is something quick about his smile in the black-and-white photos taken before Ming Yue died. Something light and lyrical about his eyes. Afterward, a weariness settled in his soul too deep to keep him at home for any length of time.

The only work 'Chinks' could get in those days was at a restaurant or a corner grocery store. Her father made a decent living running a corner market; a lot of Chinese people in their building bought their Asian groceries from him rather than a Safeway, Kroger, Lucky, or Albertsons. Liang spent his mornings stocking shelves, rotating stock, grinding meat. Ann's father sometimes drove the kids to the store in their 9-seat Mercury Marquee station wagon that often refused to start again once it was shut off. They were the happiest times, when the loneliness that seemed to be part of Ann's soul was kept at bay.

Before Ann was born, her mother did the books late at night. Liang's store carried things like vegetables, chops, tofu, milk, bread, ice cream, TV dinners, cereal, beer, and cigarettes. Those were Kool-Aid days; sometimes Liang offered his customers free smokes. When she thought about it now, Ann could almost hear the sticky-sweet buzzing of bees in the alleyway, the barking of loud dogs and louder motor cars.

Her mother's life, sewing and singing and rocking. Ann's life, cutting open bodies, weighing organs, trying to find answers to the hideous questions hiding in others' souls. Oceans apart.

We are given glimpses of our destiny, Ann thought, *and many of us spend our lives running away from it.* Was that what she had been doing since her divorce? Seeking to immerse herself in darkness in order to find the light? Or had she always been drawn to darkness, and was just now picking up where she had left off before her marriage? She stared at the rain-streaked window, the fat drops falling into the open part where she had raised it.

She was exhausted, but the diary had been dusted and released to her that morning. It lay on her bedside table now, where she'd been meant to find it the first time. She picked it up and began reading. The diary of Farrell Neff, who'd been given a hasty trial and publicly executed for Nell's disappearance despite the fact that her body had never been found and he'd proclaimed his innocence up to the end.

September 7, 1902

I want to remember yesterday forever. When I am old, I want to return to this moment and live it again and again and again and never let it die. I put my mouth between her legs. Her sex was sweet and wet and musky. Her sigh as I touched her sounded like a taffeta comforter slipping off a bed.

Her flesh was a soft, mutable tremor, the forbidden taste was heady—I stroked her with my tongue, nipped her tiny, pink kernel of joy with my teeth, tasted her essence. She writhed beneath my explorations and clutched the top of my head, and my hair, with her slim, silken fingers while she spread her legs. The bud beneath me tightened and soon spasmed, spilling her juice on my lips, my face, the soft skin of her inner thighs. For a moment, we were both still. Her eyes were closed, a smile dancing on her lips. I inched my way up so that I lay next to her, raised myself up on an elbow so I could look down at her. I pushed her heavy, golden hair back from her face and ear and leaned down toward her face. My words were a diamond whisper, an uncut thought brought into being by heat, innocence, and the power of the moment. "Do you want to know what you taste like?" I murmured. She opened her eyes slowly, big green pools of shattered brilliance and guilt.

She did. I lowered my mouth to hers, my lips sharing the musky taste that came from between her legs. I asked her if she liked it and she said it was strange.

I placed my hand on her chest and felt her heart still hammering from when she had climaxed. "It's not strange. It's beautiful."

She closed her eyes briefly, her golden lashes licking the edges of her cheeks, and opened them in a brief moment of courage. I thought then that it was courage because she frowned slightly, that same frown she always gets when she isn't quite sure something feels right, but she wanted it to. "I want to taste you too," she said.

I was surprised, and aroused, but just then heard the front door below slam open and shut and then heard my father's strident voice.

The moment was gone. I told her to get in the closet. I heard my father speaking to someone and knew then that my mother was home from the institution. "I'll get you a drink of water," I heard him say—his remedy for everything. My mother didn't respond. Nell threw some clothes on—I don't know if they were mine or hers or a combination and hid in the closet.

I wasn't sure what to do. Fear and elation crawled over me in batches, alternating like the tides. I dressed and carefully went downstairs, greeting my mother—her eyes dark and worn and vacant—with the guilty taste of the girl I loved still in my mouth. As my father came into the living room, he seemed surprised to see me. He looked more tired than I'd ever remembered. He asked me why I wasn't in school but didn't really seem interested. When I was 7 or 8, he would get really angry with me. He'd stare at me purposefully as he began to remove his belt with the Indian-head belt buckle. It was the same belt he'd once used to beat a mule senseless. He hadn't cared then that I'd seen him do it. I was horrified. The old mule couldn't get up. What sort of man could do that to a poor defenseless animal, then shoot it? I ran around to the backyard and wretched. I'd never been so achingly sad in all my life. He found me.

The first few blows to the backs of my knees burned and I nearly buckled. I remember urinating, something that incensed him even more. I screamed, begged him to stop, the senseless bark of the shotgun still ringing in my ears, and thought of other things. "Ready to say you're sorry yet?"

"No!" I remember screaming.

He whipped me harder. "You ready yet?"

"No!"

I thought about the stars hanging in the tattered night sky, the rooted trees, and felt like one of the brown leaves blowing in the wind. The air was a soothing blanket that wrapped itself around me and carried me far, far away from my father, from the belt with the mean Indian face. The pain no longer mattered. It was like I was floating above my body, watching the scene from above. Eventually my father stopped, winded and sweating, leaning against the stone base of the well to catch his breath. Then he was gone. That was when I knew my father and I were different; I thought, I could never be driven to hurt another living thing. Yet I had sprung from his loins. How could that be? I'm nothing like him. I knew the next day he would say nothing about it. He would forget it until I did something else that made him angry.

I studied my mother the day she came home from her 'oasis,' sitting on a straight-backed chair, looking like a wooden statue. Sol lucet omnibus. The sun shines for everyone. But not everyone feels its warmth. She was better off in the hospital, maybe even happy there. And yet she couldn't stay there forever. I mean, how many of us can really stay in a place of escape forever? I thought of Nell, hidden away in my closet while all this was going on. I wished I could keep her there forever. I am dangerously obsessed. I wish I could call back the thought, the wish, because it feels like it will one day come back to haunt me. I can't explain it. Sometimes life is so raw, so brilliant, so alive, that I think I can't stand it. Especially when I'm in the presence of people who are half-dead, who've forgotten how to live.

"Did you know I was born in Rome?" my mother asked, her eyes lucid.

I was surprised.

"I went back there once, when I was 19," she said. "I fell in love. He taught me to swim in the Tiber. I learned how to recognize the sound of Saint Peter's bells."

She turned her head and looked out the front window. "We kissed beneath the water fountain, watching water and time. I thought he was going to propose. He said he had a special surprise for me and that I was to meet him there the next day. I waited…he never came. I waited every day, at the same spot, for two weeks. Then I packed up, went home, and married your father six weeks later."

My mother asked, "Do you know what heaven is? Being close to someone you love and who loves you back with the same intensity. If God gives you that gift, even if it doesn't last forever, it's everything."

"You're upsetting her!" my father said, returning with a glass. He took her hand and led her docilely into the bedroom. She was telling me not to feel sorry for her. She was telling me, in her own way, that you choose how you are going to live your life.

September 19, 1902

I haven't written for a while. My room is on the third floor. I can look out my window and see her house down the street, ornamenting the corner with its grace and vitality. The light jogs off the cornices and jags into the yard below—creating gauzy streamers of gold-green air. I feel an odd comfort knowing she is close.

I spend a lot of time here. It's always dark. I like it that way. My father probably thinks I am doing what most teenagers my age do in the dark, if he thinks about me at all.

I decided to try a little experiment today. We were having dinner. Nobody says much at the table. My mother has never known how to talk to me. The only thing that can be heard in the dining room is the hurried scraping of utensil against plate, the clank of serving spoon and ladle as my mother doles out the food.

In the silence that starts at the oaken legs of the table, swaths the arms and necks of our high-back chairs, and spirals with a dead clatter toward the ceiling, I put my fork down and asked them why they are still together.

My mother's eyes, normally like violaceous grapes too long on the vine, came alive for an instant. She didn't answer me at first. Her lips were taut, glasslike—at that moment, her sharpest feature. I was afraid if she frowned, her face would shatter into a thousand pieces like glass. I told her that she and my father never talked to each other.

She stabbed at the mysterious meat on her plate and looked away. "We're married," she half whispered. "Married people don't talk."

I chose that moment to tell them I was in love with a girl. I blurted it out, the words driven through the air like the white, fluffy threads of a dandelion on a hot, brisk summer wind.

I told them I had kissed her.

My mother just stared at her plate. I could see my father was trying to get his mind around this.

He looked like he had stopped breathing. "It's that damned school. That damned school with its fancy teachers and fancy ideas and…"

My mother excused herself, saying she had to lie down.

Father stood, walked around his chair, and turned, gripping the back of it until his knuckles strained white. Then, with the flick of a wrist, he reached out and slapped me. Hard across the cheek. He stood before me, a caricature of blasphemy, saying all with his eyes. Then he spoke. "Whatever you're feeling, it's not love. Never speak of it in this house again."

In that moment, the dull, olive green walls hummed and bobbed with condemnation; the remnants of the uneaten meal stood stiffly on our plates, reminding me of my misshapen family. I cannot imagine the moment I was conceived. I know nothing of my birth. Nothing of my childhood before I came into my own memories. She never speaks of it, nor does my father. I write this from a dark room, the only light a drizzle of stars held by the velvet joist of the northern sky.

Later, I'll walk to the window, as I've done many times before, and throw open the upper sashes that lay close against the small square panes, the movement like a reptile blinking its yellow eyes in the night. Does she know I'm awake, thinking about her? Can she feel me winding myself about her?

Ann stopped. Something wasn't making sense. The diary was elegant, intelligent, deeply emotional. She'd read in one of the newspaper articles that Farrell had been the son of a farmer. She continued to read, pulling the little lamp on the table closer.

April 1, 1903

I haven't written for months. I don't know why. I love to write. I love words. Where do words go when they die? I don't think they ever die. I mean, you can't call them back once they're spoken.

April 5, 1903

April is the cruelest month. I don't resent March because March is always unpredictable and you know that going into her. But April; April is a different story. She catches the sun in your eye then darts behind snow clouds. She breathes warmly against your cheek and then disappears, laughing, in the final sting of winter's ice-clad breath. You hope for the sun's warmth, expect it more and more each day, then wake up to find snow curling and twisting and piling itself on tree branches one last time. It reminds me of ice-cold fingers tangled in dark hair.

Her middle name is April. Her daffodil-blonde hair skates around her shoulders hinting of the sun; her startling blue eyes hold silver-gray crystals of warmth; her smile holds the promise of new beginnings. You can see them if you really look. I suddenly find I'm in no mood to write about anything more. I'm sick of the gray shadows skidding across the sky. I'm sick of the cold. I'm sick of the boredom. I think I'll go down to the lake. It won't be frozen now; just gulps of brown toffee water shifting to the surface and breathing again. I like to sit on the bank and feel the wind reveal it secrets. When the wind stings my skin, I have the strangest feeling I've lived before, and it wasn't good. Like I am shades of all those who came before me, shadows and twists of things. Lately, when I look out across the lake at blonde shadows scratching black water, I feel a premonition. I don't know what it is, but it makes me shiver. It makes me fear for April and the coming of spring.

April 13, 1903

I came home from school today to a real mess. Mother. She was sitting cross-legged on the living room floor. My father wasn't home. She was laughing and crying and pointing, looking for all the world like a little girl who's just done something naughty. She'd plastered one of the front windows with stamps from father's prized stamp collection. At first, the pattern looked random, like mud splattered on a sidewalk. But when I looked again, I recognized some of my father's choicest stamps. Old, valuable. Stamps from Italy, Africa, Egypt, England now traveled in smeared, incandescent arcs over and around the pane, creating cuts and jags of colorful, sticky rainbows. Worthless now. The stamp books, guts opened up and flayed like a fish freshly caught, lay scattered around her on the floor. She pulled up her knees and rested her arms on the tops of them, looking at me. I'd never seen her look like that—almost like a young girl again. Maybe that's how she did look as a young girl. She cocked her head to the side, her dark hair unbound for the first time in years and trailing over her shoulder like a wave cresting a waterfall. The sunlight fell on it, widened in spirals of red-gold, drowning out the gray that had begun to appear. Her eyes were refulgent. She never took them off me. She had stopped crying. "I don't love your father. I never did." She took in great gulps of air, as if she had just remembered, after all these years, how to breathe again. I was silent. I felt that anything I said would have been trivial, insignificant, compared to her confession. I knelt on the carpet in front of her and took one of her hands. The warmth of her hand shocked me. It was like reaching out from a dark lake in the fog, lost, and finally finding purchase on a solid ledge of shore. I moved next to her on the floor. She smiled weakly and turned to look at the fire blazing in the hearth. Then she did something she'd never done before. She leaned against me, her head on my shoulder. Her words were soft, crawling across the stale air of the room. "I don't know if I can do this anymore." I squeezed her small hand gently. Just then a shaft a sunlight divided the room; I was enfolded in light, she in darkness. We were silent for a while. I looked at the smeared glass, the circles of stamps and felt that, for the first time, we had traveled beyond the walls of that room.

"Abeunt studia in mores." It's strange, this woman who rarely speaks has woven Latin dictums and phrases and interpretations around her soul like expensive bracelets. Suddenly, I understand why she always had a stack of dog-eared Latin books on her bedside table. They're different colors and sizes and the order shifts almost imperceptibly. It's my mother's only rainbow in an otherwise dim and colorless world, the pages curled and yellowed from constant thumbing. I noticed her eyes too—they were not like dull, dark grapes. They were shining deep blue and gold specks—ocean marrying beach.

I heard the words again in my mind. I had heard them before but suddenly realized their meaning. 'Zeal develops into habit.' This woman who'd married a trolley driver, a farmer, a man for whom language was dead. 'Zeal develops into habit.' Was she warning me? My Latin teacher had often told us that hours of earnest application would one day pay off. Not for me, of course, a student who could rattle off declensions and grasp meanings too easily. I did not study as hard as the others; therefore, I must have cheated on my exams. But languages seemed to come easily to me. I knew it; none of my teachers cared enough to know it. The day I was ten, as my mother tucked me into bed, she slipped a worn volume between my palms. "You might enjoy this some-day." That was before she had slipped further into the deep well of her worn world. "Don't tell your father." I never got any gifts that special again. When I was twelve, I came across it in the bottom of a desk drawer and started reading it.

Maybe because it was the one true gift my mother gave me, or maybe because it was a secret we had shared, I started to treasure it. It let me see my mother as I hadn't seen her before, a young girl secretly studying the dead language of poets, Roman orators and playwrights in her bedroom after her father went to sleep, much as I was doing when I was twelve. I could see her whispering the beautiful words, giving them life, letting them drip off her tongue and run through her veins like liquid rubies, master-ing finite agglomerations of dry-as-dust facts while other girls her age were out doing things with boys.

In that moment, in the rosy blue light of almost-spring straining through the thick glass panes and patches of stamps, she was a tabula rasa, an empty slate—before she'd been stamped with all of father's impressions, something pristine. I felt sudden anger looking at those stamp books. My father collected useless things. Things more interest-ing to him than I or my mother have ever been. Silently, I scooped them up one by one and laid them in the fire. My mother and I both sat cross-legged on the floor, watching the flames dance and curl and lick the stamp books until they were nothing but blue-black ash on the hot stone base of the hearth. "Ars est celare artem." I put the meaning together quickly. "It is art to conceal art." My mother nodded. Nothing more was said. A few days later, she admitted herself to a hospital of sorts for another 'evaluation.' I was left with my father.

April 29, 1903

Ashes to ashes, we all fall down. I'm so tired and yet I can't sleep. A glittering, sil-ver void, she somehow fills me with color. Where will all this lead? I never live in the present. I'm always thinking, this moment will end just like all the others. Everything will end. It always does. Is there anything we can hold onto?

A fistful of dust. A fistful of ashes. In the end, who has more than that? There's always someone with more and always someone with less. Things could always be worse; they could always be better.

She breaches me like I'm some sort of offense. I've watched her in the shadows, drawn to the light in the parlor beyond her front window like a moth, only, I know I'm caught there, endlessly fascinated with the light, circling and fluttering until my obsession will eventually kill me.

I wonder what goes on in those rooms. They circle each other with laughter and love. Through the windows, I hear the heavy clank of china as the table is set, the drift and bubble of contented voices on the spring air, the delicate chafing of utensils against plates warm with food. My own house is like a cathedral when the last candle has been snuffed out, the voices an incantation that never changes. They live; we exist.

May 1, 1903

A few days ago Nell and I sat on the roof of the Oak Hotel talking about Arvid Hinrich's suicide. I'd wanted to sit on the roof from where he'd jumped; I talked her into it. I wanted to see what he'd seen the last moments of his life, his body stretching out flat from the rooftop. The buildings, formerly a hat shop and shoe store, were combined this year and made into an inn. I edged closer to the precipice and looked back at Nell. She looked positively pale. I learned she was afraid of heights.

I thought of the German American boy, who spoke little if any English, whose ears stuck out of his head at perpendicular angles, and who smelled like the bad side of a barn. It wasn't his fault that people made fun of him. I felt sorry for him. They were so cruel. Cruel enough to make a young boy jump two stories to his death.

Fall: break down; buckle; cave in; crash; dip; dive; flop; plummet.

They said the top of his skull cracked open and popped off and his brain, mostly intact, was just lying on the ground beside it. I don't believe it. When he first came to school, some of the kids would pass him in the hallways, calling him "pig ears" or "cunt sore" and he would smile shyly, thinking they were just saying hello and being friendly, until they started to laugh and then he would hang his head and walk on. I hated them for that.

Nell brought some colorful exotic flowers from her mother's garden. I'd brought dandelions and a picture of Teddy Roosevelt. I wanted to say goodbye properly, and I liked the thought of the hardy weed because it grows up anywhere it wants to and doesn't care who gets disturbed about it. It's strong and it always comes back, no matter how many times it's pulled from the ground. I wasn't sure why I'd brought the picture.

As I blew the silver-gray threads out over the ledge and watched them float and scatter, I thought about the one time I'd tried to befriend Arvid by sitting at his empty lunch table with him. He'd looked at me like a frightened rabbit about to bolt. Before I could say a word, he stood and there was a wet stain on the front of his trousers. He had been so scared he'd wet himself and everybody laughed. That's how this school had conditioned him to react. Severely. I'm thinking that time is a hard, filthy disease coated in sunshine. It's subtle; we don't realize how it's moving over us every second of the day, taking something from us that we can never get back. Nell actually said something beautiful as she plucked the petals off one by one and let them go zigzagging to the ground. "Here's to the two friends you gained in death that you didn't know you had in life." Of course, then she laughed ignobly, stripping the moment of all its richness.

I didn't tell Nell, but that day that I dangled my legs over the edge and gave her a fright, after I said goodbye with the dandelions, I went to Arvid's grave. I will never forget the sight of his poor mother, shoulders hunched, as she wept in her dark, tattered coat, mumbling things in German, a black, sorrowful speck against the uncaring earth. She turned and saw me. Her skin bistered, raw. She struggled for the right words between sobs and great gulps of air. "You fend of Arvid's?" Her words were like little, cold, misshapen darts. I just nodded. I wanted to be, I thought. But did I really? After she left, I felt like I had to do something, so I put the picture of President Teddy Roosevelt by his stone. I don't know why. It just felt like the right thing to do. Someone had placed a photograph of Arvid as a baby on the ledge of the stone. He was sitting in a tiny sled, covered in a soft baby blanket, a dear woolen hat covering his large ears. He was a beautiful baby. I cried. I hoped no one saw me.

We're all broken, spotty beings, in one way or another.

Broken: *disjointed; halting; hesitant; damaged; fallen apart.*

Some of us just give up. I can't imagine ever doing that. But I didn't live his life. I had an odd thought kneeling down by his grave: I wondered, was he smiling when he leapt into the air, knowing he was already free? Was this last act a little joke he played on all of us?

Jester: *person who jokes; antic; buffoon; droll; harlequin; wag.*

Why, why, why? I read the obituaries in the newspaper today and the only thing I feel in my being is the question, why? An 18-year-old colored man named George died on Court Street. Allen Davis, 34, originally from Dallas, died. And Josephine Salvo, aged 3 months, died of heart disease. I've pasted a copy of Arvid's death notice below.

Arvid Hinrich Died Saturday

Due to Accident

Fifteen years of age, Arvid Hinrich died in a fall from the Oak Hotel Saturday and was pronounced dead at 1:15 pm. The funeral will be held in the Doylestown Presbyterian Church on Tuesday.

41 words. For a life. I counted them. I tried to love and caress each individual letter, to draw them inside me, to feel what was in the spaces between the letters. Nothing. What did he do after school? What was he like as a boy? Like me? What were his dreams? Did he ever go to Willow Grove Park and inhale the sights and sounds and smells, the sticky-sweet cotton candy, the mechanical laughter of a carnival world, the jolt of a roller coaster clanking up a wooden track? Life. Cui bono?

I whispered to Arvid in the cooling night air. "Life. It's a long hard pull, and sometimes you just have to stop and take a rest." I remember thinking I had one wish for Arvid, in heaven or the next life or wherever he was, that he would know he'd mattered. That he wasn't unimportant. Currents of air high above me chose that moment to collide and rumble. As I ran out of the cemetery, it sounded like a thousand drawers slamming shut around me.

32

Kevin walked down the freshly polished gray-and-maroon tiled floor, glad to be home, and quietly opened one of the wooden doors with a window. It reminded him of high school. The rehab group was already in session; a tall teenager with movie-star looks and disheveled dark hair was standing up, reciting the standard lines: "Hi, I'm Brad, and I'm a drug addict." He wore a black DKNY T-shirt, dark jeans low on his hips, and Converse sneakers. He had a baby binky on a chain around his neck.

Jim Brooks, the group's counselor, introduced Kevin. Jim's cheery voice grated on Kevin's nerves. He gripped Kevin's shoulder warmly and said, "This is Kevin, a former drug addict and a schizophrenic. He's agreed to talk to us about his experiences and the phenomenal success he's been having with an experimental therapy used to treat schizophrenia. Everybody, let's welcome Kevin, a street educator who helps addicts and counsels other schizophrenics.

"And Brad, don't say 'I'm an addict.' It's OK to say 'I have an addiction.'"

In reality, Kevin was feeling manic, panicky. The only reason he'd agreed to this sort of thing was so he could find the next one, the next one to *die*. He scanned the group and smiled, then launched into a bunch of lies about how he'd been a teenager addicted to drugs in New York City, how he'd slept nights in Central Park, too tired and stoned to care if he was attacked. The movie-star kid raised his hand.

"What kind of drugs?"

"Crack mostly, but I took anything to keep me in my fantasy world, where it didn't matter that I didn't have a home or a family or clothes or food."

"Heavy," the kid said, his amber eyes curious and flirtatious. "Ever turn tricks?" he asked.

"Yes. I was so messed up, it didn't matter who it was, as long as I had money to score some crack." The group listened attentively. "I took anything not to feel," he paused for dramatic effect, "*alone*." The group murmured, nodding in agreement.

"I wanted to die, but then somehow, I ended up in a rehab that helped me to stop drinking and drugging. I still heard voices, I still had blackouts, but now...I don't need to turn to alcohol or drugs to deaden my pain, my fears. I've been taking a revolutionary break-through drug called Lucinate X. It quiets the voices. In fact, I've been living drug-free for a year. Lucinate X has helped me so much that I'm a counselor now."

The group ooohed and aaaahed as if on cue. Kevin produced tears, said things he didn't feel. He talked to each group member and seemed loving, kind, sane. What he really wanted to do was light up a cigarette and drink a bottle of DeWars. He slipped a hand through his hair and sighed. "So much shit to deal with, I know. It's useless trying to figure out why things are the way they are. It's better just to go with the flow, find a way to get cleaned up. There's no future in drugs." Kevin almost threw up at his own words. *What a crock.* He paid special attention to Brad. The shadow side of himself was having irksome thoughts. *It doesn't matter who you kill—it doesn't matter if it's a good-looking teenager with an addiction to drugs who wants to sleep with you.*

Brad started to cry and Kevin was mesmerized by his eyes, his lean waist, the way his elegant fingers drummed the steel leg of his chair.

"I just…I just feel so goddamn *alone*," Brad said.

Kevin nodded, playing the father figure now, stretching his arms leisurely above his head. He thought about sharing a cigarette with him. He thought about what was beneath his jeans, thought about how it would feel to fondle him.

The group consisted of an elderly man with yellowed teeth, an overweight woman with bags under her eyes and nervous hands, two men who appeared to be in their twenties, both with ponytails, Brad, and a thin woman who looked to be in her forties with a sad face and spiked red hair. She was dressed all in black and had a pierced eyebrow. Her shirt said "Jameson Irish Whiskey." She wore loafers but no socks, and had a space between her two front teeth. They were all so transparent. They all wore the look that said, *What the fuck am I doing here?*

The thin woman jumped up suddenly and started crying. "I don't want anyone to call me Kelli anymore. I don't like my name. I don't like Regis's co-star, Kelly Rippa. I want everyone to call me Dorothy, you know, like Dorothy in the Wizard of Oz?" Then she sat down and hugged her knees to her chest, trying to disappear inside herself like a turtle curling back into its shell.

The session ended a short while later and Jim thanked Kevin. Kevin walked slowly, turning to look knowingly back at Brad, then walked toward the smoking room, a dingy, glass-enclosed room decorated with old lawn furniture in various stages of decay and lumpy pastel ashtrays that looked like they were from the sixties. Brad appeared a few moments later.

"You look like you could use a smoke," Kevin said, offering him one. He lit it and Brad said nothing.

"First day?" Kevin asked.

"Yeah."

"First day is always the toughest," Kevin said.

Brad inhaled, exhaled. Smoke twirled. Between puffs of smoke, he said, "Speed freak." He wiped at his nose with his hand. "That's what I am, man. A speed freak. When I couldn't get it, I'd steal Valium from my mom's purse. Pretty pathetic, huh."

Kevin put his arm around him and said soothing things.

Brad looked up at him with unmistakable sexual desire. "I'll feel...so *naked* without it, you know, the speed." He looked down at his bright red sneakers. He smiled shyly and dimples appeared in his cheeks. "I'm also...um...addicted to sex. With men. I miss my boyfriend, but I'm no good to him. No good."

"I'm not here to judge," Kevin said, discreetly running his hand slowly down Brad's back as he withdrew it. *I ain't no choir boy, either.* "Sex is a good amnesiac," Kevin said. "I've been there."

"You know how it happened, I mean, the first time?" Brad blew a puff of smoke. "I was high as a kite. Cop thought I was going for his gun. He pistol-whipped me. I *liked* it. Said he wouldn't charge me with assault if I jacked him off in the back of the cruiser." Brad looked up at the smoke spiraling toward the discolored ceiling. "I was fourteen. My dad is a goddamn district attorney in Washington."

Kevin sat in a lopsided orange-and-white lawn chair. "I don't know man. I don't know if I can do this," Brad squeaked. "I need him. Rick. One last time. One last high. One last fix."

"It seems impossible, but it's really just one day at a time," Kevin said, feeling like a lame version of Oprah and enjoying it immensely. Brad was now openly displaying a silver chain with letters spelling b-o-y-t-o-y that had been hidden beneath his shirt during group. Kevin imagined twisting the chain around his neck as he fucked him.

"They told me I have to remain sexually sober for *twenty eight days*. How the fuck am I supposed to do that?"

"You ever hear that song "Your Own Backyard"?"

Kevin started to sing it. He had a good voice. He could be anybody he wanted to.

Drugstore cowboy criticizing
Acting like he's better than you and me
Standing on the sidewalk supervising
Telling everybody how they ought to be.

"I'm not a drugstore cowboy," Kevin said. He left, having given his phone number to Brad and telling him to call if he just needed to, you know, talk.

33

Ann had taken one swallow of coffee when a new message appeared in her e-mail. The subject line read *Fool's Mate* and the sender was *chaos@hotmail.com*. She clicked it open and read:

I knew someday I'd find you again. I had to be sure it was you.

Fool's Mate. Do you know what this is Ann? Can I call you Annie? I feel like I'm getting to know you. It's a blitz-like chess move that can end a match before it begins.

I have a proposition for you. A, shall we say, unusual proposition.

I have a lot of buttons left on my jacket and I'm getting kind of bored. I propose a game, Annie, between you and me. I want to test your intellect. I want to see if I can catch you first. You want the killings to stop. If you'll be my last victim, I won't kill after I kill you. I'll save the rest of the buttons for you, Annie.

What do you think? I'll even give you a clue about where to find the next victim. You're wasting your time about New Orleans. That was just practice. Here's your clue: You'll find him where moonlight sparkles on stones of faith. I did him a favor. He was strung out bad. Pills. Valium. Speed. And a juicer on top of all that. Good-looking kid, too. A shame. I hope you'll come out and play with me.

Ann picked up the phone and dialed Chief Hyde. "Get some units out to all the cemeteries within a 15-mile radius of the city. Just got an e-mail from our killer—told me where he's dumped his latest victim. I think it's for real. I'll meet you at the Court Street cemetery. We can start there."

"Annie, be careful. Our guy could still be out there waiting for you."

It was 10:10 pm. Ann felt like she'd had a bucket of ice water dumped on her head. The cemetery was within walking distance. She printed out a copy of the e-mail, strapped on her Glock, grabbed a flashlight, and ran out of the house into the shadows along Main Street. It was stupid, reckless, careless. But she had to go; maybe there was still time to help somebody.

34

The whole time Ann was running down Court Street, the phrase bumped around in her head. *Where moonlight sparkles on stones of faith.* Despite the coolness of the night, sweat jumped from her pores. Every sound—a car horn, wind rustling the leaves, her feet pounding pavement—seemed louder than life. She was operating on pure adrenaline now, her mind, her muscles, synchronized. She was sure the killer would pick the cemetery closest to where she lived. She felt it in her bones.

When the shot splintered the bark of a tree immediately to her left, pure instinct made her roll into the hedges and simultaneously unholster her Glock. Her impulse had been to return fire, but she couldn't. She would've risked hitting someone in the row of houses or in a passing car. Breathing raggedly, she scanned the street, the darkened and softly lit windows of houses, rooftops. *Holy shit; the bastard was out there, close enough to take a head shot. Where was he? He'd started the game without waiting for a reply.* Keeping low to the ground, she took cover behind a big tree. Silence.

Shaking, she took off running into the yard surrounding the cemetery care-taker's Italianate gingerbread home. She scrambled over the thin black iron fence that wrapped itself around the perimeter of the cemetery and darted between headstones and heavy vaults. She didn't see any blue-and-whites; where was Hyde?

Crouched against the base of a large headstone, she listened. *Hurry up Hyde.* Then she saw him and another detective. She signaled with a quick flash of her light: GET DOWN.

Then she saw something else in the shiny, wet moonlight. *No…No, no, no!*

Forgetting her personal safety for a moment, she crawled over to the body lying on a patch of ground between several headstones. The boy's arms were out-stretched, his body making the shape of a crucifix. She felt for a pulse. There could still be time. She felt a faint thrumming like a sweet drumroll against her fingertips. Jesus! He was still alive!

She stood up and started yelling. "Hyde! Over here!" Officers with flashlights came running. "Where's an EMT? The kid's still alive!"

EMTs lugging equipment arrived a moment later and bent down over the boy, who was wearing black jeans and was shirtless. His feet were bare. "I felt a pulse," Ann said. "It was weak, but I felt it. We've got to save this kid."

Had the killer finally screwed up? Thought the kid was dead? Ann knew with a sickening feeling that the shot fired above her head was only a warning; if the killer had wanted her dead, she'd be dead right now and the EMTs would be bending over <u>her</u> body.

"He's not breathing," one of the EMTs said.

Ann barely breathed herself as they lifted his tongue and pushed it to the side with a blade then expertly slipped a tube between his vocal cords and into his trachea. "I'm in," one of them said.

They attached an ambu-bag to the end of the tube and started squeezing, forcing air into his lungs. One of them bent over the boy's stomach. "Placement is good."

"C'mon, kid. C'mon back to us."

Resuscitation efforts continued, followed by another round of drugs. They'd been working on him over a minute already. *Come on, kid, fight, fight!*

Even in the moonlight, she could see how young, how beautifully shaped he was. She inhaled sharply as her eyes tumbled over the track marks on his arms. A faint hope began to form. If he was an addict, a habitual drug user with high tolerance, the killer may have miscalculated the dosage of Lucinate X needed to kill him, if, in fact, he'd used it as he had with the other victims. Ann clung to that small hope. She took in everything about the scene, the position of the boy's body, the shapes of the closest markers, the names inscribed on the stones. Then her eyes fell on something flapping slightly in the night breeze.

Staying out of the way, she walked over and bent down on her knees, examined what was taped to the headstone. It was a color printout of a piece of artwork. Ann got closer. *The Temptation of Saint Anthony. Salvador Dalí.* Someone had scribbled a note on it. As she was reading it, the boy came back from wherever he had been, sucking air, tasting life again.

"The only thing that the world will not have enough of is exaggeration." Ann had studied surrealism. Dalí made no secret of his wish to kill modern art. She wondered if that was significant. She motioned to Hyde and he lumbered over. "Check this out."

"You all right? I heard a shot," Hyde said.

"Dalí's thirst for scandal was unquenchable," Ann said.

"Who?"

"Dalí. The artist who painted this picture. The thought of not being recognized was unbearable for him. He used to walk through the streets of New York ringing a bell whenever he thought people weren't paying enough attention to him. Seems our killer identifies with him.

"Get a crime scene unit over to Court Street. Bullet may be in a tree."

"Jesus, you almost get shot and you're standing here reciting facts about some freakin' artist? You all right?"

"I'm fine. I don't think he really wanted to hit me or I'd be dead."

She handed him the copy of the e-mail. "He's raised the stakes." Hyde took a few steps.

"Stop!" Ann said. "Don't move."

A crumpled ball of aluminum foil was inches from his shoe. "What?" he asked.

Ann feared the worst. "Methamphetamine. Crank." Had Hyde stepped on it, he'd probably be missing several toes. "Could be rigged with an explosive chemical."

"Jesus."

Watching the boy being loaded onto a gurney and into the ambulance, Ann felt she had stepped into a Dalí painting. Even in the presence of the other officers and paramedics, she felt alone, awash in a thumping blue vein and red flash of light, the wail of siren, outside of the voices barking off gravestones. Was she foolish to hope the boy might live to tell them who their flesh-and-blood killer was? The lump of foil turned out to be just that: a lump of foil. The worst thing it had probably contained was a tuna hoagie.

35

It was late. Two weeks had passed. Ann scribbled on her notepad and sipped her coffee.

Heroin: Harry, horse, stuff, junk, smack, scag.
Heroin=boy on the street; coke=girl.
Large quantities of heroin found in Brad's stomach, along with Lucinate X. Still comatose; insensible; anesthetic; lethargic; impassible.

Truth was, she liked a full house, always had. She didn't notice the loneliness so much. Bo and her daughter had moved in and Ann had finally convinced Nai Nai that she should come and live with them too. Nai Nai had finally agreed, more for the sake of Bo. Soon, she would move in too. And though Ann didn't like to admit it, she felt safer with Bo's German shepherd Dingo in the house. Now all they had to do was figure out a way to make their home, their lives, ordinary again.

One night Bo had raced over and spilled her guts about the lump she'd found in her breast. She was dealing with breast cancer and a rebellious 14-year-old, Nai Nai would insist on doing household chores a 60-year-old would find exhausting, and Ann was quite possibly being stalked by a homicidal lunatic. Yep, things were as close to ordinary as they could get.

She'd come downstairs sometimes to make a cup of tea and find Dingo in the corner of the living room, staring at the top of the stairs. She called to him, but no amount of cajoling would move him from the spot. Also, he would not go upstairs. There were other things too; things Ann had pushed to the back of her mind. The smoke alarms would go off for no reason. She'd felt cold spots on the stairs.

She'd researched the property's records extensively, and now papers were scattered about her feet, including several newspaper articles and handwritten notes Mark had found beneath a floorboard he'd torn up from the dining room. One article, published in 1901, had caught her eye. Nell's family would have been living in the house at the time; her father, being a doctor at the time, would have been interested in and familiar with eugenics, a movement that urged healthy, young Americans of 'good' stock (northern European descent) to marry and have large families. The article reported how followers of eugenics thought this was the only solution to avoid the "race-suicide" that would result if 'swarthy' immigrants invaded the country and started reproducing.

Teddy Roosevelt was one of the staunchest supporters of the movement. For fifty years, from Teddy to the Nazi Lebensborn program, there had been exhortations to healthy young couples to have big families.

It made Ann's stomach turn to think about the present-day ultrasonography used to determine the sex of fetuses in India and China, about the use of selective abortion to control gender. Geneticists in several nations, notably Great Britain, urged the Chinese government to rescind eugenic features of the law.

Ann scanned another article from the 1930s about "fitter family" contests at fairs, where the best human stock was displayed like pigs and cows and awarded blue ribbons. She took another newspaper and spread it out on the floor. She stared at the date. *April 14, 1976. The Philadelphia Inquirer.*

A man serving a life sentence for killing a teenager escaped yesterday from a state prison in Bucks County, authorities said. Officials would not describe how Kevin Rice, 25, who was convicted in the 1971 slaying of Althena Dey, escaped from the 2,168-prisoner facility.

"He was discovered escaped today. It's under investigation by our Special Investigation Division," said a spokesman for the state Department of Corrections.

Rice, a criminal with a long history of mental illness, tried to rape Dey. When he failed, he was driven into a rage and killed her.

Local, state, and federal law enforcement agencies were notified about the escape and told to be on the lookout for Rice, who is 6-foot-2 and 190 pounds and has sandy brown hair and blue-green eyes.

Right next to the picture, which someone had blacked out with marker, was a horoscope for TAURUS:

CHOOSE to be a hero and stop avoiding an inevitable confrontation. There is much to be gained by calling someone's bluff.

It was 11:40 pm. Ann went upstairs, threw on a pair of jeans and a sweatshirt, turned on the house alarm, and drove toward Mark's house. She knew where he lived, but had never paid him a visit. It was overdue. She knew she was taking a risk. But adrenaline and curiosity zipped through her veins. She popped Frank Sinatra's greatest hits into the Jeep's CD player and hummed along to *I Get a Kick Out of You.*

36

The headlights of Ann's Jeep swung over Mark's front lawn as she parked along the street and a feeling, however faint, of relief and familiarity settled over her. She switched off the ignition and headlights. Mark's house was a beautifully restored maroon and gray Victorian with a wrap-around porch. She wasn't surprised. She knocked at the front door, heard footsteps, and then he stood before her, a towel around his waist, his hair glistening and wet from the shower.

She stared at his broad chest, the firm skin, his strong, muscled arms.

"Basically, the human race sucks," she said.

He opened the door and she stepped in. He gently wiped the tears from her face. Until then, she hadn't realized she'd been crying.

His place was modestly furnished; his TV tuned to ESPN or some other sports channel, a suited sportscaster droning scores quietly. Ann could see Mark's muddied work boots and discarded jeans on the mudroom floor; the kitchen had a pressed tin ceiling. His bedroom was on the first floor and he disappeared into it to change. The home looked like it still had its original woodwork; two stairways led to the second floor. There was a big fireplace with a reproduction of Van Gogh's *Wheatfield and Cypresses* hanging above it, and, surprisingly, a grand piano in the octagon corner of the living room.

Mark came back into the room barefoot, wearing a pair of jeans and a button-down shirt he hadn't bothered to button. "This is a pleasant surprise," he said, toweling off his hair and throwing the towel on a nearby chair. "I just wish you were happier to see me."

He patted the off-white couch and she sat down next to him. He pulled her into his arms, and her face touching his warm skin, the circular embrace of his arms, was so natural. "I am happy to see you." Ann looked at the piano. "I didn't know you played."

"Yeah. Kind of surprising for a carpenter, huh. My mom's influence. Twelve years of classical lessons. She wanted me to be something different from my dad. But it's not so bad, building things with your hands."

Ann stared at his face, his eyes, his lips. She'd imagined this moment many times. She needed to reach out to someone, to him…to know they wouldn't draw back, get hurt, die. It was a lot to ask of anyone. She nudged his shirt off his shoulder and pressed her lips to his flesh. He closed his eyes.

"Would it surprise you if I said I think about you all the time…that I want to know all of you?" she breathed. Ann closed her eyes, almost afraid to hear his answer. She'd taken down the barbed wire from her heart for a brief moment, and maybe she'd misread him, made it all up in her head.

He responded by putting a finger beneath her chin, tilting it up slightly, and kissing her. Slowly. Deeply. "No," he said. Ann opened her eyes. His were even greener up close.

"I'm not going away," he said softly. "I'm not going to disappear. I'm not going to hurt you."

He seemed to read her mind. Ann laughed as he picked her up gently and carried her into his bedroom. He laid her down and lit a candle on a table by the bed. It was dark, but moonlight threading through the wooden blinds at the window mingled with the candlelight.

"You sure you want to make love with a guy who likes Yankee candles and reads *Country Living* in his spare time?"

"Never more sure," Ann said.

◆   ◆   ◆

Later, as they sat in front of the fireplace, Ann wearing one of Mark's oversized shirts, he held her while they watched the flames dance. Even in April, Victorian houses could get very chilly, but Ann felt warmed to her toes. They sipped Coronas.

"This is a beautiful house. It suits you."

"It was built in 1881," he said. "It took me years to restore. The original owners were married on the front porch."

"That's so romantic. I love it." Her eyes roamed his bookshelf and her stomach lurched as they fell on a particular book. *Dalí: Madman or genius?* She squeezed out the question from somewhere deep in her lungs. "What's your favorite Dali painting?"

"Persistence of Memory."

Ann let her breath out. "Mine too." She took a sip of beer. "Remember I told you about the girl who disappeared from my house in 1903?"

"Yeah. Creepy."

"I wonder if she comes back."

"Don't tell me a seasoned, analytical professional like yourself believes in ghosts."

"I'm not sure. Have you ever seen one?"

Mark laughed. "Of all places, in the Lehigh tunnel."

"Really?"

"Yeah. It's hard to explain. I was driving out of the tunnel and I saw a bright mass of light moving across the road in front of me. The air got really heavy and it felt cold all of a sudden. I think that's the closest I've ever come to seeing something like a ghost."

"Maybe somebody was killed there and they don't know they're dead. Do you think Nell knows she's dead? Maybe her spirit's trapped in my house."

They were quiet for a while.

"Mark?"

He rubbed the back of her neck, her hair, with his strong hand.

"Ummm hmmm?"

"Thanks for making me feel so…alive."

37

Lying next to Mark in his bed, the candle flickering low, listening to the even sound of his breathing, Ann opened the diary pages again. Farrell was getting into her soul. Mark was getting into her soul. There was no date on the top of the page, and the strokes of ink looked hurried, flamboyant.

I was lying on my bed, curled up in my nothingness when she appeared in my doorway. My mother, who exists these days in a soup steam, must have let her in. My father wasn't home.

I sat up and she put her finger to her lips, handing me my coat and scarf, which lay on the floor. "Where are we going?" I asked. She just smiled and whispered.

"It's a surprise."

Nell's changed in the past few weeks. Something about her is different. I didn't know what it was until we got to the lake. It was long past 9 pm; the woods and the darkness had joined hands, the mirrory shadow of the lake cradled in its palms. As we stood at its edge, listening to water lapping the bank in unfaltering, rhythmic strokes, I took her hand. She pulled away mysteriously. "Not yet."

She turned her back to me and to the wide mouth of the lake. "Follow me."

My heart was thumping wildly in my chest; despite the coolness of the night, I was beginning to perspire beneath my coat. I followed her into the woods, carefully stepping over exposed roots, occasionally losing sight of her when she ran ahead of me. Then she would call out to me and I would follow the sound of her voice, the sound of twigs snapping sharply beneath her feet like bone. It was some sort of game.

Finally, we came to an abandoned wood structure deeply surrounded by trees and brush. The lone window had three square panes; one was missing.

She entered the structure and I waited outside, unsure of myself. Then she threw her coat, her scarf, her skirt and her stockings out the door. "Come in," she taunted.

By now, I felt as if I was going to burst with anticipation. I picked up the stocking, inhaling the sweet, dusky scent of her, and stepped into the darkness. I couldn't see her. "We're going to play a game," she said.

Then I froze as another person stepped out of the darkness, clad only in pants. Him. What was he doing there? He worked an unlit cigarette in his long fingers and stared at me without speaking.

Nell, naked from the waist down, stepped into the dim moonlight filtering through the cracked jag of window. "You can't tell anyone about this. Not a soul."

"About what?" I asked. I was trembling now. "Nell, what's this about?"

She laughed, rolling her eyes seductively over his bare chest, then over my body. "You don't know yourself," she said. "That's why we're here. I'm going to enlighten you." She stepped close to him and kissed him fervently as he cupped her from behind. "We're going to enlighten you."

Then she stepped back, taking off the rest of her clothes. My eyes strayed to her perfectly rounded breasts, the flat plane of her stomach, despite my effort to look away. She stepped back in front of him and undid his pants, removing them. She took a match from a matchbook on the windowsill and lit his cigarette.

"The test of passion. Is it worth getting burned?"

He took a long drag on the cigarette and blew out a gray fringe of smoke. His eyes never left mine. I looked at him—everywhere. I was curious. He grew hard right there in front of me.

"I'll go first," Nell said. She stepped into his arms. He brought the cigarette down on her arm and caught her lips at the same time. My stomach did somersaults. Finally, he broke the kiss and she stepped away smiling, a red, vatic welt on her arm. "I've passed the test. It's always worth getting burned. You'll see."

She flipped a silky strand of hair behind her ear. "Now it's your turn," she said, looking at me. "Take off your clothes."

I did what she said.

"Slowly."

Fear and excitement warred in my stomach. I stepped awkwardly in front of him, my nipples hard and cresting the wiry hairs of his chest.

"No," Nell said, taking the cigarette. "I'm the master. You obey my commands."

I slid into her arms, and we became a warm tangle of skin. I closed my eyes and held out my arm. She pressed the hot tip into my skin. At the same time, her lips caught my mouth; they seemed hotter than the cigarette burning my arm. I moaned; I knew for the first time that pain was the rough understanding of pleasure.

"I knew you'd like it. You passed the test," she said. "But it's just the beginning. These marks will be a reminder never to tell. A few days from now, you might think about telling someone what happened. The pain will remind you not to tell."

I expected it to be his turn next, but Nell shook her head as if reading my thoughts. "Kneel down. Face the window."

As my knees and hands scraped rough, uneven planks of wood, affection, love, something welled up inside me for the blonde-haired girl who was even now forcing me to expose myself in ways I never had before.

Then he came to stand in front of me. Very close. I caught the musky, male scent of him, something I'd never known before. She stood behind me. "Your initiation begins now," she said, a harsh edge in her voice.

I stared at his crotch, felt the bristly hair between his legs brush my face as he put it in my mouth. "Suck him," Nell said.

"I don't know how…I've never…" He gently guided my head toward him while Nell stroked my back with her fingers. I gagged a couple times and saliva dripped down my chin, but he was patient. He taught me how to taste him, how to turn and twist my mouth around him. Soon, I was lost in the new sensations within and without my body; of being open, of being closed, completed. He groaned, his guttural outbursts of pleasure reaching deep into me. At the same time, Nell slid a finger inside me and my body jerked. She slid it in again and again, and as she did, I sucked harder. She withdrew it, sucked it, and almost seamlessly, they traded places.

"Don't be afraid," she said.

My body was hot, aching with need. I didn't comprehend her words. I gasped and cried out in pain as he thrust what had been in my mouth between my legs. She caught my lips with the salty taste of him still on my tongue—the musky taste of myself, the sweetness of her lips, the pain and stinging between my legs blending into something indescribable. I was determined not to cry in front of them and choked back tears. And then a strange thing happened. The pain was replaced with pleasure.

"Virgin no more," Nell breathed against my neck. "I tasted your innocence as it left your body. So sweet."

He moved tenderly now, holding himself back, afraid he would hurt me. "Jesus, Nell," he said. "You didn't tell me she was a virgin."

His voice was raspy, an angry whisper as his flesh filled my own. I rested my head on Nell's shoulder. "It's OK," I said to him. I spread my legs wider. "I'm OK. I need you to…I need to feel you…"

It was all the encouragement he needed. He moved faster inside of me, the muscles in his arms straining with his thrusts.

"I can't…I don't think I can…" He shuddered, collapsing on top of me, curling into me like a spoon. I felt a hot, warm liquid inside me, running down my legs. Something hot and tight twisted violently in my body and I climaxed, calling his name. As our hearts thundered back toward normal, nobody moved. Nell had gone still. She stood and dressed, giving us the elegant curve of her back. Her voice was brittle, cracking like thin ice in the cold night air. "You weren't supposed to come inside her," she said.

He helped me to my feet. "Did I hurt you?" he asked. "I'm sorry…"

I reached up and touched his face, seeing him for the first time though I had seen him many times before, but always as an extension of Nell. Someone who loved her; someone she ignored most of the time. Now I saw only him. Only Farrell.

Embarrassed, I withdrew my hand and quickly dressed. I was expecting to feel humiliated, ashamed, afraid. I didn't feel any of those things.

"Fuck you both," Nell said, shattering the silence and my thoughts. She left us there, and I wondered who had been truly initiated that night. Farrell made love to me again. I asked him to. I let him. He told me I was beautiful in a way Nell could never be. I liked how he didn't withdraw from me right away; how, instead, he wriggled free from my flesh like a tooth coming loose from a socket. I fell asleep in his arms naked as the day I was born, draped only in the spectral gauze of moonlight and the tender caresses of strong, callused hands. As I drifted off to sleep, unable to fight the contentment of my body, he sang an Irish lullaby...

Oft in dreams I wander
To that cot again,
I feel her arms a huggin' me
As when she held me then.
And I hear her voice a-hummin'
To me as in days of yore,
When she used to rock me fast asleep
Outside the cabin door.

The memory was green-gold; I pressed it into my soul like a leaf between pages of a book. The leaf—patched and potted, streaked and fractured—is one of a kind; there will never be another like it. Somewhere in my soul, I know that. Somewhere in my soul, I ache. Somewhere in my soul is the knowledge that I have never known who I am and what I am. I don't know why it hurts, not yet anyway.

My name is Ruth. But I am not Ruth. I am shades of all those who came before me. I am shades of Ruth. Shades, tints, and stains.

Ann put the journal down. She stared at Mark's broad chest, the tangle of sheets around his legs. *It wasn't Farrell's journal.* It was *Ruth's* journal, a girl who loved Nell. And Nell, bright, beloved daughter of a wealthy doctor, was not who she pretended to be. Are any of us?

Then what did "FN" stand for?

38

Ann sat around a scarred conference table with Chief Hyde, homicide detectives Randall and Lynch, and Tony, discussing how to handle the e-mail threats. Randall had always been easy going and accepting of her position; Lynch had never warmed to her, and in the first five months on the job, had barely spoken to her. He chewed on a sloppy lemon Danish and looked uptight, given Tony's presence.

Lynch fixed her with a snake-like glare. "Yang, you really evade a bullet on Court Street?" It wasn't a compliment. It implied she was a daredevil and a show-off, like it was glamorous to get shot at. "You seem to be good at attracting psychos." He crumpled up the tin foil he'd brought the Danish in and looked at Ann. "Watch this." He threw it into the trashcan. "Go boom!" he said, and laughed.

Ann ignored him. "I think I should call his bluff," she said to the group. "I think I should respond." Hyde lumbered over to an outdated-looking coffee maker and refreshed his cup.

"I think we should talk about this a little, Ann. This guy is organized. He leaves us with outdoor crime scenes and virtually no clues. He knows things about you. Everyone in this room needs to be in agreement before you contact him."

The door opened and a grinning Wade, the computer guy, stepped in flashing a sheaf of papers. He actually had a pen clipped to the pocket of his shirt. Lynch traced a finger around the rim of his half-empty Styrofoam cup. "Could just be her ex," he said casually. "Taking advantage of all the publicity just to jam up her nerves." Lynch always spoke like Ann wasn't in the room.

"It's not Peter," Ann said. "He doesn't have the balls for this, and besides, whoever sent the e-mail practically told me where to find the next victim. Despite the fact that Peter's a blood-sucking lawyer, he fainted once at the site of blood, so I doubt he'd make a good homicidal lunatic." Randall and Tony laughed.

Wade sat down and papers were ceremoniously dumped on the table. "Good news is we have city, state, longitude and latitude of the computer used to send you the e-mail. Doylestown Public Library."

"Shit," Hyde said. "So, the bad news is despite the expert spider techniques used to search the databases, we have a public computer connected to the Internet?"

"Yep. See, we start our probes with a time-to-live of one and increase by one until we get an ICMP 'port unreachable,' or the host, or hit a maximum number of hops, which defaults to 30," Wade said. Blank stares.

"Speak English, tech boy," Lynch barked.

"Computer host names are names given to individual computers. Each host name corresponds to an IP address. Anyway, look at the header," Wade said. "The information next to 'received' shows the routing IP by which the e-mail was sent and the time it arrived to the mail server. This particular e-mail originated from a computer with this IP address." He pointed to a bunch of numbers. "If several routing IPs were listed here, the e-mail would have passed through multiple recipients. This is like a personalized traffic report showing the route the data takes to get to a remote server, and the bottlenecks and hazards along the way as your data passes from router to router."

Ann studied the message. At 8:42 pm, the killer had been in the public library, sending her the message. How long had it taken him to put the boy in the cemetery, backtrack to the library, get over to Court Street to watch her tear out of her house? She'd checked her e-mail at 9:20 pm. Plenty of time.

"When does the library close on Thursday nights?" she asked.

"Probably around 9. I'll get someone down there right away to check their user and message logs to see who was logged into that particular IP at that time," Hyde said. "And maybe the librarian on duty will remember something."

"The library doesn't have key-sniffing devices installed in the computers," Wade said. "Too bad. If they did, the user's keystrokes would be registered, creating a record of everything typed at a particular terminal. He might as well have been in a cyber café in Nigeria."

Ann fingered the edges of the report. "The guy has to know I have protection now; my street is crawling with undercover cops. I still feel in my gut that I should respond, draw him out." Ann felt a little safer knowing one particular cop, Brody, an officer with "double-D" biceps who had a picture of his little girl in her softball uniform taped to the inside of his cap, was one of the officers assigned to watch her street, her house.

"I agree with Ann," Tony said. "But I don't like it."

So far, Ann had kept a tight leash on her paranoia. She didn't want to end up being one of those people who stuck a gun in their pocket just to take out the trash.

"I'll be with her when she responds; I'll help her draft the e-mail," Tony said. "I think I'm pretty much inside this guy's head now."

"Then it's decided," Hyde said, not even trying to hide the fact that Tony's vote was really the only one that counted.

Lynch sneered. "Go get 'em, Rambo." He was the classic white guy who had a problem with women and blacks, and constantly wanted to prove his badge was bigger than anybody else's.

Ann looked at Lynch. She knew his wife sometimes dropped off his bagged lunches at the office, usually tuna salad or a ham sandwich, a thermos of iced tea, and homemade chocolate chip cookies. Sometimes, detective work paid off. "Lynch, why don't you join us. I'll make tuna salad and iced tea and you can have milk and cookies too, with extra chocolate chips." Everyone but Lynch laughed.

39

In the dream, Ann was running, roaming, shifting, her strides splashing up mud. But she wasn't Ann. She was Fen, the one who'd found her aunt murdered. She was five years old, and late for dinner. Her parents were away, so her sister was in charge. Fen figured she'd cut her sister a little slack because her sister might be worried if she came home too late from a friend's house down the street. Fen trotted along the side of the road. A car came along, the driver slowing down to look at her. She felt a strange chill when she looked at him. His eyes were mean and black, like the pits of olives, his arms muscled beneath his dark T-shirt. She couldn't tell what color the man's shirt was. It had splotches on it, like he was sweating on it. The man smiled slowly.

He was clean-shaven, his teeth white, his hair long. There was something malevolent in his smile, and Ann ran faster. On his arm was a colorful tattoo—a butterfly with fangs. She raced up the drive to the house and sauntered in the back door, taking her muddy shoes off in the laundry room. The lights were on in the house.

"I'm home!" she shouted. She heard a thump upstairs. She noticed several pictures askew on the walls and large, muddy footprints on the hallway floor and up the stairs. For a moment, she froze. Then she ran upstairs.

Jia Li was in the hallway, half sitting, half lying on the floor. Blood ran from the corners of her mouth and down her T-shirt. There were red spots burgeoning up through the cotton, spreading like crimson roses, red flowing from her legs, splashed on her underwear. Dazed, she kneeled beside her, holding her. She was trying to speak. "Butt...Butterfly."

"Jia Li," she sobbed. "You're going to be all right. You're going to be OK." She knew it was the man she'd seen in the car. Just now. Jia Li had told her so. With one word. Butterfly. The man with the butterfly tattoo who'd smiled so horribly at her, knowing he'd just attacked her sister. She ran to the phone and called the police.

All of a sudden, she was older, a woman standing over a metal slab in the medical examiner's office. A body lay on the slab. A body with the tattoo of a butterfly with fangs on the left arm. As Ann stared at the wasted, withered body, the eyes flew open. She gasped. They were the color of a diseased liver. "I've come back," Ivey said. "Your turn is coming." Ann woke with a start.

The readout on the digital clock read 2:20 am. It had been a while since she'd had nightmares about Ivey. Ivey had been arrested for possession of marijuana several months before the attack and sentenced to a community clean-up crew. He'd wandered off to a nearby neighborhood and stolen a car, her aunt, Jia Li, the unfortunate victim of his sick mind and violent tendencies.

It was Jia Li's small sister, Fen, who had found her and whose testimony had helped nail him. The memory of that tattoo forever painted on Fen's five-year-old heart. Fen had picked Ivey out in a line-up as the 'mean' man who was seen driving slowly down the road by her house. He'd had on a T-shirt and the tattoo was clearly visible. He was arrested the next morning. On April 3, 1964, Ivey's jury found him guilty of manslaughter. Two months later a state circuit judge sentenced him to death in the electric chair. Thank God they'd found him early in the investigation—a key to success in any criminal investigation.

Ann remembered reading about the crime when she was older, reading about how Ivey had laughed in the judge's face and told him to "rot in hell" and that he'd be back.

Ann had known long before she'd become involved in solving violent crimes that no matter what she did, it would never be enough. She could never bring her aunt or anybody else back. She wondered if she was getting too close to the cases, getting too far into the minds of serials. As long as she could think like them, but not get into their minds, she *would* be OK. She would.

She listened to the quiet of the house, knowing Bo and Nai Nai were sleeping. Nai Nai's snoring could wake an elephant. Janie was spending the night at a friend's house. Ann threw a robe and slippers on and went to the kitchen. There was nothing in the fridge, so she ripped the tab off a can of Lime Diet Coke, poured it into a glass, added ice, and padded out to the living room with the diary. She still had to find something in that diary.

May 3, 1903

In her usual tactless way, Nell suggested a game. We each have to find out three things about Arvid. Whoever finds the three most interesting things wins. It's just a dumb game for Nell but something far more meaningful to me. I really do want to know about Arvid.

I decided to take a casserole to Arvid's mom. I almost lost my nerve when the front door to Arvid's house opened and she stepped out. She motioned for me to come inside.

The house is small, dusty, cluttered. Dishes stacked up by a small sink. She put a kettle of water on the sooty stove. "Kaffe?" she asked. I nodded. A little white dog yelped and followed at her ankles everywhere she went. "Ich schiddel dich, Bubbelly!" she said, gently pushing it away with her worn boot. She struck a long match, bent down and lit the stove, rubbing her hands together. The house, it's cold, the room…it's like January in a jar. This is a different woman than the one I saw in the cemetery; this is a strong, practical woman. She pulled something down from a shelf and set it on the table. "Lebkuche?" I knew it was honey cake. It looked delicious. "Yes, please," I said. She wiped her hands on an old apron that hung from her slim waist and I noticed her greasy hands. A chicken sat in a pot on the stove, a cutting knife and carrots next to it. The kitchen smelled like garlic and onions and fried potatoes and churned butter. Her eyes were wet—greasy and churning with thick tears of grief.

"I'm sorry about Arvid," I blurted, hoping she'd understand.

The woman stopped and simply nodded, bobbing her black head of hair.

A loud screeching noise startled us both. Arvid's mother turned and closed her eyes for a long moment, taking a deep breath. "Grossmudder," she said, bustling out of the room. Some time later, she emerged, sweat beading on her brow, guiding a very large, old woman into a chair by the stove. Grossmudder's body was grossly overweight, her head almost disappearing into the folds of her neck. Her face was pinched, her dark eyes darting everywhere. Drool had started to form on her lips. "Gemiess! Gemiess!" she shouted, shaking her fat, crinkly fist at Mrs. Hinrich.

Mrs. Hinrich spooned some broth, vegetables, and chicken into a bowl and brought it to the old woman. She looked so tired, like her life had been bleeding out of her for a long time. Then she cut me a slice of honey cake, poured me some coffee, and left for a moment. The old woman looked at me curiously with her mean eyes as she spooned bits of broth and stringy chicken into her mouth with a shaking hand.

When Mrs. Hinrich came back, she was carrying a black book. She poured herself a cup of coffee and sat down at the table. It was an album with photographs. Of Arvid. She showed me the photos, lovingly curling her fingers around the frayed edges of each. There was a picture of Arvid as a very young boy, smiling uncertainly, holding up one of his hands. His hair was tossled. "Raspberry torns," she said. The old woman practically shouted, "Ich hab mich verschunne in der hemmbieredanne!"

Mrs. Hinrich shook her head. "She remempers."

There was another picture with Arvid smiling, a small finch sitting on his arm. "Hunnich. Dats what he called bird." She pointed. "Honey." The old woman raised a bony finger and pointed to the floor. Mrs. Hinrich sighed. She rose, grabbed a hickory broom, and started sweeping even though I didn't see any crumbs. The old woman's tongue poked out her mouth, licking its sides like a horse flicking its tail. There was a shelf above her head, a miniature landscape of shoemaker wax, brushes, and old shoes.

Mrs. Hinrich softly patted the woman's ample thigh, which was the size of a large tree trunk, then sat down again and continued going through the pictures. "She's vaiting for Arvid ta come home from da school. She dasn't know...he's..."

I nodded, feeling so sorry for both of them. "But he never come home again..." Mrs. Hinrich burst into tears and I hugged her. I was wondering why I'd brought a casserole to a woman who wouldn't feel like eating for days. Why do we always try to pull our lives back together with kitchen crockery?

A vowel is long when it's doubled. A vowel is long when followed by an 'h.' Almost without exception a vowel is short when followed by a consonant. Listening to the sounds of the two women, to their movements, the shuffling of their tongues, it struck me that Arvid was the long vowel in their trio and now that he was gone they were like two consonants bumping into each other without any sense.

Bpdtk. Bpdtk. January in a jar.

Mrs. Hinrich pushed more cake toward me. "Versuche der Kuche moll."

The old woman spat her soup into the bowl and threw the spoon down so it clattered on the floor. "Leppisch!" she shreaked. She looked at her soup. "Motherfucking damn cunt sore!" she screamed.

Mrs. Hinrich suddenly laughed. "Arvid, he teach her bad vords. He very vunny joking."

That was something I didn't know. I got a completely different picture of Arvid at home.

We'd finished looking through the album so I rose to go. I took Mrs. Hinrich's hand, said thank you, and left her to deal with the old woman. As I was passing by the front window I saw the old woman reach out and grab Mrs. Hinrich's breast, twisting it. Mrs. Hinrich batted her hand away and I thought, there are things I don't know about this family. Wondering. It's like trying to remove the pit from a cherry. A hard, slippery thing.

I hurried home. I was pretty sure I'd won the 'game' but this was not something I would ever share with Nell—or anyone.

Mrs. Hinrich had looked young and beautiful in the pictures, her eyes shining with uncut promises. Now she was like an ox broken to work. Work, work, work, work.

I took the long way home, enjoying the solace of the wooded path, the gold wax of sunlight pouring through tree limbs. We are all imperfect. We all do what we can.

May 4, 1903

Do our lives really belong to us, or are they just smudges of color that eventually fade into some forgotten place? I think about all the places our tongues go when we string words together. Horseflyhorseradishhorseshoehorsestablehorsewhiphotairhotpunchhotwater.

Motherfuckerdamncuntsore. Words are sharp, bittersweet, funny, jolting. Words have power. I am reminded that a word, a gesture, a small parting of the lips can change a life large and small. With our tongues, we seek our way: north, south, east and west. I think it's interesting that for the Pennsylvania Germans, troubles start early in life with the short e, the long u, the short o, b and p, d and t, g and k, etc. From sounds that are as common in German as they are in English.

I think today is Tuesday. I am unsure of the date.

I found an old set of paper dolls the other night that I used to play with when I was a little girl. The box stuck out at an odd angle from a top shelf of my closet, a forgotten paper world suddenly given swift passage of time. As I dug my fingers into the assorted papers, I found myself holding a pretty, cardboard blonde with green eyes. As I ran my fingers over six cutout dresses, the years slipped away with lightning speed. I used to pretend she was going to grow up and marry a preacher, a man who understood the power—and the importance—of words. In my childish way, I was dreaming of a man who was the complete opposite of my own coarse father. With haste, I changed her into each outfit. It made me inexplicably sad. Gone were the simple joys of childhood, often found wandering a peach orchard alone or climbing a pile of crumbling stones or feeling ice cream running down my chin, sticky and sweet, in the middle of summer. I ran my finger over her cardboard hair. No preacher to save you now. Just foolhardy adventure to tear at your dreams.

I've been thinking a lot about Farrell. I've come to the conclusion that there are a lot of things I like about him; the slow, deliberate way he walks; the smell of wood smoke on his skin; the worn stretch of his clothes across his shoulders; the rough gentleness of his hands. It makes me angry that Nell can't see any of it! I think of the way his fingers felt inside me, pushing, opening, filling me in a way I didn't know I could be filled. I especially like something he said to me once. "Beauty is mesmerizing but soulless." I know he was really talking about Nell; he is still drawn to her and I think he despises himself for it. I think about my mother, in love with that boy, in Rome. Did she feel this way? Did she die that day when he left her all alone at the spurting water fountain? Did they walk together on crisp, clear mornings along chestnut-tree-lined avenues by the banks of the Tiber? No aim to their walks? I read somewhere that Rome has the highest number of fortune-tellers of any city.

A sudden thought occurs to me: genius doesn't sweat in creating a masterpiece. Do I believe that?

Paper: Something made of pulped fibers like wood, cotton, or flax.
Papyrus: Something made from the cut sections of the flower stem of the papyrus plant, pressed together and dried.

I remember folding the blonde doll and her clothing and wondering why she wouldn't bend the way I wanted her to.

Joint: connection, coupling, joining, junction, seam, union.

Yes, I want a man who understands the power of words. And gentle hands don't hurt.

I once read about an ancient Japanese purification ceremony dating back to 900 AD. Unwanted paper "hina" dolls and folded paper objects resembling kimonos were put into small boats and set adrift on the sea. This was in order to wash them of "keg-are" (defilement) and to pray for the expulsion of "byoma" (evil diseases). The ritual was performed by breathing on the dolls, rubbing them against the body to rid it of impurities; the idea being that the sea carried the infected dolls away. It still goes on today.

To fold: to wrinkle, ruin, crease.

Why did I love something soulless? One of my paper-doll histories. I've decided we all have them. Do we all search for the perfect lover or do we all use that as a guise while searching Rome for Mary?

The thing about Farrell: I am washed color; he is strong lines.

40

Ann found loose pages, out of order.

February 1903

Around 6 pm, I walked from the market grocer where I sometimes do bookkeeping for old Mr. Heilemann to catch the electric trolley home. The temperature was cold, barely above freezing. Thick snowflakes were beginning to fall and shown contemptuously in light flung modestly from the gas street lamps. The entire trolley line is twenty six miles long, but I was only taking it through the downtown streets of Doylestown. The fifteen-minute ride cost three pennies. As I got off at Market Street, I noted the Coca-Cola sign in the window of a small saloon. It made me thirsty.

"Drink a bottle of Coca-Cola, five cents at all stands, grocers and saloons."

Wonderful how when you see something like that you want it. Even if you hadn't wanted it five seconds ago. The street lamps hissed and sputtered as I passed a big sign for the future home of what was to become one of the first automobile dealerships in town. They will offer something called a steam mobile trap, Cadillacs, and electric runabouts as well as light touring cars. The trolley is smoother and faster than the old horse-drawn carriages, but a lot of people still ride in their buggies. Change is slow. I wonder who will buy the cars. Nell's family will, simply because they can.

As the snow covered the city like a woolen blanket, I thought about Farrell. I thought about how we'd skated on the frozen lake together, the block of ice like a giant fist holding us up, just the two of us. We didn't need any words. As he laced up his skates he watched me skate figure eights on the crisp sheen of ice. He just sat and watched, saying nothing. Then he skated by me to the other side of the ice, challenge in his hazel eyes. We raced and laughed until the wind caught our voices and carried them away. We fell laughing in a heap of snow on the bank. I loved the silence of the snow, how it quieted everything around us, so we could only feel the beating of our hearts between us. We watched a pewter sky, the clouds a silver gavel about to strike the horizon. Then he led me silently by the hand to the old, boarded-up wood shack.

That seems like weeks ago and I've hardly had a word from him. I walked the long, dark path to our cottage sitting humbly at the rear of Dr. Schaffer's property like a servant squatting over something spilled. Lights and candles blazed in Nell's windows and I wondered if she was home. I caught the faint clink of China and imagined they'd be having tea and brandy about now, talking about politics, neighbors, furniture, whatever rich people talk about. I'd had no dinner, and jealously, I thought of the plates of food they were probably enjoying right now—consommé of green turtle, broiled shad, filet mignon, and sorbet, followed of course, by the finest cigarettes, canton ginger ices, cheeses, Madeira, and cigars. I've heard that Nell's father owns another house in New Jersey, on wide macadam streets, and that all of his children get brand new bicycles every year and the whole family makes trips to the theater in New York at Christmastime. The gossips often talk of Nell's mother Francine; well of course, she's accustomed to absolute social dominance and she's wealthy. Her own father was a doctor and quite rich. Most recently she suppressed a revolt led by several elegantly coiffed and dressed ladies who thought it was their job to plan and decorate the town buildings for the holidays. Francine told Mrs. Cox, leader of the tiny revolt, "I do hope that this community will not become disgusted with our sex." I have to say I liked her for that, even though I don't generally like rich people.

In the time it had taken to get home, snow had started to accumulate on the path. It crunched beneath my feet in a familiar way and something inside me longed to be a little girl again. I laughed, catching a snowflake on my tongue. The cottage ahead was dark, as I knew it would be. My father is rarely home these days; my mother is in the asylum, her life a curtain drawn shut to keep out the sun. She's given herself an enforced period of rest and suffers from what is called "melancholia." I noted the dark shape of the water pump, which my father had covered in horse manure to keep it from freezing. A sharp wind scoured the alleyway. Clumps of stiff horse manure rose like piles of gauzy cotton in the drive. The hall was dusty and smelled of kerosene, an exchange of air forever stale.

I lit a candle and climbed the stairs to my room. I set the candle on my windowsill. My room is always cold, so I lit a fire in the hearth on the north wall. Wind scratched at the windows. When the fire cracked and lisped, making my frozen skin tingle, I watched snowflakes float down from the sky and dance and twirl before they were sucked away by the wind. I thought of Nell. I haven't heard from her in weeks either. I feel forgotten.

As if my thoughts had conjured her, I heard her voice. I closed my eyes and willed her away. But the voice was real. I turned my head, and she was standing in the doorway to my bedroom, light snowflakes caught in her blonde hair, her eyes a sparkling manipulation of green-gold rings. She'd let herself in. She'd done it before. I didn't mind. But I turned back to the window, ignoring her. I was still angry with her.

I felt her hand on me then, stroking my hair. "My little pet," she whispered, and she almost sounded contrite. But there was an edge to her voice and I was wary.

The way she accented the words, it reminded me of the uniform rising of a group of schoolchildren from their backless benches, reciting some clump of dusty literature in a group like parrots. I felt caged. I shrugged her hand away, indicating I did not wish her attentions.

She left me then and I thought she'd gone. I watched the snowflakes again, suddenly aware of how tired I was. It struck me with force how much I missed Farrell.

I turned to rise and stopped short. She was standing there, half clothed, her walking skirt in a pile on the floor. Her feet were bare, glistening, pale; she'd kicked off her boots and she'd worn nothing beneath her skirts. No expensive rose-laced corset; no pale white stockings embroidered about her trim ankles. I wondered if she'd been watching out her window and seen me pass by in the darkness.

She removed her silk waist, settling into my bed after closing the door. I watched the alluring sway of her rounded backside as she walked to my bed. An odd thought struck me: what creature, male or female, can resist the beauty of a woman's form? It didn't matter if it was right or wrong: there was grace, wantonness, and fire in the curve of a hip, the tilt of a breast, the smoothness of a thigh, even if there is baseness in the soul. I watched as the peaks of her rose-colored nipples jutted and rose stiffly, begging to be sucked, needing the warmth of an eager mouth. She slid her hand between her legs. "Come lick me, pet," she said.

I was powerless to refuse. I was ashamed at the liquid heat that rushed to my core, the sudden wetness between my legs. I didn't want to but I did! I was lost in her heat, the gift I thought she was giving in reconciliation for having ignored me. She closed her eyes and as she came, her fingers slid from my hair and caught in my sheet, gripping it tightly. It was then I noticed the ring. I stared in shock. My breath caught. It was lovely. Yellow gold and bright green tourmalines seemed to laugh at my inelegance. Tiny seed pearls sat erect on a rectangle with hour-glass shaped filigree cutouts.

As her flesh quivered and surged and clutched at my fingers, I looked at her face, expecting her eyes to be closed. She was looking at me and there was laughter in her green eyes. The laughter of a skater scraping freely across ice. The laughter of someone who knows better. I knew who'd given her the ring. She'd wanted me to see it. And what better way to show it off then for me to see it on her fingers as they curled in a fit of passion? I felt a raw hurt. Farrell. How long had he saved his money to buy her something she'd wear for a week and then callously discard? I felt jealous that he hadn't bought me anything. I remember once he'd said, "Ruth, you aren't a girl who needs trinkets. I like that. You're happy with a sunset, an icicle, a frozen swirl of snow. I wish Nell could see the beauty of those things and..." He stopped talking because apparently, I hadn't adequately disguised the look of pain on my face. I skated away from him then, removed my skates, and stomped off. I'd seen a gorgeous locket in a jeweler's window once that I'd wanted as a young girl. It was yellow gold with a finely detailed repousse bird and flowers on one side and scalloped scrollwork on the other. It opened to reveal glass inserts with a picture of a lady in a big feather hat on the left, and a place for hair locks on the right. Beauty is a false assurance, isn't it? While we experience, possess, and own it in some measure, we feel nothing bad can happen. I told myself it wasn't that I wanted expensive jewelry. It was just that I thought Farrell understood me. I thought something was different between us. That we shared something he and Nell could never have. Was I wrong? Why is it so hard to be good to the people we love while we're here? I think something in me is finished. But maybe it has just begun.

March 1, 1903

Days apart. Days together. Nell wasn't wearing the ring today. I wonder if she's already forgotten it—just a rude piece of gold among the others. She told me today she never wanted to marry. "All the people I know who are married are miserable, Ruthie." I hate when she calls me that. It's demeaning somehow. But I was surprised at what she revealed; I thought it was the ultimate goal of all rich, young women to acquire a tasteful and wealthy husband to whom they would be forever subservient.

"I mean, think of my poor Mama, married for 17 years and pregnant for 8 of them. Marriage is a lottery among slaves, and women are the slaves." I could hear the far-off clip-clop of hooves in melting snow.

I laughed. I don't know why. She looked at me, her eyes like the spiked, hooded undergrowth of an evergreen's branches in deepest winter, but she didn't smile. "I can't remember the last time my Mama smiled. I'm different. I want a new man for every week of the month. Or a new woman," she added, taking my hand in her own as we skirted the great bulk of dark brown ice that was now the lake. "There's so much to discover in each person who tantalizes you. You wonder, how do they make love? Can they make me feel more passion than the last?" She was silent for a moment.

"Do you love me, Ruthie?"

I was not prepared to answer. I know the truth in my own soul, and I fear she can feel it. She just smiled at my silence as we walked. We would soon come to the town and part ways, as Nell has a 'reputation' to uphold. If only her father and mother knew what a rotten core she has. Instead, I asked a question of my own. "That night in the wooden shack, why were you angry with us?"

As we walked through a labyrinth of trees subjecting their green crystal-like leaves to a dull sun, she kissed my cheek delicately. She squeezed my hand warmly and gazed into my eyes. "My dear Ruthie," she sighed. "You aren't supposed to like it so much, because then you orgasm, and then you can get pregnant. If you just let the man have his pleasure, you can't get pregnant." She brushed her white-gloved hand over my nipple, which rose to her touch beneath my dress. "I mean, even now, what if you are growing Farrell's baby inside you? What would you do?"

My mother has never talked to me about sex, except that I've heard her say to my father that it's a constant annoyance, and why does he persist in wanting it so often?

I must have had a frozen expression on my face, because she leaned over and kissed me with a shocking warmth, letting her tongue trace my lips then delve inside my mouth. "Ruthie, I like you, but I could never love you. Love is an impossibility that men strive for. Their species is born to drive and possession. I don't say this to hurt you. Ask yourself, do you know anybody who hasn't killed what he or she loved in one way or another?" She stroked my hair and whispered. "Don't love me, Ruthie. Don't."

Then she skipped off through the trees, a slice of pale blue fabric among the greenery. I felt like throwing up. Why am I so desperate to please? So desperate to love? I don't think Nell is afraid of anything in her nature, and that's what scares me the most.

March 6, 1903

It's been a few days since I've written anything in my diary. Where should I start? It makes the most sense to start with Nell's calling card. Four days ago I received a knock on the door and found a card of heavy stock with ornate scalloped edges slipped beneath our door. We don't have a silver tray in which to catch cards—who would ever make a social call at our house? I lifted the ornate illustration of a bird with exquisite blue feathers and found Nell's elegant signature beneath. It read "come at once. tell no one" and gave an address in Ambler, twenty-two miles by trolley. The passage had already been paid.

I slipped on my coat and as I rode the trolley I wondered what I would find. What was so urgent that Nell should call me to her side at once? The countryside was flashing before my eyes. My boots were soaked through. I hadn't eaten breakfast and my stomach growled angrily. Belatedly, I thought about Farrell: shouldn't I have told him? But it was too late for that. If Nell was in some sort of trouble, I was the logical choice; no one knew of our relationship. I'm a piece of coal to be sacrificed to the fire in a situation requiring warmth. I've always known that.

It took forever to get there. When I got off the trolley I found myself in front of a building with a grocery on the first floor and an opera house on the second with a façade of cast steel and leering painted faces. Both looked deserted. There was an alleyway between and a flight of stairs leading up, so I took them. My muddied shoes made ghostly echoes on the steps that seemed to fill every nook and corner of the auditorium in which I found myself. The inside of the building was dull cream with accents of maroon and federal blue, a stenciled pattern along the walls. A satin curtain, ripped at the edges, dangled above a dusty stage. I almost heard the breaths expelled in exclamations of past wonder, almost heard the hot words the actors flung at each other while they danced to the cutting strokes of piano keys, their voices cajoling and scraping the painted and pressed tin ceiling. The stage was flanked by four boxes of carved cherubs, cherry bark rolls of childlike ecstasy in the wings. Big scrolls of hand painted scenery hung in the background and covered three windows in the rear of the stage. A set of wide steps on either side of the stage led up to the dressing rooms. I heard coughing coming from one of the rooms and I raced by rows of empty mahogany chairs and a row of metal support posts down the center of the auditorium, past a wide room with a big, cold cast-iron stove.

It was dark and I stumbled up the stairs. I opened the door and saw Nell in the soft light cast from a lamp with a pewter base and a milky glass dome, in a dirty bed, the light lending no warmth to the horrid room. She had a bloodied sheet pulled up to her chin and was trembling, delirious. Her clothes—a long brown skirt, a white shirt with a delicate ribbon strip around the neck, a corset cover laced with little ribbons, a black petticoat, and black stockings were slung over an oaken chair; a new pair of patent leather low shoes rested at its base. A table was laden with sharp bloodied instruments and Nell was moaning.

"I'm here, Nell," I said, stroking her damp hair. "I'm here. I came."

Her forehead was hot to the touch and her eyes were glazed. "I had no choice," she said weakly. "He was the only doctor who would...help me."

"Nell, where is the doctor?"

She laughed hysterically. "I haven't seen him. After he did this to me, he disappeared. Fortunately, I had the foresight to send the card before the...operation."

"Nell, we've got to get help. I'm going to send for your father."

"No!" she screamed and I was startled.

She looked into my eyes and a shiver tickled my spine. "Who do you think did this to me?" Then she started rambling incoherently. I only understood fragments. "He checks my neck every month...he knows my monthly cycles...I am never to tell a *soul…it would kill my mother if she knew…They think I'm on holiday with cousin Isabelle."*

My God, her own father had raped her! Her own upstanding, wealthy father, a doctor whom people trusted! I felt as if I would have a sinking spell but somehow remained upright. "I won't call your father. Don't worry pet," I said. "I'm going down the street. I saw a chemist's sign. I'm going to see if he can get someone to help. No one will know." I kissed her clammy cheek and ran to the chemist's. The kindly old man with whiskers sprouting from his neck and cheeks like sage grass took over from there. I told him I'd heard some strange noises coming from the opera house and found a girl there suffering from the administrations of a quack and could he please help her? I told him I had no idea who she was. A cart was sent for and Nell was taken to hospital. I left her in good care and returned several days later to see how she was faring. The plan was that Nell would send a note to her parents about how much she was enjoying her holiday with Izzy. When she had recuperated, she would return home, none the wiser. None except me. I was shocked when I first stood by the small bed in which she lay. Did she know she was lucky to be alive? She looked so small, so fragile, and there were shoe-polish circles of dark gray beneath her eyes.

She would not speak to me. She would not let me touch her. "Nell, what is it? Are you all right?"

She looked at me and in her eyes I saw despair, something I'd never seen before. She moved her parched lips slowly. "Did…I say anything…about…why I was there?"

I stroked her hair and she didn't move. "I know why, pet. I'm so sorry for what you went through." Then I lied. "You don't have to tell me who the father was." Relief washed over her face like sun skidding across ice long abandoned by skaters. "The doctor," I said, "did he tell you…"

"What? That I will never have any children? That that butcher also removed my ovaries and had you not come, I would have bled to death?"

She rolled away from me and gave me her back. Her shoulders shook with sobs. "I'm a stub of a woman, Ruthie. Who will want me now?"

"It's not true, Nell. Don't think like that, please. You'll grow healthy again."

I am so angry at her father I could kill him. What sort of sick, demented soul would do this to his own child? I've never thought much about Nell's father, but now I can see his eyes, and they remind me of oiled wood.

"Remember what you told me about your mother?" I asked. "There's another way to think of this. You won't have to endure pregnancy after pregnancy. You won't have to be any man's slave. You don't want to marry anyway, right?"

"Oh Ruthie," she sighed. "You are so naïve."

She lay quietly for awhile then said, "It's getting dark. You'd better go. You don't need to come back again. And don't ever tell anybody."

"I won't. But I want to stay with you."

"No. Leave me be. When I'm well enough, I'll come home."

"If you need me…"

"I don't need anybody."

I walked into the shadowy feel of dusk wanting to wash the scent of her, of the hospital, of the cheap stump of tallow candle by her bedside from my shabby clothing. I thought sadly of the little baby that would never be born, despite the strange coupling of its parents. Light from street lamps hissed and convexed in odd angles and I felt something tear at my soul. I am unraveling, frayed, dreamed up.

April 11, 1903

It seems impossible, but I think Nell may be in love. Or perhaps just infatuated now with a man who spurned her advances in the garden, who would not drink the milky threads of moonlight washing the bejeweled fingers of the trees. She told me about it. How could she think this man, who turns out to be quite honorable, would keep her behind curtains? I'm not surprised, either, that Nell felt completely comfortable and unobserved in the dark garden behind her parents' house, propositioning a married man with the flick of her eyelashes or the coquettish turn of her head. But she would not have needed these feeble gestures; everything Nell wants is naked in her eyes. There can be no misunderstanding. Nell fears nothing. I'm sure of it. Even the bold Mary Watts, her gossipy housekeeper, who has spent time hop-picking in London. I would've thought Nell's 'operation' would have had some affect on her person, but clearly it has not. In fact, I think it has pronounced those qualities in her that repulse and attract at the same time. She has no fear now of conceiving, and it has made her more bold.

The man, a surgeon and acquaintance of her father's from Philadelphia, was dining at invitation of Mrs. Schaffer. He was staying in the house, his invalid wife at home with the nanny and the couple's two daughters, Sophie and Gertrude, ages 7 and 11. At dinner, Nell was smitten with him, his dark looks, his gold-brown eyes. Said they reminded her of warm brandy. The guest room window faces the garden pathways; Nell crept out of the house after everyone was asleep and walked in the gardens, staring up at the window where she knew Thomas lay in his bed. Her glorious blonde hair was unfettered and hung to her waist, like roses escaping a trellis. After she'd stared longingly at his window, she told me she disappeared into the mossery. The Schaffers' gardens have to be seen to be believed. In the winter, they look wild;

withered exotic stalks of plants trailing their fingers where they should not, stroking the
ground with their dead petals. In the spring, they are more than magnificent. A large
cast-iron stag stands midway up the path; there's an ornate fountain and a ginger-
bread-decorated gazebo in the center of the garden. Mrs. Schaffer spends a lot of time
alone there. She contends that plants never die; they just sleep. She knows everything
about plants; she has exotic specimens imported from Australia, South America, and
Africa. No one has a garden to rival hers. Everyone is in awe, always asking her for
seeds and cuttings, which she generously shares. In the summertime, the carpet of
plants is arranged such that it looks like a clock when viewed from the upstairs win-
dows—a bright clock with electric-blue, goose-egg arms. Nestled in the gnarled trees,
colorful flowers, and burgeoning hedges are secret rendezvous areas. I've watched the
Schaffers and their guests conduct nude scavenger hunts when citrus floats on the air
and flowers bark with color. They think the world sleeps, that servants never watch
them. They talk as if we don't have ears; they move as if we don't have eyes. Now the
salvia, ageratum, cockscomb, geraniums, and golden feverfew are open in all their
glory to the hints and suggestions of spring.

It was not long before Thomas joined Nell in the mossery. At first, he said nothing.
He would not look at her. She stared at his handsome profile and put her small, whit-
ish hand on his trousers. He pushed it away, clearly alarmed, and Nell said she
thought that was funny. "What do you think of mythology, Thomas?" she asked. Nell
would think nothing of using his first name like that.

"Mythology is tragic in its view, Miss Schaffer."

"Call me Nell, Thomas."

"Wherever the mythological mood prevails, tragedy is impossible. A quality of
dream."

"Do you think I'm beautiful?" she asked.

"It is not a question of beauty. Beauty itself is a myth."

"Why did you follow me here?"

"I don't know. You seemed…troubled."

"Troubled?" Nell laughed. "Of all the people you know, I am surely the least trou-
bled."

Nell told Thomas she thought he was beautiful, one of the most beautiful men
she'd ever seen. After she'd extolled the virtues of his warm, dark eyes, his long, lean
fingers, the powerful tug and stride of his shoulders, the saintliness of his occupation,
he was quiet. "Perfume and whitewash, Miss Shaffer." She looked into his eyes and
there was a longing there so deep and wide it made Nell shiver. Mistakenly, Nell
thought it was desire for her. After she told me how he responded, I knew at once it
was desire for his invalid wife, for things that could not be, for the warmness of nights

long gone, of touches gentle and words sacred and ordinary at the same time, spoken in scrapes of whispers, cuts of love.

"*O, that this too too solid flesh would melt,*
Thaw and resolve itself into a dew!" *he said.*

"*You speak in riddles Thomas. Why don't you stop reciting and kiss me.*"

He readjusted his position but did not reach for her.

"*Do you love your unacceptable wife?*" *Nell asked.*

"*Yes.*" *He seemed hurt by the description of his wife, but did not say so.*

"*But surely you have needs…surely you hunger for passion…*"

He stood. Nell told me she stared up at his face, which seemed hardened by moonlight yet softened by sentiment for a woman lying in a bed with nothing more to give him.

"*Einmal habe ich geträumt.*" *He spoke German and Nell was entranced. She had to ask me what it meant. I told her. "Once I dreamed."*

Nell and I argued then. She told me she was going to make him love her. Make him dream again. I told her you can't make someone love you. I can see her now, sitting in that garden, staring at the weeping trees as if they were wish-fulfilling rivers, not knowing she cannot give him what he needs.

May 13, 1903

I'm watching a crinkle of wave kiss the shore and pull back. A water-and-foam imprint that only I see before it's gone. When I'm old, I will forget the fragile fingerprint, the careless, joyful way the water reached for and hugged the sand then withdrew. I love it here, so alone, so peaceful, the world stretching away from me in rafters of blue. This place is a treasure, a place where I can slow my life down.

I sit and scratch sea star shapes of ink on these pages because I don't want to forget this feeling, I don't want to lose it to the wind, a memory born of time, salted away. Maybe I don't want to grow old? I can see tiny shapes farther down the beach, the timid shapes of small children dipping their feet in the ocean for the first time, their mothers holding their hands as water licks skin and dampens clothing. Their voices drift like dreams at dawn.

Sometimes it's good to be alone to think about the people you love, to dream about them, because who will tell our stories years from now, when we are gone? Ocean City—named by four Methodist ministers who met 23 years ago beneath a cedar tree and decided to build a tabernacle in a thorny thrash of sea and beach and swamp.

Tabernacle: a house of worship; a large building or tent used for evangelistic services.

I look at lunging waves the color of carved jade, the golden, fat coil of dust-like sand, the streaked thread of sky and cloud, feel the sharp snap of salty wind against my face and arms, and wonder, why did they think they needed to build one?

This is the only place where I feel like I'm being born again. I feel old and young at the same time. From where I sit on the beach, I can see parts of the Sindia, tall masts and her tiller post, sticking out like an ancient finger pointing the wrong way. The four-masted ship is sinking beneath the sand more each sun-lathed day. Last year the ship reached Cape May and a howling winter gale and churning seas battered her for 4 days, ripping her sails and rigging to tatters and spinning her around broadside to the beach, driving her toward Ocean City, her final resting place. I read an account in the newspaper. On her last, fateful journey, she traveled to Shanghai and then to Kobe, Japan, before setting sail for New York City. There's speculation that items were looted from Buddhist temples during a rebellion in China and stored in her hold—gold, porcelain, fat Buddhas, jade dogs. Yelping pieces of art—symbolic, sacred, sitting like fugitives from fate in the callused hands of greedy men.

Art: abstraction, carving, skill, creativity, imitation.
Art: deceit, astuteness, duplicity, guile, slyness.

I love this salty air, this beach, this solitude almost as much as I love words. I whisper to the wind, "I love you Farrell." I'm not really alone. I see him, his broad shoulders and strong arms glazed with salt water as he emerges from the sea, his skin ruddy with the cold and wetness of it, his dark hair soaked and curling at his nape. Immediately I want to touch him, warm him. He alone understands my need for solitude, my need for him, that they are not opposed; at least, I think he does. He carries in his hand a seashell he has scrimped from the hardscrabble waves. It glints an iridescent blue and pink in the waning sun. I know I will forever treasure this moment of my life, unfractured and pure. Because I know, in my soul, that I will never love anyone as deeply as I love Farrell. He sits beside me on the sand, reaches for my hand, places the shell in my fingers, a bone-and-flesh wish for more. When this moment is gone, will someone dream it back to life, dream back all the things we shared?

May 15, 1903

It's been warmer. I've never really minded the heat the way some girls do when it makes their fancy dresses and underclothes stick to their skin or the curls on top of their heads go riotous in mutiny. My hair's straight as a poker, black, and not much affected by weather. I never much thought about it one way or another until Farrell pushed my bangs out of my face and told me he liked it, that it was full of fire. Shortly after we made love in his father's fading barn, a really strange thing happened. It was frightening, beautiful, and resolute in a kind of irresolute way. I can't talk about it now. I have to be sure it really happened.

May 18, 1903

Sweat drips from the back of my neck down the hollow of my back. I feel like I'm glowing, changed. It was only a few days ago that I went to see Farrell. I found him in the barn. The air hung heavy and taut around us. The sky had been dark for three days, threatening to unleash itself for hours, but not a drop of rain. My clothes stuck to my body. He noticed. He was wearing trousers and no shirt, pitching hay with a pitchfork. Sweat glistened like yellow afternoon on his skin. He stopped, and leaned on the top of the pitchfork, not saying anything. We just studied each other. I swear I could feel the electricity in the sky; I've seen lightning hit the roof once or twice and watched it dance and skitter across the heads of nails. He put the pitchfork down, walked over to me, and just wrapped me in his arms. "Do you hate me?" he asked, his voice raspy and thin.

"Hate you?"

"Yeah, I mean, what happened...it wasn't...how I wanted it to be with you."

For a moment, I just absorbed his words, took his breathing inside of me.

"Then show me how you wanted it to be."

He was tender and passionate and I loved the way that errant stalks of straw stuck to his arms and his hair when we were sated. On my way home, I passed a group of tattered looking boys greasing the trolley tracks. I'd seen them before; the car slides off the tracks into the dirt and can't go over the railroad. The streetcar company has to send out a crew of men to put sand on the rails so the run can go on while women with pretty parasols and men in suits look chagrined.

Sometimes I scold them. The boys. That day, I didn't care. Something in me was completed. I was practically skipping home when the sky ripped itself open like a grocer's bag of apples. I was drenched in no time. Carelessly, I began to run. What happened next is almost embarrassing. It's the thing I haven't been able to write about yet. I slipped and hit my head on the smooth, slippery skin of a rock.

I woke up confused in my own bed. It was hotter than a depot stove. A bowl of untouched gruel sat on the table next to the bed. My father was stomping up the stairs with a pitcher of water. When he saw that I was awake, he almost dropped it.

"You're awake."

"Apparently."

"How do you feel?"

"What happened?"

"Nell found you by the lake, unconscious. You hit your head on a rock. You have a nasty gash on your forehead."

Immediately, my fingers went to the gash. I felt the ragged edges of torn skin and panicked. *"How long ago was that?"*

"Three days. You've been delirious. Nell's been helping to take care of you."

"But..."

It all came rushing back. I'd known somehow that I'd hit my head. But it was Farrell who carried me back to the barn; it was Farrell who pressed cool cloths to my forehead and bandaged my gash; it was Farrell saying he loved me and always would. Wind that tasted of green apples pressed against my throat; strong fingers slid themselves across my skin, through my hair. Everything was blurry. But I felt a peace I'd never known; Farrell was there, but he was...different. With each gentle stroke against my skin I finally understood that not everything is up to me. It was like he was a future Farrell, someone he would always be, someone he would become. And he told me something. Dreams die hard. And maybe they don't have to die at all. Even if we do.

Suddenly, I had to know if it had happened at all. I had to talk to him. But you don't just run up to someone and say, hey, did we make love over and over in the barn three days ago and did you tell me you love me and that dreams don't have to die? Yes, I'm sure I would be carted off to the asylum, given a room right next to my mother. Nell, fortunately, broke the tight space between my father and me. I didn't feel sore between my legs, like I had that first time Farrell had entered me, bruised me with his passion. I wanted to feel that belligerent, angry, passionate, fanning pain that dulled sweetly and hung on to remind me that we'd been one; that I belonged to him.

Nell had brought me freshly baked scones with nut butter but I just couldn't eat them.

"Farrell," I breathed.

"He's here," she said, and just like that, he appeared, twisting his worn hat in his hands. My father had left the room and then Nell went down to fetch some lemonade.

Tears streaked my eyes. *"I had the strangest experience. I dreamt that you found me, not Nell."*

"I had the same dream," he said, surprised. *"I wish it had been me."*

His eyes were the brown of corded wood on a fire, smoldering. He's my life, my soul, and he soothes the part of me that has been charred. *"Was it real? Did we..."*

The words were barely a whisper. "Yes," he said. "It was real. It will always be real between us." He traced the cut on my forehead with his fingers.

"What happens next?" I said.

Nell stepped through the doorway and the glass of lemonade she was balancing on a tray slid to the ground and shattered into tiny jagged pieces. I felt a sharp, wet, silky feeling in my gut—a foreboding I couldn't shake. Tempered with the knowledge that I am following my heart. That can't be all bad, can it?

"If something happens, come back for me," I whispered loud enough so only he could hear. What a strange thing to say. I wonder if I knocked myself loopy on that rock.

May 24, 1903

I went to see my mother today. She was wearing a standard issue gown and sitting at a table. She wasn't wearing any shoes, and there were large, dark circles beneath her eyes. I felt like shaking her and asking her, why aren't I enough?

Some people trap themselves in the past. It's like a bitter root and they can't let go. Her breakfast, sloppy creamed ham on toast and coffee, sat cold and untouched on a plate before her. I hugged her and the nape of her neck was cold. She sucked on a cigarette. She didn't ask about the gash on my forehead; she didn't ask about my father. She just looked at me and said, "I want my shoes."

That's when I knew she was already dead, that she'd rather live in this colorless, stale world than be with her own daughter in the real world. As I looked around at the children, the aged and infirm shuffling through the hallways like ghosts, I told myself, remember to blink. In every society that has left records there has been madness.

Monique blew a puff of smoke out the side of her mouth. She is simply Monique to me now. She is so thin, thinner than I've ever seen her.

"You know what they have me doing here?"

I didn't say anything, just listened. "Folding fucking towels. Day in, day out."

I thought she liked that, since she spent every other minute at home folding and refolding all the household linens.

We walked on carpeting as worn as old skin to her room. She was one of the "milder" patients, so she got a roommate. Her roommate was a plump woman with ginger-colored hair curled up on the other bed. Despite the warm spring we're having, her room is drafty and heated by steam, the radiator arranged to heat two rooms. The rooms open onto the hallway, and I could see further down the hall that the radiators were protected by heavy iron netting. Monique lit another cigarette. "Let me tell you, this is no fucking picnic." After she finished her cigarette, she curled up on her bed like I wasn't there. She reminded me of a brittle leaf, streaked and veined—a dead dream, weltered and unscholarly, and my heart hurt from loving her so much. "Can you bring me some eggs or some borax next time? I need to wash my hair."

A nurse shuffled in and placed a small dark tablet under her tongue. "What is that?"

"Glyco-heroin," the nurse said cheerily. "It'll help your mother to break her addiction to opium. It's a new tablet that dissolves under the tongue. It's coated in chocolate." She leaned closer to me. "And it will regulate her bowels."

She pulled out three more tablets.

"How many of those things do you give her?"

"Now Deary, I'm the nurse." She was about to give them to my mother and I stood up and knocked them out of her hand. I don't know why. I don't like the tablets.

"Why don't you shove them up your ass?" I screamed.

The ginger-haired woman sat up and laughed. "Uptight nursie wursie needs a gin. Needs a gin." There was the grammar of dynamite in her smile and a bone yard of sorrow in her eyes.

The nurse's lip crumpled and her chin dimpled. She smoothed her dress. "Well then," she said. "I'll come back later."

Heroin: Sedative for coughing; used to treat addiction.
Heroine: Latin heroina, from Greek hērōinē, feminine of hērōs. A mythological or legendary woman having the qualities of a hero, or, a woman admired and emulated for her achievements and qualities.

Monique is trying to stop time, reverse it, back it up and freeze it. The blue-black tangle of her hair, it's like watching ink dry on a page…and then disappear. I blamed my father for so long, but now I realize Monique made choices. She chose to stop living, to stop thinking about what she needs and wants from life. It leaves me wondering, is there a set of connections between experiences that outlives us?

Glance: Hit off something. Bounce; brush; careen; carom; graze; kiss; strike.

I find myself thinking about Farrell. I know Nell will hurt me. But the way Farrell looks at me, I don't know if he'll heal me or destroy me. I realize that's what I like about him. I think his convictions could be dangerous.

May 27, 1903

SHE IS GONE. GONE!

I heard and felt the cinching of the press as a noose around my own neck, saw the black belching of ink and smoke as the paper unbound Farrell's life—my life. I read with dread and fear as the short clerk in suspenders pasted the bulletin to the window of the newspaper shop:

Was Farrell Neff, son of Otto Neff, responsible for the disappearance of Miss Nellie April Schaffer on the night of May 26? Farrell stoutly maintains his innocence. He denies he had anything to do with the crime. Says he was at his father's farm during those hours and that he never saw Miss Shaffer that night. He talks freely, does not hesitate in his manner, and appears to be somewhat educated. If he is covering up, he is more intelligent and rehearsed than a Shakespearean actor.

No, no, no. It can't happen this way.

June 3, 1903

I had to turn away from the eyes of these pages. My hands were shaking so badly, I couldn't write. The two people I loved most, and most imperfectly, are dead. It might as well have been by my hand. I'm not sure now if Nell's death was intentional or an accident. I can't separate memory from reality. I don't know if I did it on purpose. Before I die, which will be shortly, I'll lay it all out to the best of my ability.

In Nell's death, I am oddly more awake and alive than I have ever been. Perhaps it is karmic and fitting that, as in our lives, we were an entanglement of languor, desires, hatreds, and loves, because it was an entanglement, and a thin, silky scarf the color of blood, that caused her death, that stretched out from my hand and her neck as she turned, too quickly, on the top of the stairs. Nell. Beautiful angel. Threads of her blonde hair washing over the pine boards like the outstretched wings of an angel, eyes unblinking and frozen in copious grief and surprise. Like the green sea, white-capped and frozen in time. No breath escapes from the mouth that both caressed and abused me. In a way, I am frozen too. No! I want her to see me! Her neck and one of her legs both convex at odd angles. A tug. A raised voice. A fall. Bones snapping. I will never forget that sound. After her broken descent, I carried her in the darkness down to my father's cellar, where there is a secret room that only I know about. It's back behind his curious jars and when I discovered it I was only 7 years old. I never told anyone. It's a hollowed out crawlspace, really. I took Nell there and set her down so her back rested against the wall.

Tomb: box, burial chamber, coffin, crypt, grave, pit, vault.

She still wears the scarf. I'd borrowed it and she wanted it back. She was going to meet someone she said, her eyes flirtatious. Farrell? Thomas? Someone else? My father has been gone for a few days, off to visit my mother in that God-awful institution. I will be gone when he comes back. Dead. But here, under his roof, with the girl I loved. And the thing between us that he could never accept.

Passion is like mythology. A story. A legend. A laceration across the soul.

Passion: Craving, craze, drive, fad, fancy, fascination, idol, infatuation, mania, obsession.

I've always loved words. And the power of them. But people look at my worn blouses and frayed sweaters, my scuffed boots, the fringe of my black hair, which falls like a shadow across my face (it's OK, I prefer it that way; I've never really liked my face), and my faded stockings, pale skin beneath, and they judge. I don't have anything to offer the world, they say. What a waste. I'm an ephemeral blight to society. A man's sweaty, filthy, grunting eruption inside a half-dead woman with no prospects for respectability. A drop of semen that, unfortunately, they say, grew into a human being.

Here's what happened with Farrell. After I ran to tell him what happened with Nell, that she was dead, he calmed me down with soft words that I can't remember now. I kissed him. He told me he loved me. That he never loved anybody like he loved me. It was an accident. It would be OK. Then I came back. I didn't leave my house for a few days. I didn't hear from him. I got lost in my sorrow, confusion, guilt, and, yes, relief. The source of my jealousy was dead. By my hand. I could've saved Farrell. A week later I once again entered the outside world. I hadn't bathed for several days. I hadn't combed my hair, I hadn't eaten. I walked along sun-glistened walkways, passed the Episcopal church with its stained-glass windows, felt the warmth of the sun burning me with a numbness I could not fight. I walked aimlessly for awhile. I found myself in front of a large tree not far from the cemetery with its iron rails and the jailhouse. Its oaken limbs stretched and twisted in the sky, Farrell's lifeless body hanging from a rope that had been tied to one of them. I collapsed. I don't know how long I lay there. I don't know how I ended up on stranger's settee. It didn't matter how many covers they piled on me or how much warm tea they tried to force down my throat. I couldn't get warm. I knew I would never be warm again. The man who found me, and his wife, they are regular people like me. Good people trying to do the right thing. While they were busy in their tiny kitchen, I overhead them talking about Farrell and how he'd been accused of Nell's disappearance, given a hasty trial, and hanged! Someone had overheard an argument between Nell and Farrell. He'd threatened her in some fashion regarding a man she'd claimed she was now seeing, a much older, married man. I couldn't breathe. I nearly vomited on the wooden floor by the settee. Then I pushed open the heavy window drapes, opened the sash, and crawled out into the yard, blinded by the harsh light of a vengeful spring that did not love me. I could've saved him! He was always stronger than me. Washed color. Strong lines. I bled over his lines until the shape of him was erased. He knew the truth and yet he didn't reveal it, even to save his own life.

Turn of century: Saint James' Society mails free samples of heroin to morphine addicts who are trying to stop using it.

1903: Discover my mother is a heroin addict. Her withdrawal from the world is better explained.

June 3, 1903: Many heroin addicts in the United States. I will commit suicide. I will do one more thing. Write "FN" on the front of this diary. "For Nell." I think Farrell would approve.

Shade: screen, shadow, dimness, blackness, cover.

My name is Ruth. But I am not Ruth. I am shades of Ruth, of all those who came before me.

I'll put this journal in a safe place, away from our bones as they age and leak our secrets to the locked air. After I take the packets of heroin, I imagine I'll hear the lapping of waves against the boat and it will be peaceful after the pain passes. I'll think of the little hina dolls and wrap my fingers around Nell's cold, lifeless ones. Infected lives to be swallowed up by the sea. I'll wrap the scarf around both of our necks. A symbol of blood and brokenness between two souls. Perhaps it will bind us together in the next place, wherever that may be. We'll become a gray tangle of bones wedged against a wall. And I'll know. Dreams tell us we're not who we think we are. It is over.

41

It was Wednesday evening and Ann was in her office with its depressing gunmetal grey walls. She held the receiver away from her ear, preferring not to lose her hearing due to the "hold" music, a much too upbeat version of "I've Got You Babe" followed by John Denver's "Sunshine on My Shoulders."

Finally, she heard the music click off and Narcotics Chief Steve Bruno pick up.

"You <u>got to</u> get better hold music."

"I've requested the complete Bette Midler, but so far, the office hasn't approved."

"Jesus," Ann said, laughing. "You got anything more for me on the stomach contents?"

"An NK3 receptor antagonist. In development to treat schizophrenia and other CNS disorders. Experimentally, it's available to severe schizophrenics through the drug's Pennsylvania producer, InnoPharm. It controls what the patients hear in their heads but it can cause heavy duty damage to the liver."

"I know all that Steve. An NK3. Blocks a receptor in the brain for dopamine," Ann rambled. "It reduces the number of D1 receptors, which can result in working-memory impairments. Blackouts too."

"When it's chewed, it delivers a heroin-like high. InnoPharm offers it in a 120-milligram dose."

"So patients can abuse it, become addicted," Ann said. "Has there been any fallout?"

"Wasn't tracked until earlier this year. Fallout has been fairly contained, but the DEA said the pill is creeping into larger East Coast cities. DEA says there have been several overdose deaths and more are likely.

"I talked with some hot shit VP of Marketing at InnoPharm; he said doctors are *unnecessarily* concerned that patients will turn around and sell it once it's prescribed. Of course, he went on and on about how innovative the drug is. Swears legitimate users haven't been known to get addicted."

"The victims weren't schizophrenic," Ann said, taking notes on her notepad. "So why did they have high concentrations of Lucinate X in their systems? What's your theory?"

"The killer likes to play games? Likes to get high? Maybe he's a schizo himself who otherwise leads a normal, even respectable life on the outside?

"I also talked with the VP of Clinical Affairs who recently resigned. Clifton Barks. Whistle-blower. An interesting chat. He told me if someone was given a double dose, even if they had no underlying predisposition to seizures, they could quickly become unconscious and could have a fatal seizure. Company wants to launch it anyway. Doesn't want to lose sales or positioning in the market."

"Jesus. What about his background?"

"Already checked him out. He had an affair once, but otherwise he's clean."

"Thanks."

"Anytime."

Ann hung up and rubbed her temples. It was 8:15 pm, she hadn't eaten anything except a bag of stale pretzels from the vending machine, and she was still surrounded by mounds of paperwork. Her congenitally cheerful secretary, Mamie Pratt, bobbed her severely dyed blonde head into Ann's office. "You want takeout? I'm ordering Italian."

"No thanks, Mamie. Go home. I'm leaving soon. This place gives me the creeps at night."

Mamie laughed, knowing that nothing ever gave <u>Ann</u> the creeps. She walked away and Ann jotted down a few notes.

Existence: Actuality; animation; being; breath; continuance. What makes this guy tick? We all have the faces we show the world. We all have the faces we wake up with. Lucinate X. Brass buttons. Strangulation. Pennsylvania. The Big Easy.

Ann realized she was adopting the style of the diary she'd found. Ruth's diary. The girl who loved words. Strange. She thought of the present-day killer, a twisted, sadistic individual who looked 'normal' to the world, and it was like an oily substance in her soul. Why couldn't they dredge up a single forensic clue? The buttons. The notes. The Porsche that he'd painted black. None of it had yielded anything substantial. She heard Mamie order a meatball sub and cheese fries and her stomach grumbled. She opened her desk drawer to put her notes away and stared.

"Mamie?"

"Yeah?"

"Can you come in here a second?"

"Sure."

Mamie waltzed in, a lollipop stuffed in her mouth.

The drawer was jammed with pages torn from magazines. Men's magazines. Ann put on a latex glove, pulled them out, and unfolded them, ads for condoms, sex toys, and triple X movies.

"Was someone in here today?"

Mamie shook her head, looking pale. "Your office was locked. I <u>know</u> it was locked. That's weird. <u>Really</u> weird. I mean, who'd do something like that?"

Ann decided she would take the pages to the lab for testing.

"You're sure no one came in here for anything?"

"Positive. I didn't see anyone."

"Were you here for lunch?"

"Oh." Mamie said. "Well, I did run around the corner to get a sandwich, but it only took like 5 minutes."

Somebody had gone to some real trouble to pull all those ads out of magazines and put them in her desk drawer. Someone with a fetish. Someone with a message. On the last ad, someone had written in black sloppy marker YOU KNOW YOU WANT IT. AND ONLY I CAN GIVE IT TO YOU RIGHT, LIKE YOU DESERVE. And then in smaller letters, FUCKING CUNT.

Then, a thought: sexual dysfunction is a potential side effect of the majority of anti-psychotic drugs on the market. If the killer was taking LUCINATE X himself, he could be experiencing sexual problems. *Great. An out-of-control, drug-addicted, sexually dysfunctional, raging, homicidal, psychotic lunatic had maybe, perhaps, very probably, been in her office.*

Thoughts about the investigation, the anonymous notes and phone calls, the sex ads, the victims, Bo being diagnosed with breast cancer, bounced and snapped in her head like illegal firecrackers. What she really needed was someone to talk to. *Mark.*

42

"When I was a little girl, upset because I didn't have the things that other girls had, my grandmother would tell me the story of Sheng Bo," Ann said.

Hands on warm, sticky flesh. Moving with butterfly wishes in a man's hair, over the soft, glorious crown of penis.

"Tell me," Mark rasped in the darkness.

"Sheng Bo dreamed that he crossed a river, where someone brought pearls to him and asked him to eat them."

Tongue-crying-silver-sparking-heat. Fink, fine comb, finery, fingers, finish off. Smell of a man. Mouth filled with stretchy hard flesh, the fine tickle of coarse hair and sweat on her chin.

"Sheng Bo cried," Ann breathed. "And his tears turned to pearls that covered his chest."

Slim, feminine fingers awakening rivers in a man. Stretching north and south with clemency. Coarse, raw grace in the thrust of square hips, the eruption of pearly seed on wet mouth and erect nipple. Faith brought me here, she thinks.

"Then he sang a song. 'Across the river I was given the pearls. Returning, returning, the pearls are all on my chest.' As time passed, he felt less afraid. Three years later, as he was leading his army into battle, he had completely gotten over it. What did he have to fear?"

Lipslynchingprogressplayactingwithlife; ligaments sewn up with sighs.

"He told others about his dream and how it had turned out to mean nothing. That same day Sheng Bo was killed in battle."

He flips her over so she's on her knees. Bent elbows. Fingers gripping sheets. He fucks her deep, from behind. The wetness from an eager mouth and a straining cock, sliding, slippery; the touch of him against the far wall of her womb a catholicon for the traffic in their heads.

She is not worried about how she smells; she's a dancing girl...

Dancingsilversemen

Locolocuslocutionandlodge

She sees his face in the dim starlight, the roughness of skin and desire cranking hard against swollen need and random dust motes. She is motion, a provoked stimulus, a need and a motive. Who needs blond bracelets dangling on wrists and pearl earrings

167

threading lobes when there is such hate in the world? Stroke. Stroke. Stroke. She comes. Spirals. Erasing hate with each wave of heat.

43

Bruce had enjoyed dinner in town with some of his colleagues and had returned to the office to find Gerdie gone for the night. Good, he thought. She always works too late anyway. He unlocked the office door, flipped the light on, and headed straight for the filing cabinet. As he was sitting in Maxwell's enjoying a thick burger and spicy crab soup, he realized what was bothering him. It wasn't that one of his clients had confessed to killing someone in a past life. That was certainly unusual and its own dilemma. It was something else. Two of his patients, who as far as he knew had never met, seemed to be describing past lives in which they *knew each other*. And one was a killer in that life.

He thumbed through the files until he found both of the cases, carted them to his office and put coffee on. It was going to be a late night.

Bruce had often wondered—could serial killers be reincarnated? It wasn't a subject he'd thoroughly investigated. He'd read theories about souls traveling in groups. About karma and debts that had to be paid. Certain sects of Gnosticism held the belief that the soul has to experience all aspects of life; Western philosophy decreed that if man does not reach a higher spiritual level, he must repeat the cycle until he does.

Bruce wanted to look over his notes in detail and listen to the tapes again before he made any decisions. He always made tapes of his clients' sessions so that they, or anybody else, could listen to them after the fact and know he was just a facilitator and not a source of any memories that had revealed themselves.

He listened to the familiar late night churning and gurgling of the coffee maker. Vaguely, he was aware of why he worked so much. He didn't want to go home to an empty house. To memories of his first wife, and the happiness they shared. He immediately brought his mind back to his clients. He knew he wouldn't have the resources to investigate a murder in another state that may or may not have happened close to 140 years ago. Now, if his patient had talked about committing a murder in his *present* lifetime that would be different.

Bruce had done some reading about hypnosis that was used with defendants on rare occasions. Usually it was used as a tool to ensure accuracy in eyewitness testimony. But it had its drawbacks. For one thing, the possibility that a recovered memory is incomplete, inaccurate, or based on some leading suggestion is a concern. There's also the possibility of hypermnesia, exceptionally exact or vivid memory, especially as associated with certain mental illnesses, or confabulation—filling the gaps with false material that supports the subject's self interests.

The courts were divided on the issue of hypnosis as a method to enhance recollection and assist in arresting an offender, let alone to contribute to a capital sentence. After all, memory isn't all it's cracked up to be. And people can lie under hypnosis. Yet hypnosis had played a significant part in many criminal cases, including Sam Sheppard and Ted Bundy, and Bruce had been just as intrigued as the rest of the nation by those cases.

What was bothering Bruce was a feeling of foreboding. Would his subject kill in his present lifetime? Bruce needed to go deeper, but he would have to be careful.

He poured a cup of coffee and sat down behind his desk with a notepad and pencil. He pressed play and listened to the most recent session he'd had with Kevin, if that was his real name. When had the subject become agitated? When had his voice changed, become more feminine, mocking? Halfway through the tape, he found what he was looking for.

I'm just home from the war. I lost my arm.
Which arm?
My left arm. I got shot up. I woke up in a barn. Even though it's gone, sometimes I still feel myself flexing fingers that aren't there, still feel my elbow flexing.
Where are you now?
I'm waiting to board a train. I'm going home.
How do you feel?
I'm feeling happy for the first time in a long time. I'm going to see her.
Who are you going to see?
Lavinia. She's been writing to me while I was away.
Jump ahead. Go to her now. What do you see?
We're standing by the lake where we grew up in Virginia. It's getting close to dusk. I'm wearing my uniform. Risky to wear it in Confederate territory, but I like to take risks. She's wearing a white dress and she has a red ribbon in her hair. A gold necklace sparkles around her neck. She is so beautiful. I can feel myself sweating. The uniform is hot, but I want her to see me in it.

There was silence for a few moments before the subject spoke again. Bruce remembered him fidgeting in his seat, his tall, muscular frame tense, his facial features knotted with tension, his fingers restlessly tapping.

What's happening now?

This isn't what I expected...she's not...

Bruce looked at his notes. He had recorded the fact that his subject was actually perspiring at this point in the conversation. *Subject still sweating, fists clenched. Visibly distraught. Seems to be struggling with something profound. Patient's voice changed to sound more high-pitched, like a female's, even mocking.*

We don't really know each other anymore, do we? I'm sorry...I...I never meant to give you the wrong impression in my letters...There's someone in my life now. He is the most wonderful man. We're to be married next week. I can't wait for you to meet him.

Subject laughed harshly.

How do you feel?

Like someone's thrown cold water in my face. My whole body stings. I'm numb. I've pushed her to the ground. The elbow of my good arm is across her throat. She can't breathe. She doesn't understand...she's dead now. She didn't expect it. I made it as quick and painless as I could. I kiss her lips. I take her ring and yank the gold chain from her neck. I don't like it. There's a swan on the chain and it's looking at me. I put it in my pocket. I make her a promise.

There it was in German. *I'll find you again, my sweet.*

Bruce popped the tape out and put the second tape in, the session with Ann.

Where are you now?

I think I'm in the South, Virginia maybe. I'm going over last-minute details for my wedding. It's only a week away. Just one week! I'm going to be moving to Washington, DC. I am so happy, because the war is over and I'm getting married!

What's your name?

<u>Lavinia.</u>

Bruce stopped the tape. There it was. The same name. The same year, possibly. The same <u>state.</u> Both sessions had occurred in the same *week*. He hit play again.

What are you doing now?

I'm running my fingers over the soft fabric of my wedding dress. It's pale blue and lovely. Blue, that means love will be true. It has a fitted bodice, a small waist, and a full skirt. It's made of tulle. The veil is a fine gauze, sheer.

Can you see your groom?

He's not here right now. The wedding will be in Washington, DC. I finally brought my parents around to the fact that I'm marrying a Yankee. They weren't happy at first, but once they met him, saw that he is a fine, upstanding man who has saved many lives they consented to the match. I think if he had been a Union soldier they would have forbid it. But a surgeon, that was a little different. They are more open-minded than others.

How did you meet him?

Subject smiled, obviously content.

In Washington. I decided to attend a lecture he was giving. The room was large and very full, and he gave a talk about his experiences in the war. There were other soldiers there, soldiers with crutches and bandages about their heads. He spoke slowly, distinctly, and with perfect ease. I was enthralled. The first time I looked at him, I felt I already knew him; the way his dark eyes sparkled with intelligence and sadness, the way he moved his shoulders, how he seemed bigger than the world. I never thought I'd see him again. Then we met, or rather, bumped into each other at Lincoln's funeral.

Tell me about Lincoln's funeral, about how you met your future husband.

I remember approaching the Capitol, being awed by the sight of the Capitol building dome—unfinished yet magnificent—poking into the early morning sky. It was overcast, a grey pallor hanging over the entire sprawling city—from the grand marble buildings to the little frame houses and raggedy, cobble-toothed streets. It seemed that everyone—and everything—was grieving.

I wished I'd come to Washington sooner, to have been among the throngs who had witnessed, just a few short days ago, the President's final speech. He had been a ray of light, a humble yet brilliant man, who had led his country through four years of war and who had preserved the Union. I could have made the trip with Meagan and her parents, but my parents didn't want me to see Meagan, given the family's Union sympathies. I thought I would have another opportunity to see Lincoln; after all, he was recently elected to another presidency and often granted an audience to civilians.

Oh how I wish I'd come sooner. Since the assassination, I've spent a good deal of time crying. Even now, it's difficult to breathe. I can smell the wafting stink of the nearby canal waters carried on the stiff spring breeze. I read about the President's speech, the dedication of a national cemetery for fallen soldiers, and the events surrounding the event in a newspaper. All the windows of the White House had been lighted with candles and the President stood in the center window of the second floor reading. Across the river, the crowds watched rockets being fired from Arlington lawn and throngs of ex-slaves sang "The Year of Jubilee."

Where are you now?

I'm standing outside the White House, in a crowd of people that stretches for at least a mile. It's strangely quiet. We're all waiting for the gate to be opened so we can file in through the South Portico, which is heavily draped—like the rest of the White House—with mourning. The great structure looks like it's being swallowed up in the wings of an enormous bat.

What time is it?

It's 9:30 in the morning, and the gate has just opened. I'm scared, but I am determined to look for the first—and last time—on Lincoln's face.

How do you feel now?

I feel some strange sort of urgency I can't put a name to—a frenetic energy and a feeling that something had begun and yet ended much too quickly. It's strange, but with the death of the Confederacy, I have never felt more alive.

I've been having the same dream over and over during the past week, a frightening dream where I hover above my body as someone snatches a gold chain from my neck.

Shit. The gold chain, Bruce thought. This is too freaky.

I also see a black coffin floating away from my house, the occupant hidden beneath the closed lid. I always had a feeling I would die young. We're moving very slowly through the dim great hall into the darkened Green Room, and then into the East Room now.

The light slips through the Venetian blinds. And then, it's there. The catafalque. A monstrous platform that bears the tall President's body and his coffin.

Even now I feel I'm moving through a dream, that none of this is real. The enormous chandeliers are shrouded in black bags. Tall mirrors over the marble mantelpieces are swathed with black cloth. My feet tread over pale sea-green carpet. I wonder how often the President and his wife entertained in this room where Lincoln's body now rests, and women, men, and children sob aloud.

I raise my eyes to the catafalque. Black velvet decorates its sides with sweeping festoons of black crepe. Enormous black satin rosettes sit on the points of each festoon. The underside of the canopy is white fluted satin. A uniformed army officer, mourning crepe hanging from his arm, is sitting all alone at the head of the coffin, weeping.

I'm feeling faint. The coffin is covered with black broadcloth. Lincoln's head is resting on quilted white satin lining. On the center of the lid there's a shield outlined in silver tacks, in the center of which is a silver plate bearing the inscription:

ABRAHAM LINCOLN

16TH PRESIDENT OF THE UNITED STATES
BORN FEBRUARY 12, 1809
DIED APRIL 15, 1865

Officers somberly direct me and several others to the foot of the catafalque, where the throng divides into a single line on each side, mounts the steps and walks beside the coffin pausing to look down at the face. The lid is folded back; only his face and shoul-

ders are exposed. I am sobbing. No one says a word as they pass, not even the bandaged and limping soldiers taking a last look at the face of their honored Commander-in-Chief.

What happens next?

Ann wipes her eyes.

I stumble down the other side of the ledge and faint. When I wake up, a doctor is holding me in his arms and he has the most beautiful dark eyes I've ever seen. People say brown eyes are so plain, but there are so many shades of brown, you know? It's the surgeon who gave the lecture. He takes me to his home, and we sit on a bench over-looking a swan sanctuary he's created to provide a peaceful place for himself and for his patients, mostly soldiers, to heal.

Is this the man you will marry?

Yes. Yes!

As the sun fades, he reads to me, parts of a poem by Longfellow called 'Resignation.' I can't keep my eyes from him. The way his lips move, his thick, dark hair, the way his dark eyes speak to me:

There is no flock, however watched and tended,
But one dead lamb is there!
There is no fireside, howso'er defended,
But has one vacant chair!
There is no Death! What seems so is transition.
This life of mortal breath
Is but the suburb of the life elysian,
Whose portal we call death.

Though we only know each other for a short time, he asks me to marry him before I go back home. He gives me a ring and a beautiful necklace, a swan made of mother-of-pearl and black onyx on a gold chain.

What are you doing now?

I'm at home. I'm going over the guest list and the menu. We're going to have five kinds of cake—orange, coconut, fruit, gold, and silver cakes. And scalloped oysters, pressed chicken and beef biscuits and butter.

Subject paused, seemed thoughtful.

I hope I may be a blessing and a help to my husband. He is so dear to me, and I wish for his sake that I was a thousand times better than I am.

Do you see this man in your present lifetime?

I'm not sure. Maybe.

What else is happening?

He's a saint. He's agreed to the Italian musicians for the wedding. Two will play harps and one the violin. I want to walk down an aisle strewn with yellow rose petals. I'm sure when I go to Washington, I'll miss my home. Life is very strange. One goes on from day to day, occupied, content, interested in one's present life, then some small incident will raise the curtain on the past and it is all there, so vividly that one wonders which is the most real—the present or the past. But Washington will be exciting. I'll have my own garden. There will be parties and social functions and we will travel. My husband-to-be is a surgeon; he knows a lot of high-profile people in Washington.

Tell me about the wedding.

Subject agitated.

I…I don't see that. I kiss my mama on the cheek, and with flour on my hands, I go to meet a friend of mine just returned from the war. I haven't seen him for 4 years.

Where are you going?

To the lake. It's not far. I grew up by it. I tell Mama I'll be back for dinner and give her a quick kiss on the cheek.

Who are you meeting?

A boy. He fought for the Union. He is afraid that he will not be received well by the others because of it. Even his own family. His father…he is a monster. We agreed it would be best to meet in secret at the lake.

He's changed…he wears a uniform. He is taller than I remember. He is…missing an arm! I am glad to see him. He has always been a good friend. I tell him I'm getting married.

Subject's hands clenched into fists; she started to thrash and scream and clutch at her neck.

No! No!

What's happening now? Remember, you are not living that lifetime now. You can remember then let go.

Subject whimpering, crying.

I'm…on the ground. He is lying on me, his elbow is crushing my throat. It's so hard it hurts. I can't breathe. I don't understand! There is a sudden wind; all around us are the white fleecy threads of dandelions…so many, floating, drifting, caught on the wind. It's surreal. They are blowing up from the edges of the lake, little wishes lost in time. It's like being in a snowstorm only it's June. When I was a child, and I saw one, I used to try to catch it and make a wish. He…he's killed me! I don't understand! I am floating, floating above my body! He's taking my jewelry…he carries my body deeper into the woods by the edge of the lake and slips it into the water. I'm only eigh-

*teen…and I'm dead now. He took it all, took it all away from me…the life I was sup-
posed to have with Jake!*

Who took it Ann? What is his name?

Subject quiet. She just shakes her head from side to side.

*You are not living that life now. I want you to go ahead and release all that pain,
the fear, the utter disappointment. Can you do that Ann? Do you understand?*

Yes.

Bruce stopped the tape. A quiet rain was tapping on the roof and gold flashes
of lightning lit the sky outside his window. This was either one hell of a coinci-
dence or a potentially deadly situation.

He didn't like the fact that Gerdie thought she'd misplaced a copy of one of
Kevin's sessions either. Had she really misplaced it, or had Kevin taken it? What
if history was about to repeat itself and he did nothing? But what of patient con-
fidentiality? Kevin hadn't seemed upset by the revelations of his session. He confessed to reading a lot of true crime books and to being a Civil War buff, and that
could perhaps explain some of his 'memories.' But two people describing the
same event?

The best course of action now would be to bring him in again, to push him
more deeply into a trance and regress him again. See if he had kept his promise to
Lavinia in other lifetimes. If Ann was in danger now, he had to find some way of
warning her…

44

Summer was at the end of its candle…its glorious final burst of come-on fall. Derek leaned into the bike and let long stretches of nothing fill him. Tall trees and smoothly banked roads—that was all he'd ever wanted. Silence always surrounded him; he preferred silence with a backdrop. It was rare to pass a motorist, even rarer still to see another human being on the back roads of Vermont. If he did pass them, he didn't really notice them; they were visored, charcoal shadows behind the windshields of their cars.

Summer licked the earth spilt green; tree branches arced into the sky then dipped and dropped in resplendent green-gold showers toward the earth—like fireworks falling quietly to the ground after bursting. The late afternoon sun, a shimmer of blonde behind the petals of leaves, glinted off Derek's copper magnetic bracelet, the chrome of his bike, bounced off his helmet visor. Wind pressed familiarly into his long, lean body; the Big Dog hummed and vibrated beneath him.

The bike had been an extravagant college graduation gift from his pharmaceutical executive father. They'd made an agreement. He had a year to get the wanderlust out of his system, to do whatever the hell he needed to do, as his father put it, before he came back and settled into some kind of respectable job. Work was all his father had ever known; Clifton Barks had never had any dreams bigger or shinier than the tiled floors of a lab or the chrome and steel of a corporate headquarters building.

The Big Dog Wolf, mirror silver, felt like a part of him now; the 110 rear-wheel horse power, 6-speed transmission, 54-mm inverted fork, PM scream wheels with matching rotors and pulley knew him better than his father ever would.

The past year had been the best of his life, given him something to dream about besides *her*.

He'd graduated with respectable grades, but he knew from the first day of freshman year that he didn't fit in. He hadn't ever fit in anywhere. He'd accomplished a lot for being deaf, more than his father had ever expected of him; even managed to avoid the dreams and headaches for a few days at a time now. But they—she—always came back.

He smiled, thinking of how his mother had stripped the zigzag wallpaper down from the dining room after his headaches had begun. *She* understood sudden sparkles of snow and rings of flashing silver.

The dreams and hallucinations had started when he was twelve. It was bad enough that he was deaf—imperfect and flawed in his father's eyes from the day he was born. Then the dreams started. He always dreamt of a beautiful girl in a white dress. The next day, the migraine would start. She would flow around his eyes like ice-cold milk, making him seek darkness. The dreams hadn't been as frequent during the past year, but the closer he got to the end of his ride, the more they bothered him. Then he'd have to hole up in some cheap motel for a few days, avoiding light like he was some sort of freak.

Nautoscopic hallucinations. That was the medical term for what he had. Sometimes <u>she</u> walked beside him or suddenly appeared next to him. He could never hear people approaching, so it was unsettling to see her. Thing was, now she was *talking to him*. And he could *hear her*.

He would watch her lips in fascination, out of habit. *You can't go home. Come to me. I'll help you find what you're looking for.* She'd beckon him then vanish in a thin trail of whispering silk, a serous image floating off the edges of his mind.

Last night she'd told him to go to a place called Doylestown. A community in Pennsylvania. She'd never been that specific before, and he'd never felt pulled so strongly in any direction. He was already past his father's deadline; he wasn't sure of the exact date, but he thought it was July. As the sun sank into the bruised clouds edging the horizon, he knew he would keep going until he found her. But what would he do then?

Maybe he was going crazy. He wanted no part of his father's suit-and-tie world with its antiseptic meetings, egos, and agendas. His father had started out as a clinical scientist; now he was some sort of director of research. He split everything into two categories: experiments and money. Derek was just another one of his experiments, and one that required a significant cash outflow.

The summer always seemed endless and dreamlike to him, but now he felt like he was drifting, riding in circles. He wasn't sure he knew *how* to go back to his real life. Using the short messaging service on his cell phone, he'd typed a few messages and sent them to his father's cell phone. But his cell never vibrated with any return messages. Derek wondered if Clifton had even informed his mother that he'd called.

Once Derek had stopped at a pay phone and punched in his home number. His father had answered—and through the expensive hearing aid that Derek rarely used, his father's voice sounded odd. The impatience, the coldness, had always been there, but now…Clifton had never been an emotional man; affection was a puddle of rain he refused to splash in. That was it. What he heard in his father's voice. *Defeat.* He'd never heard that before. He quietly set the receiver back in its cradle without saying a word.

Later that summer, Derek had finally given up and winged the black, compact cell phone into the woods. Damn thing always needed recharging anyway at the most inopportune moments.

He'd find a place to get a cup of coffee and the girl would lead him where he needed to go. Strange, but most of the diners and coffee places he'd seen along the way were closed. He'd hole up for the night. He always carried his Imitrex injections with him, in case the headaches started.

Afterwards, his bike would point him south and take him where he needed to go, with corybantic fury.

45

Thursday. 11:30 pm. Tony and Ann sat in the dining room, coffee cups half empty, Dingo curled at Tony's feet. The only light in the room came from the computer monitor's screen.

There had been no phone calls, no e-mails from Chaos since his challenge. The silence, the waiting, was even more worrisome to the pair. Nai Nai, Bo, and Janie were all at the hospital; they would stay overnight. Ann planned to join them again later. Bo had had chemotherapy and was very tired. She had an infection and they were trying to bring the fever down, figure out the source of the infection. Ann remembered sitting at the kitchen table, Bo asking quietly, "Am I going to die?"

"No," she'd said firmly. "I'm going to be your rock. You're going to get better. You're going to keep yourself busy and involved with living. Your daughter needs you."

"I hope I won't have too many 'chemo moments,'" Bo said, laughing weakly. "I've seen what these women go through. Now I'm one of *them*."

Tony and Ann had discussed how they would respond when their guy contacted Ann again—and he would, Tony was sure.

"You want to get a pizza?" Ann asked.

"Pepperoni?"

"You got it."

Ann had connected to the Internet over 4 hours ago. Teams were in place. A trace, a phone call, and they could have their guy. "I think our Freak Show is scared," Ann said. "I don't think he's going to show."

Ann flicked a button on the remote and changed the channel to a Happy Days rerun. She felt pent up. Since she'd been shot at, she hadn't been taking her nightly runs. She missed the feel of her muscles burning and straining, her feet pounding the pavement beneath the shadows of trees, good music thumping in her ears, sweat pouring down her back.

Just as Ann was about to pick up the phone and call for delivery, her machine burped at them telling her she had mail.

She looked at Tony. It was from "Chaos."

Tony placed a call as soon as it was opened; they started the trace.

DO YOU STILL WANT TO PLAY WITH ME?

Ann typed in the short message she and Tony had agreed on.

I'LL PLAY YOUR GAME. NAME THE TIME AND PLACE. She hit "send."

They waited, seconds feeling like hours. He replied.

YOU KNOW BETTER THAN THAT. DO YOU THINK I'M THAT STUPID? IT'S NOT ABOUT A TIME AND PLACE. IT'S ABOUT YOU AND ME. LET THE GAMES BEGIN.

That was it.

Tony's cell rang and he answered. He nodded his head. "Got it."

"Stay here," he said. "Keep everything locked. We got a location. An apartment downtown. Team is responding now. I'm going to bring the fucker in myself."

"Be careful," Ann said.

46

Show up: expose; discredit; invalidate.

Kevin woke with a start. He'd been in seven treatment programs. Two mental wards. Had six social workers. A dozen different counselors. Where was he now? It was pitch black in the room. He was lying on a couch. He could make out the edges of a desk, some shelves. My God, he was in *Bruce's office.* And there was something wet and sticky on his arms. They stung. Burned.

Blood.

He jumped up and felt his way along the wall, to the light switch. No, couldn't do that. Not supposed to be here. "Doc! Doc! You here?"

No answer. He wandered into the reception room. The files. He'd come for something. What? He scratched his head. *The tape. The tapes.* Evidence. No bodies lying about. Had he killed the good doctor?

He rummaged through the drawers of a tall black filing cabinet until he found what he was looking for. Then he saw something interesting. A file labeled "Ann Yang." He took it too.

47

The phone rang. The sound startling, like glass splintering. Ann picked it up. "Hello?"

"Ann, it's Mark. Listen, there's something I need to tell you."

Ann's fist unclenched. "Mark. Thank God."

"I wanted to tell you about her...I just didn't know how."

God. Was he married?

"Someone who's important to me, someone I want you to know about."

"Mark, listen, you don't have to tell me..."

"Yes, I do. I want you to know..."

Click. The line went dead. The lights flickered and went out. Very carefully, Ann reached for her Glock. It wasn't there! Dingo's ears sprang up and he growled from low in his belly.

48

Tony stopped his car in the middle of Main Street. Squads drove in from both directions, blocking the street. Red light washed off brick and stone while Tony, Lynch, and Randall ran up the stairs to the second floor apartment, guns drawn. People stopped and watched, curious.

Tony banged on the door. "Police! Open up!"

Nothing.

They called again then shouldered the cheap wooden door off its hinges, flattening themselves against the walls. Lynch raised his flashlight and slowly swept the room. A definite Bachelor's pad. A sofa and a TV sat in the center of the room; half empty bottles of DeWars littered the floor next to a plastic laundry tub filled with smut magazines. Underwear and socks in piles. A few loose books on a bookshelf. A computer. They swept the place; nobody home.

Hyde came up the steps carrying mail he'd retrieved from the box downstairs. "Kevin Rice. #201B. Now all we have to do is find the fucker and we got him. Lynch and Randall, you stay here. He has to come back sometime. Tony..."

Tony felt chills. The e-mail had been a distraction. "My God. Ann," he said, racing down the stairs.

49

Kevin sat on the roof. He had on sneakers, jeans, a T-shirt, and the jacket. The jacket gave him power. After all, he'd worn it 139 years ago when he was a captain in the Union army. And she hadn't been impressed. She would be impressed now. She would wear it to her grave.

Lavinia. Ruth. Ann. All the same soul. The sound of the powerful motorcycle was a Godsend. He chopped his way through shingle and wood then dropped down the hole he'd created. He was standing in the shadows in the front hall when he heard her talking on the phone. He took care of phone wire. He took care of the lights. Then he waited in the shadows again.

In his car in the alley, he had the box with the souvenirs.

Great claps of thunder rent the air. Rain pattered at the windows. Flash of lightning. Flash of brass. For a second, Ann saw the silhouette of a soldier standing in her living room and thought she was hallucinating.

Flash of lightning. A face. *His* face. Surprise. Cold, dead surprise. She felt utter disbelief flowing through her body.

"Annie, my Annie," he said, his voice a soft shadow floating through the room. "Why couldn't you have loved me all those years ago?"

She had to think. Had to try to reason with him. This couldn't be happening. How could she have been so stupid? And how could she shoot someone she thought she knew so well?

Because he'll kill you, Ann. You know that, deep down in your soul.

He stepped forward, became more visible. In his hand he held ragged-edged papers. "I have something that belongs to you. Pages from your diary, Ruth." In his other hand he held an ax.

That's why there had been some pages without dates, months between entries. "You shouldn't have fallen in love with Farrell," he said. "He was a pantywaist. How could you not know that I was your true love? I was Nell, Ruth. And I'm back. And you killed me."

He stepped closer. His face was expressionless, his eyes blank. Not a trace of emotion.

"I remembered living in this house. That's why I bought it. I only lived here a few years though. I sold it and tried to move on to other things. Oh, I tried. But you haunted me Ruth. You've always haunted me. I found the diary, but I left it here. I only took part of it with me. I knew some day you'd come back for it."

He started to cry and wiped at his eyes. "Why couldn't you love me? It's not my fault I lost an arm in the War. I'm still a man.

"What's the Chinese word for 'forever', Annie?" He started laughing hysterically, and Ann bolted toward the back door, throwing a dining room chair in his path. At the same time, Dingo lunged for his throat.

She turned the lock, yanked open the door, ran toward Nathan's cottage. She banged on it. No answer. She could see him coming down the path. *Dingo. No.*

Then she heard sirens. *Sirens.*

She turned the knob on the cottage door. Unlocked. She ran through the house, down the cellar stairs, barricaded herself in with the long wooden latch. Sweating, breathing raggedly, she looked around. Shelves. Felt along them in the darkness for a weapon.

He was outside the door now. "I've killed you before, you know, many times," he said. "And it just keeps getting better."

Frantically, her hands swept the shelves, knocking over jars and cans, splintering glass at her feet. She felt a flashlight, flipped it on. Weak light. She heard a sound at the door, a sound like paper rustling. Then she heard the heavy swing of his ax. She felt so confused. Could she have been Ruth in a past life? She didn't want to die. She backed up, searching in the corner. A pile of bricks. Old bags of coal. She picked up a brick and waited. *Come on, Tony.*

He kept hacking at the door until she heard it splinter and crack. She turned the flashlight off and backed into the corner until she couldn't go any further. Her arm fell through part of the rotting wall. It was stuck, jammed. She yanked at it, pulled it out. She went still, her fingers gripping the brick so hard they bled. It was quiet. He was in the room.

"Annie, I know you're in here. I'll find you."

She heard a loud crash as he swung the ax in the darkness, hitting the metal shelving.

She heard his footsteps. He was close. He would swing again. *Not yet. Wait a few seconds more.*

When she felt his presence close, heard his breathing, she stood, switching on the flashlight and cracking his skull with the brick.

When he fell forward, knocking the flashlight out of her hand, she heard shots and yelling.

Bodies. Running footsteps. Tony's voice.

"Tony! My God, Tony!"

Tony was there. Bright light. Ann shielded her eyes. Tony had blood on his hands, his shirt. Ann was crying. Tony checked the man's pulse. "He's dead, Ann. Kevin's dead."

"Kevin?" she sobbed. "That's Bruce Miller. My hypnotherapist."

"Shit." Tony held Ann in his arms, trying to calm her down, as he took her outside.

"Ann, it's Mark. He must have thought you were in trouble."

"Mark? What? What's wrong with Mark?"

She fell to her knees when she saw another body on the ground between the cottage and the house. Nathan was working over him frantically.

"No…" her voice wouldn't come.

"We thought he was…someone fired a shot. It was dark."

Ann got up, ran over to Mark, and fell beside him. "Mark, no. Don't die! Oh please. Don't die…"

50

Mark walked down a brightly lit hallway and was ushered into a small waiting room. The entire room, including the marble bench, was white. There were no windows or doors. The clocks ran backward. He sat down, wondering why he was clutching a child's crumpled gray baseball hat in his hands.

A door opened in the wall and a small man in a white suit appeared. He looked furtively around before dropping his eyes on Mark. His voice was a colorful waltz in the chalky endlessness of the room. "*He'll* see you now."

Mark stood, wondering who 'He' was. Where was he? He slid through the door, which had no handles, into another seemingly endless room, also white. A tall, striking man with dark hair sat behind a marble desk streaked with thin lines of blue. He appeared to be daydreaming, his arm stretched away from him, his eyes—of a color unlike any Mark had ever seen or could ever describe—studying his short, immaculate fingernails. There was a nameplate on his desk. It read "Ernest."

"What do you think, Mark? Cotton candy blue? Rose petal pink? Scrambled-eggs-in-the-morning yellow?"

Mark stood there, twisting the soft cap in his hands.

The man flicked his wrist and his fingernails became small, iridescent rainbows in exactly the colors he'd mentioned. Another flick of the wrist and the rainbows became streaks of lightning headed toward morning.

"You know Mark, God loves rainbows. I send some out every day. But people don't notice those things anymore." The man swiveled around in his chair and indicated the chair in front of the desk. "Please, sit down. Make yourself comfortable."

Mark sat down. "Who are you?"

The man smiled, a little sadly, arching a winged brow. "People don't think about us too much anymore." He held out his other hand and another man, in another white suit, appeared with a blue envelope. He handed it to Ernest, who opened it, glanced a few times at Mark, then sighed. "I see." He set the papers down.

"What? What do you see? Where am I?"

He stood up and Mark was surprised to see he was wearing a white T-shirt, a pair of stone-washed jeans, and cowboy boots. He heard the distinct twang of a guitar and closed his eyes. He opened them, but the man was still there. Ernest picked up the papers and started reading. "Let's see, this says you left the seat up 2,477 times in your lifetime, ran more than your fair share of yellow lights, went through the express checkout in the grocery store even though you had <u>16</u> items, called your sister a worm head, and threw a mud pie at Sally Schneckers, the scrawniest kid in the class, breaking her glasses. After which you went behind the school and threw up. Oh, my. And you told your grandmother once that you couldn't clean her house because it was the Sabbath."

"How…how do you know about those things?" Mark suddenly realized what he was listening to. "Are you actually listening to *Garth Brooks*?"

Ernest ignored him, appearing to be deep in thought. "This is an immedicable situation. I'm afraid you'll have to go back."

"Is this heaven? Are you an angel?"

"You haven't learned what you're supposed to learn yet. Looks like you have three choices. You can go back as a hamster, a dung beetle, or," he shuffled through some more papers on his desk then frowned. "My God. Oops." He sheepishly rolled his eyes heavenward. "Or you can go back as a *woman*."

"Go back? You mean I'm dead?"

The man placed his arms on the desk and stared at Mark. "Well, what's it going to be?"

"Did you say *hamster*?" If he wasn't dead, Mark would be sweating buckets right about now. He'd had a hamster once, as a kid. He'd tried to make it perform circus tricks. It got loose once, in the basement, where his mother was storing all the boxes of Girl Scout cookies waiting to be delivered. The hamster ended up in the sump pump, minus a tail.

Think. You're in the presence of an angel. An angel who wears Levi's and cowboy boots and listens to Garth Brooks, but an angel nonetheless. Dung beetle. Wait, that last choice…a woman?

"These are my choices? This is what's written about my life?"

Ernest fell back into his chair in a fit of laughter. "And they say God doesn't have a sense of humor." He picked up the papers and began to read some more. "It also says here you saved a lot of lives. You were a surgeon in the great War. You were an Egyptian servant who became a healer, an archeologist, a nurse in the ER, a veterinarian, just to name a few of your occupations. You also take care of your daughter very well. Visit her in the hospital every day. You have a soul that needs to reach out and touch people, a soul that wishes to ease suffering. A very noble, very old soul. It also says your heart aches for someone, someone who's been very important to you in many lifetimes. Someone you've loved and lost in too many lifetimes. Someone without whom you feel incomplete, no matter how many lives you save or how many wounds you heal. You just risked your life to save hers."

Ernest looked at him now, well, earnestly. "We have some decisions to make. I was just pullin' your leg about going back as a hamster."

"What about the dung beetle, and the, ah, woman?"

"You need to lighten up. Don't be such a fatalist. I'll explain everything. But first, follow me."

In an instant, they were standing before a shiny black Ranger FX4 with 16-inch aluminum 5-spoke wheels, P245/75Rx16 all-terrain OWL tires, and platinum wheel lip moldings. "Get in."

Mark opened the door and climbed into the passenger seat. Ernest got in the driver's side and turned the key in the ignition.

"Please forgive me, but this isn't what I thought heaven was like."

"What'da expect? Blaring trumpets? White gowns? Puffy clouds?"

"Well, yeah, kind of."

Ernest revved the accelerator. "Listen to that engine purr. Like butter." He looked at Mark's hands. "Better hold onto your hat. We have some old roads to drive, my friend, some old roads." He turned his attention to the dashboard but continued to talk. "There's no one chasing her anymore."

"Her?"

"The soul of the woman you love. He's pretty much beyond redemption.

"But the first thing. You have to remember in order to forget." He jerked the truck into gear and slammed the accelerator down, tires spinning, cotton-candy-blue chunks of gravel flying through the air. "I love that part, man. I love it," Ernest said as they drove off. By the time they reached their destination, Mark was a boy again and they sat in a field of dusted clover, engine idling, listening to the sound of a wooden bat cracking, the white whine of a baseball sliding through the air, a father's voice high and triumphant singing on the wind. "That's it! That's my son! You did it!"

Mark sat beside him, a dangerous possibility, a marvelous past. Fat, marvelous tears climbed out of his eyes, tears that nearly cracked his soul in two. He looked at Ernest. "I'd forgotten," he whispered, sobbing. "I'd *forgotten*."

But Ernest was gone. Suddenly he was running the bases, crossing home plate, jumping into his father's arms. His father was *real*. He could touch him. Feel him. Hear him. Smell him. As he hugged his father, he felt an old sadness falling away from them both. *I love you Dad.* Then he heard the revving sound of a motorcycle. A Big Dog. A young kid with a copper bracelet and an oceanic smile looked at him. "C'mon kid. It's time to go."

In the time it took to walk over to him, Mark was a man again. "Where are we going?"

"I'm getting my wings. You could say it took me a while to realize who I was...that I was...gone. I died in a motorcycle accident." He patted his shiny bike. "Isn't it cool they have Big Dogs up here?"

He kicked the stand up and Mark hopped on. "I'm taking you home. Where you belong."

"What's your name?" Mark asked.

"The Protector. I had issues with my old man too."

They rode into a perfect blue sky, into oceans of cloud, burnt sun, and cool moon.

51

When Mark woke up, he was in a hospital bed. Ann was sleeping in a chair beside the bed, her head resting on his arm, her fingers laced through his. The room was dimly lit.

For a moment, he just breathed, inhaling the scent of her, the feel of her, the sight of her. *He wasn't dead.*

She moved in her sleep and he stroked her hair. "I'm home," he whispered.

She woke. "Mark! Oh my God, Mark. You're awake. You're alive. I don't know what I would have done…" She broke down in sobs.

They clung to each other. Then Mark remembered what he wanted to tell her.

"I wanted to tell you about my daughter."

"Your daughter?" Ann's eyes shown bright through her tears.

"That's what I was going to tell you when the phone went dead. Yes. Susanna is a beautiful girl. She's fourteen and she's been in and out of mental hospitals her whole life. Schizophrenia. Manic depression. Her mother left when she was one. She couldn't handle her."

"Oh Mark."

"I should have told you…before we got close."

"It wouldn't have mattered. Did you think I couldn't handle it? That I'd run away?

"Mark, you know me better than that. I…I love you."

Mark closed his eyes and cried.

As she tried to quiet the sobs from his body, she told him about Dingo, who'd fought valiantly but died, the diary, about how Bruce had lived in her house at one time under Kevin's name, how he was a schizophrenic. When a woman named Jeannie had read a newspaper article about Beverly Wilcox's disappearance, she recognized the description of the car. She'd overheard her boyfriend Kevin on the phone, agreeing to sell a similar car. They'd found strands of Beverly's hair in the front seat. They found a fingerprint he hadn't managed to wash away on the glass of the windshield. But the murderer was dead. The young boy who'd been in a coma was dead.

"He really thought he lived before, Mark. He really thought he was a soldier who came back from the War to a girl who didn't love him. He thought I was that girl.

"As a doctor, he had access to Lucinate X, an experimental therapy used to treat schizophrenia. He volunteered at rehabs, hospitals. That's how he got the drug. *That's how he picked his victims.*

"You know what they found in his car?" Ann shivered.

Mark shook his head. "What?"

"A box containing *fingers.* Skeletal. Some decaying. They were his souvenirs. And a gold chain with a swan on it."

"So he was a freak. Found the diary. Started living it."

"But that doesn't explain the past lives I remembered under hypnosis," Ann said.

"No, it doesn't."

"My God, to think I trusted him…thought he was a legitimate hynotherapist…"

He stroked her hair.

"You know the girl who disappeared from my house, Nell? Her father was a doctor. He was into eugenics, conducting secret experiments. He raped his own daughter. I think he thought she was the perfect woman and wanted to create perfect descendants.

"And there was a newspaper article I found in the house from 1979 about an escaped murderer named Kevin Rice."

Suddenly, Ann kissed Mark's lips tenderly, over and over. "When you're better, I want to hear you play the piano. I want to meet Susanna. I want to go to the movies and stay up late talking and do things that *normal* couples do."

Mark smiled. "It's a deal."

That night, she fell asleep in Mark's arms again. *Thin cotton sheet. Warm man. Smell of hospital, hope, healing. Some things are meant to be.*

Epilogue

When the cellar of the cottage where Ruth and her family had lived was being repaired, they found two skeletons. The skeletons sat in repose, a gray tangle of bone wedged against a wall. They had waited so long to tell someone their secrets. They didn't need to wait any longer. Their skulls rested one against the other, the bones of their fingers entwined. Hanging between them, and wound round both their necks, was a silk scarf. The color of blood. A fiat of conscience. It had been a hundred years and a knot of lives. Now they could rest in peace. *Hina dolls. Japanese stick figures made of paper or wood or bundled sawdust or wheat starch. Lavishly clothed. Heads bent low, elegant arms outstretched. Sent to sea on cold boats. Touching themselves. Washed clean.*

The solving of the over 100-year-old disappearance and the present-day murders would mean another term for Ann as county medical examiner. It was November and a fire crackled in the hearth; Mark sat reading a newspaper in the dining room he had restored. "Hey, check it out! Another article about you!"

Ann walked over behind his chair and started to knead his shoulders as she read it.

Dr. Ann Yang is seeking a second term as Bucks County Medical Examiner. Her opponent, Democrat Dr. Brian Kitch, said his medical background is more well-rounded than Yang's, who once put her career on hold for 'personal' reasons. Last July, Yang solved a 100-year-old murder that took place on the grounds of the residence she now lives in and was also responsible for stopping a serial killer who'd killed at least three victims in the area.

"The citizens of this county need and deserve a state-of-the-art forensic facility," she said. "We've done a lot to improve the office; there's a lot to be proud of."

Voters will decide if the Republican gets a second term in office in Tuesday's election, or if Democratic newcomer Kitch will get a go at the job. Kitch said his record and experience should be enough to put him over the top.

The Democrat said that his more generalized experience as a family practitioner could be important in ruling on cases. "It's not that she's done a bad job, but when she got married, she put her career on hold for personal reasons. She may be behind in current forensic thinking and technology."

"Pompous ass," Ann said aloud.

She silently congratulated the reporter for his next paragraph, which made Kitch eat his words.

Yang says in the not-too-distant future, autopsies may be performed using comput- erized scanning rather than scalpels. A Swiss forensic pathologist and his colleagues at the University of Bern's Institute of Forensic Medicine are working on a virtual autopsy—a minimally invasive procedure that relies on high technology rather than sharp instruments. Bodies are not cut up and juries can view computer simulations rather than photos of cadavers. And it doesn't destroy key forensic evidence.

"The images can be stored on the computer, e-mailed to others for a second opinion or posted on a website. It's technology like this that will save future lives and give fam- ily members, who may be squeamish about traditional autopsy methods, or whose reli- gion forbids it, another option."

Kitch countered that the technology would be expensive, and out of the reach of most county budgets.

Yang said the cost would come down and the technology could well be comparable to how important DNA evidence was in the mid-1980s.

The medical examiner job pays slightly less than $50,000 a year. The medical examiner's office is responsible for investigating any deaths where there's a potential the cause of death wasn't natural. Yang said her staff generally tackles about 600 cases per year, about half of which require autopsies.

It was deep Fall; bright red and orange leaves danced in the wind outside the windows. The house was renovated, the skeletons in the closet literally let loose. Ann was sure she would win the election hands-down. But she was mulling over another idea. Tony said she'd make a good FBI agent. Ann had argued, her point being that the killer had been right under her nose the whole time. Tony's response had been enlightening. "It happens to the best of us. We all think killers should have stringy, greasy hair, crooked teeth, and wear nothing but AC/DC T-shirts. But killers are some of the most normal looking people you see on any given day."

There *were* lots of houses in Virginia that needed fixing up. Mark and Ann wouldn't be getting married, at least right away. First, they would build a house together. If they could build a house together, then maybe they could build a life together.

0-595-32664-1

Printed in the United States
32353LVS00006B/142-156